Also by Leonora Nattrass and available from Viper

BLACK DROP
BLUE WATER
THE BELLS OF WESTMINSTER (2024)

SCARLET TOWN

LEONORA
NATTRASS

VIPER

This paperback edition first published in 2024
First published in Great Britain in 2023 by Viper,
an imprint of Profile Books Ltd
29 Cloth Fair
London
ECIA 7JQ
www.profilebooks.com

1 3 5 7 9 10 8 6 4 2

Printed and bound in Great Britain by
CPI Group (UK) Ltd, Croydon, CR0 4YY

A CIP catalogue record for this book is available from the British
Library.

ISBN 978 1 800816992
eISBN 978 1 800816985

In Scarlet towne, where I was borne

'Barbara Allen's Cruelty', *Reliques of Ancient English Poetry*,
vol 3, collected by Thomas Percy, 1775

AUTHOR'S NOTE

THIS NOVEL IS INSPIRED by the true story of an election in the market town of Helston, West Cornwall, in the late eighteenth century. Prior to the Great Reform Act of 1832, Britain's electoral arrangements were a shambles. Qualifications to vote varied arbitrarily from place to place and Cornwall, once the prosperous centre of tin mining, sent forty-two MPs to Parliament while Manchester, Leeds and Birmingham sent none at all.

An educated guess puts the national electorate before the Great Reform Act at about 5 per cent of the adult population. Afterwards, it rose to 9 per cent. More working people got the vote under further reforms in 1867 and 1884. Universal manhood suffrage only arrived in 1918, after the bloody fields of the Somme and Passchendaele, while it was 1928 before women got the vote on the same terms as men.

CAST OF CHARACTERS

THE DOCTOR AND HIS CIRCLE
Dr Pythagoras (Piggy) Jago, newly appointed surgeon
and physician in Helston
Tirza Ivey, his housekeeper
Bitterweed, his cat
Laurence Jago, Piggy's cousin, just returned from America
Marie-Grace Jago, Laurence's mother
William Philpott, journalist, all-round controversialist
and Laurence's employer
Nancy Philpott, his wife
Their six children

THE DUKE'S PARTY AT THE ANGEL INN
Francis Osborne, 5th Duke of Leeds, former Foreign
Secretary, and patron of Helston
Catherine Osborne, his wife
George Osborne, his son
Sidney Osborne, his infant son
Sir James Burges, Under-Secretary to the Foreign
Office and the duke's candidate for Parliament
Charles Burges, his son
Anne Bellingham, stepdaughter of Sir James's former

4

colleague, George Aust, acting as governess/companion
to Charles Burges
Thomas Wedlock, the duke's elector
John Scorn, the duke's elector

THE HELSTON CORPORATION AT THE WILLOWS
Thomas Glynn, Mayor of Helston
Sarah Glynn, his niece
Stephen Lushington, chairman of the East India
Company and the corporation's candidate for
Parliament

SUNDRY PERSONS
Richard Hitchens, High Sheriff of Cornwall
Thomas Roskruge, Helston coroner
William Wedlock, curate at St Michael's Church,
Thomas Wedlock's grandson
Eleanor Scorn, John Scorn's granddaughter
Cyrus Best, Eleanor's lover
James Julian, grocer, Cyrus's uncle
Loveday Landeryou, the Scorns' maid
The choir of St Michael's Church
Jeb Nettle, choirmaster and sexton at St Michael's
Toby, the Sapient Hog
Mr Nicholson, Toby's manager

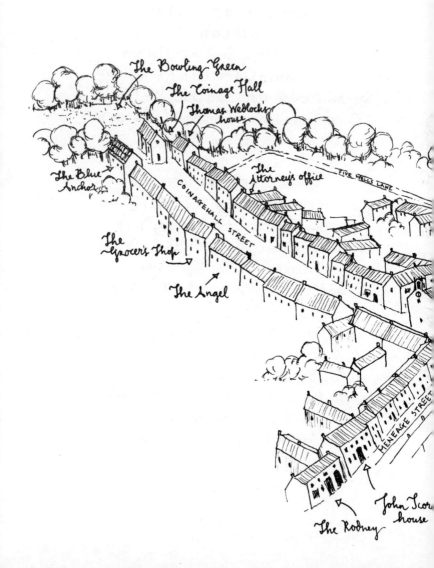

The Bowling Green

The Coinage Hall

Thomas Wedlock's house

The Blue Anchor

The Attorney's office

FIVE WELLS LANE

COINAGEHALL STREET

The Grocer's Shop

The Angel

HENEAGE STREET

John Scor house

The Rodney

Helston,
West Cornwall,
1796

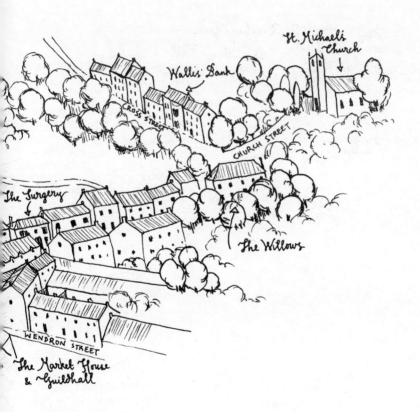

St. Michael's
Church

Wallis' Bank

CROSS STREET

CHURCH STREET

The Surgery

The Willows

WENDRON STREET

The Market House
& Guildhall

FRIDAY
27 MAY 1796

All in the merrye month of May
When greene buds they were swellin'

I

EVENING

IT WAS GONE EIGHT o'clock, and the last rays of sunlight slanted between the buildings on Meneage Street, illuminating a rash of vivid silk ribbons in the hats of the crowd. We were swaying down the narrow road through such a throng it frightened the horses. They jibbed in the shafts and made the whole coach judder in a thoroughly disagreeable manner.

My mind skipped to the coach roof, piled high with our belongings, and I imagined in some morbid detail the top-heavy vehicle toppling over. But I comforted myself with the reflection that though this would be unpleasant for those of us within, it would be far worse for the multitude without, who were pressing against the sides of the vehicle, their faces coming and going as they peered in at us.

But of course, I was alone in such fears. 'Party colours,'

was all Philpott was saying, in a marvelling tone. 'Laurence, what the devil is afoot? I can see blue ribbons – and red ones, too, whatever *they* may signify.'

Parliament had been dissolved, we had heard on landing at Falmouth, and a general election had been called. My home town of Helston being an egregious example of a rotten borough, Philpott had declared an immediate intention to put off his return to London by a week and linger in Cornwall to report on the town's shocking corruption for his newspaper, the *Weekly Cannon*. There were only two old voters left, the rest having died off over a long number of years, and the remaining two were firmly in the pocket of the town's patron, the Duke of Leeds, who told them who to vote for and no doubt paid them some little sum for their trouble. This having been the case for many years – only the number of old electors inevitably dwindling – we had expected to find the town in its usual state of drowsy repose.

Instead, we were arrived in the middle of a noisy political meeting. The blue silks Philpott had noticed were certainly the Duke of Leeds' colours, but the scarlet red of their opponents was new to both of us. And there was something else generally strange about the whole scene that I could not, as yet, quite put my finger on.

Philpott looked entranced by the roar of laughter, screams and angry shouts magnified by the walls of the narrow street, while his wife was busy rebuking William Philpott junior for gurning back at the gawking faces beyond the window. Margaret, Philpott's eldest daughter, was now seven years old and growing dignified. The other small Philpotts formed an undifferentiated mass of shrill voices and writhing limbs, which I generally endeavoured to ignore as best I could.

The crowd was thickening and, thwarted of all further progress, the coach ground to a halt. A moment later the coachman's face appeared at the window. 'I can't get no further,' he said. 'You'll have to get out here. The Angel's only an 'undred yards further on, round the corner.'

Philpott took this news stoically and, if he showed any hesitation at disembarking in the midst of such a riotous crowd encumbered by his luggage, his wife and his six children, it was only that of a man set on braving a tiger and calculating the safest way to do it.

'Pass the brats out to me, will you, Laurence?' he decided after a moment, leaning out of the window to get at the door handle. 'Hand in hand, I think will be best. Nancy my dear, you come last and for God's sake don't let go or we shall scatter like shot and the children will all be trampled to death.'

This was not a very encouraging idea to infant minds and they squawked with alarm as I funnelled them through the door and down the carriage steps to their father, who braced himself against the tide of bodies with his stout frame and gathered his brood about him like a mother hen. Mrs Philpott went last, with one infant on her hip and clutching another by the collar. I thrust my eyeglasses more firmly up my nose before stepping down from the coach behind her. A man pushed past me roughly and I staggered back, banging my head painfully on the door handle. Meanwhile, the coachman had scrambled up to the roof and was handing down our luggage, a vast pile of boxes and bags we had brought with us hurriedly from America and which now formed a whole new obstruction in the crowded street.

Though we were out of the coach, we were so hemmed in by bodies there was no possibility of further progress either forwards or back, especially with our luggage and clutch of small Philpotts in tow. And a strange new wave of movement was now approaching up the street, accompanied by shouts and screams that verged on panic. The crowd parted to reveal a posse of running men, mouths horribly agape in blood-red painted faces. They were in some strange ecstasy beyond noticing pain or fear as they bore down on us, wildly drunk. The Philpott children shrieked again as the running men slammed into the coach, and the coachman shouted an angry reproach from his spot on the roof. One of the front horses reared in its traces and the crowd flowed, perhaps afraid the huge vehicle really would topple. The drunk men bounced off again – one of them now bleeding briskly – and swept into a doorway to our left. It was the Rodney Inn, where I had spent some discreditable evenings in my youth, and I well recognised the solemn naval captain on the inn sign gazing down with disapproval at the turmoil unfolding below him.

It now became clear that the whole crowd was converging on the Rodney and had blocked the street, being far too many to enter. There were shouts coming from inside the inn, and even over the general racket I could hear the dull thuds and thumps of drunken affray. The scarlet-painted men would hardly be welcome but would be equally hard to be rid of. Other men without party colours were hastening out of an alley beside the inn, buttoning their breeches, come from the privy. I recognised one or two of them as my mother's farming neighbours, probably come into town to witness the excitement but only adding to the general disorder.

There were more shouts from inside the Rodney, followed by a sudden and rather bruising exodus. The innkeeper, possibly fearing a fatal crush, was driving everyone out. The crowd around us flowed again and one of the infant Philpotts came adrift from its mooring and was swept away by the current. If I had been as careless as Philpott had proved in the heat of our flight from Philadelphia I might have let it go by. But being a man of more sense than my employer, I scooped it up as it passed me and set it on my shoulders. In front of us, a woman's bonnet was knocked off her head and she gave a yelp of anguish to see it trodden underfoot. Then, finally driven out of the inn, the group of painted drunks landed at my elbow. Their knuckles were as red as their faces now, and they were clearly itching for another fight. Whether I was to be their next victim was entirely out of my hands for I could not move a step in any direction nor let go of the child on my shoulders.

Next to emerge from the inn were two parties of gentlemen. Or, at least, from their general bearing I would have called them so, but there was something strange about them all the same – the same general strangeness I had already noticed while inside the coach, but which I still couldn't name. I had an uneasy feeling that there had been some kind of revolution while we were abroad, and all our old masters had been deposed. One of these curious-looking gentlemen was being carried in a bath chair, as if it were a sedan, held aloft by a pair of burly labourers one to each of the chair arms. The invalid appeared to be enjoying the turmoil quite as much as Philpott.

Three ladies were now coming out of the inn behind the gentlemen, despite the innkeeper's remonstrances that they should stay safely inside – a courtesy not extended to poor Mrs Philpott who was being buffeted about like a piece of imperturbable driftwood in a turbulent sea. She did not deserve such treatment, but I felt little sympathy for the other females present – even the creature still mourning her lost bonnet. Any sensible woman who did not fancy the crush could have stayed safely at home.

There was no doubt as to these three ladies' superior rank, however, being gorgeously attired in the same party colours we could see everywhere else. A girl, dressed in glowing scarlet with shining ebony hair and wearing an expression of barely suppressed excitement, stood slightly apart from the other two women both dressed in shades of ducal blue. The larger of the blue females was all curls and satin, the other slighter figure was rather dowdy by comparison, though still very respectable. The blue women were clearly not on speaking terms with the red, but one of the gentlemen now noticed them and bundled them all higgledy-piggledy into the marooned stagecoach for safety. As he did so, the dowdier woman in blue turned towards me. To her I would have been only one unnoticed face in the pressing crowd, but my heart straightaway exploded. It was Anne Bellingham to the life. Or now, perhaps, Anne Canning, for she had been on the verge of marrying for a second time when I had quitted England eighteen months ago.

I didn't know if I should first be sick or die of joy; and why she was here in Helston I couldn't imagine. She was wearing blue, which certainly meant she was of the duke's party. He had been Foreign Secretary when I first entered Downing Street, and Anne's stepfather his permanent under-secretary, but she had been only fourteen and I didn't remember any special connection with His Grace that might account for her presence here. Had Canning made himself useful to the duke? I looked for him among her gentleman companions who now all seemed very bent on speaking to the crowd, but he was not there.

The coachman consented to the further requisition

of his vehicle without much complaint, having – like the rest of us – nowhere else to go. One party in scarlet cockades climbed up to the seats behind the carriage roof, while the fellow in the bath chair was slid into the compartment we had lately quitted, his chair fitting neatly between the six facing seats so he could look out at the crowd. The ladies within were thrown together in a heap by his arrival, squashed against the opposite door. Meanwhile, the second set of blue-favoured gentlemen were mounting the front of the coach to the driver's seat, so that the rival parties were separated only by the domed roof of the carriage.

I felt even more perplexed now I could see the men better. One of those wearing the unfamiliar scarlet cockade had a heavy chain of mayoral office about his shoulders, but however self-satisfied his expression, he looked quite unlike any gentleman I had ever seen before. My eye swept over the crowd below, and it occurred to me that, apart from the ladies in the coach, no obvious persons of rank were visible at all. Philpott alone looked like a gentleman among these people, though he was only a farmer's son born and bred like myself. And then, at last, I realised what was strange. Philpott and I were the only men in the street wearing wigs.

I looked back at the mayor, and finally recognised him as Mr Thomas Glynn, a very wealthy man with a fine country estate, and a Helston town house opposite the church. I hadn't recognised him before because he was quite bald, a fact with which I had been previously unacquainted, having never seen him wigless. Some extraordinary revolution in fashion must have occurred since we left England; a revolution that in a crowd like this flattened all social distinctions. That was what had seemed strange. All my life, I had recognised the well-to-do by the merest glance at their heads. Now, the crowd might well be half gentry, but without a closer examination of the quality of their broadcloth, their possession of spectacles or pocket watches, or the amount of money in their purses, it was quite impossible to tell who was who. As a democratical rebel I ought to have been delighted. In fact, it made me feel almost as seasick as Anne's unexpected appearance here had done.

Mr Glynn, the bald mayor, was being handed some notes by an assistant, probably one of the town's serving aldermen. Helston was a borough in the old fashion handed down from the days of Good Queen Bess. There were a dozen such places dotted about Cornwall, little kingdoms amid farmland, moor and sea; kingdoms which were a law unto themselves – and, as I well knew, habitually wracked with violent internal division. It seemed, from the red ribbons pinned to the coats of the mayor and aldermen, that instead of bickering among themselves in time-honoured fashion, they had now taken it upon themselves to challenge the supremacy of the duke's blue cockade.

The drunk men beside us were chanting something

that sounded like *Mohawks for Helston!* while another party were retorting *Cherokees forever!* accompanied by their erroneously Cornish idea of an Indian war whoop. Glynn was waving his hands in an attempt to quieten the crowd, but no one took any notice until Philpott emitted a sudden and doleful bellow, suggestive of a bee-stung bull, and a wave of shushing swept up the street like the sound of carriage wheels through rain. In the ensuing quiet, the mayor's voice resounded off the shops and houses of the narrow street, allowing the huge crowd to hear him even better than a smaller gathering might have done inside the inn.

Glynn smiled down at the multitude of expectant faces turned up to him. For all the noise and tumult, he was in rather good cheer and not at all flustered by the size of his audience or his unlikely allies, the blood-red drunks beside us, who were now growling at their opponents like a pack of mastiffs.

'I hardly expected to see such a crowd,' he began. 'We only meant to have words with the electors, and per-haps we should have held this meeting quietly in the Guildhall. But in fact I'm not sorry to see such a dis-play of public interest. Those electors here today, with the heavy responsibility of casting their vote on Monday, do well to be reminded of their importance to the town.'

'Electors?' someone in a blue ribbon shouted out. 'Imposters, more like!'

The mayor positively grinned. 'Imposters, you say?

And what do you call the duke's electors? I'll tell you what I call them, sir: a disgrace to the town!'

'Shame!' someone else in the crowd shouted. I was pretty sure he was the town's coal merchant since his skin was a strange but recognisable hue of ashy grey. 'John Scorn, you tell 'em.'

There was a movement among the mayor's blue-ribboned rivals on the driver's seat of the stagecoach, and I now saw among them an ancient man, probably eighty, dressed in an old-fashioned merchant's suit. He was scowling with furious intensity as he raised his hand in answer to the heckler. But even as a feeble shout of *Cherokees forever* in the crowd was cut off by the apparent strangulation of the speaker, the mayor was pressing on. 'The Duke of Leeds was not invited to this meeting either, but I'm glad to see him here so he may justify his disgraceful conduct to the town.'

The scarlet ribbons growled as Glynn pointed out another man on the driver's seat with an accusing finger. By God, it really was the duke himself, also strangely naked without his wig. But though he would not recognise me from Adam, his large nose, curled lip and look of general disgust with the world made me feel suddenly nostalgic for those early days in Downing Street when Anne and I had been hardly more than children and had, as yet, done nothing foolhardy or wicked.

Whatever else I might say about him, the duke was well used to being insulted in public and only shook his head disdainfully as Glynn went on. 'I hear some say I should not be hard on the two old men,' he said. 'And I grant you, they were elected freemen fairly once, many years ago. But how can they take it upon themselves alone to return both our MPs to Parliament? They are only puppets of the duke, who instructs them who to vote for according to his own convenience. One of his candidates, Sir James Burges, was his under-secretary in government, and the other, Charles Abbot, cleaned his boots at school and does not even deign to appear in the town. The duke has no connection with Helston and the whole arrangement is an insult to us all.'

The ancient old man in the duke's party had been quivering with increasing violence throughout this diatribe and now tried to answer. But his voice was too frail to be heard and Sir James Burges, who sat beside him, pressed his shoulder soothingly. Sir James Burges! Under-Secretary of State to the Foreign Office, and my old superior, who had, in his day, made me a very unhappy man. My past seemed all laid out before me: from my smallest childhood spent in this town, through my long and hopeless love for Anne, to these titled persons involved in the circumstances from which I had fled England with Philpott eighteen months earlier. It was an exile from which I was returned a little older, a degree wiser, but vastly more lonely than I had ever been before. So lonely that the familiar faces of the men who had banished me nonsensically warmed my heart.

Meanwhile, Glynn was nodding at the elector's angry old face. 'Yes, yes, of course Mr Scorn don't agree with me, being, as we know, a very irascible man. But I see that the duke's other elector, Thomas Wedlock, is absent altogether. Likely too ashamed to come to this meeting at all.'

A new outbreak of violence in the crowd brought a momentary halt to proceedings and we were all hurled to and fro. The child on my shoulders slipped sideways and clutched anxiously at my face with his small sticky fingers, leaving my spectacles somewhat fogged. When the turmoil showed no sign of subsiding, Glynn made his voice heard again over the din. 'The world is changing and Helston must change with it. We are no longer an old-fashioned place of guilds and petty merchants. Instead, we turn our faces out to the globe, and no man represents that change more than the corporation's candidate Mr Lushington, chairman of the East India Company.'

The fellow in the bath chair inside the coach raised a hand in acknowledgement of Glynn's praise. Remarkably, it appeared that this corpulent fellow with mottled red cheeks was the chairman of the most powerful company on earth, and if such power had not brought him health, there was still something of the street fighter about the set of his formidable jaw. I searched behind him for another glimpse of Anne and saw her pale face listening earnestly to what was being said.

For a short, fortunate spell I had thought I might win her. She had loved me, I was sure, and when my star in the Department had seemed briefly to be rising she had allowed me to kiss her and talk obliquely of a future together. But that was before everything went to the devil. Living and breathing politics far more than I had ever done, she had subsequently meant to marry George Canning for his position in government as much as for love, I had been certain.

The mayor had finished his oration and the duke now elected to make reply. He made no effort to stand up from where he was squashed on the box between the ancient man and Sir James Burges, but spoke from where he sat, in the impatient, rather querulous voice I remembered very well from former days, and which had always put me in mind of a goose.

'I heard of this meeting this morning,' he honked, and the crowd quietened a little to listen. 'I heard of this meeting this morning, I say, and I hardly need to point out why the mayor has called it.' The duke had never been much of an orator in the House of Lords, but the excitement of this occasion seemed to spur him to some unusual exertion. 'They are afraid their thirty-two so-called electors begin to see the error of this whole proceeding and need nudging to vote at all. Well, they are quite right to be uneasy, for if the mayor's candidates are returned instead of my own, it will be at the expense of Helston. Nothing will be widened to the world except the mayor's own pockets.'

The blue ribbons cheered enthusiastically and the mayor looked indignant. But the East India chairman, Lushington, only smiled from his place inside the coach, evidently quite immune to the unpleasant atmosphere or the duke's jibes. What Anne made of the duke's words I couldn't see, for she had turned her head towards the duchess, but as she was wearing his colours I supposed she must be enjoying his sour wit.

'It is a nonsense to say I have no business here,' the duke was going on in the same squawking tones. 'A nonsense, I say. I have long supported this town just as my father did before me. But if these new imposters vote against me, I will certainly resign my interest in the borough. Mr Glynn will be pleased, but you townsfolk will suffer for it. You will pay the poor rates, and maintain the Church buildings, and all the rest yourselves. There will be no more superior entertainments on election day. It would be a pity to see our comfortable arrangement dissolved merely so that Mr Glynn may have the ear of the East India Company for his own gain.'

The rival groups of listeners being only confirmed in their own opinions by both speeches, the violence was getting worse. Even inside the carriage, the ladies' heads were now nodding angrily at each other like pecking birds. The drunk men kept surging back and forth, causing vast annoyance to all about them, including myself. I was suddenly as thirsty as the devil and my head, where I had banged it on the stagecoach door handle, was aching. The novelty of the meeting was wearing thin and the child on my shoulders had taken to drumming his small heels tiresomely against my ribs.

Just then, as the clock tolled from the crossroads beyond the knots of argumentative bodies, we heard louder screams and shouts coming from the same direction. Everyone, even the gentlemen on the carriage roof, turned their heads to look.

'Fire!' a voice was shouting. 'Fire at the Guildhall!'

And as if God had taken his broom to the gathering, the whole crowd was swept summarily along the street, parting around our heaped-up luggage as Philpott, his wife and I crouched about the children to keep them safe. The coachman sprang to his seat without much courtesy to the ducal party and took up the reins, seeing his chance to escape even if it meant taking the town's politicians and their women with him. As the coach swept past us I caught sight of the ancient elector's face where he sat with the duke and Sir James on the box. His old eyes were rather confused, but his face was flushed with a strange, violent passion. Ahead, another voice was shouting.

'Will the doctor come to the Guildhall? The elector Thomas Wedlock is dead.'

2

W^{E WERE LEFT} abandoned by the receding tide of bodies like a heap of stranded jetsam, and Philpott removed his hat, took off his wig, and threw it down in the gutter. 'God damn me, I have longed to do that these ten years and more. Laurence, take that monstrosity off your own head and bid your nits adieu.'

Though in my recent state of mind I had been generally inclined to dispute every one of Philpott's ridiculous observations, it was certainly pleasant to disentangle my spectacles from my wig, shove the rat-like article in my pocket, and feel the evening breeze tousle my hair. Mrs Philpott stooped down, without comment, to retrieve Philpott's expensive headpiece – which might, after all, still be of service in London if not here – and stayed there to wipe eyes and blow noses among her frightened brood.

'I wonder what the devil is going on,' I said. I meant everything – the tumult, the wigs, and most of all

Anne – but, naturally enough, Philpott thought I only meant the politics.

'Perfectly clear, it seemed to me. The mayor has resolved to challenge the duke's old voters, and has named the thirty-two Freemen of the Corporation as a rival electorate. Parliament will have to decide whose votes should count, and about time too, I should say.' He frowned. 'Though I wish your mayor had chosen another man than Lushington as his candidate. I much dislike these nabobs who earn their wealth from the plunder of the East and come back to lord it over the rest of us.'

Anne's appearance still seemed too much like a dream to speak of. 'And what about the wigs?' I asked instead. Glynn had said that the world was changing, and so it had, quite suddenly, even in my quiet home town, while I had not been looking.

Philpott goggled at me impatiently. 'I dare say that will all come clear when we have had the chance to look about us. But in the meantime we are standing here, jawing about trifles, while a very interesting situation is unfolding at your Guildhall. God damn it, you'll make no journalist if you let such things slide.' He whistled to the innkeeper who was surveying the mess outside the Rodney's doorstep with some despondency. 'Ho, my dear man! Will you give my family a bite to eat while my apprentice and I set about our business?'

As far as I was concerned, he might just as well have gone about his business without me, but when I was with him it always seemed far easier to go along with my supposed apprenticeship and keep my private thoughts to myself. In any event, the innkeeper appeared pleased enough to be distracted from the litter, and took Mrs Philpott, the luggage and the children inside with restored good humour. I thought he would be even happier by the time we returned, since gaunt, practical Mrs Philpott would probably have cleaned up all the mess for him by then.

Philpott set off down the street towards the remnants of the former crowd, now thronged about the old Market House at the crossroads. It was a Tudor affair with a jutting upper storey which housed the Guildhall, scene of all the town corporation's meetings, and tall barn doors below, which opened into a market hall lit by arched barred windows. A flight of outside steps led to the upper storey, while a square stone tower fronted the market yard, topped by a belfry with a clock on its front face, its hands now pointing to a quarter to nine. Philpott shouldered his way through the onlookers to the flight of steps and I followed him up to the door, where a couple of clerks had been posted to keep out the inquisitive and the unwashed.

To be frank, after our sea-journey and tousling from the crowd we were both of these disagreeable things. But when Philpott puts his mind to something he will not be denied, and after a lengthy period in which I scanned the crowd unsuccessfully for another glimpse of the duke's party in general and Anne in particular, we were at length admitted into the sudden gloom of the squatting old building. This would have been a foolhardy course of action if the place had really been ablaze, but it turned out the fire had been confined to a very small room – hardly more than a cupboard – where the corporation kept its records and insignia of office, the most splendid of which was, at present, safely around the shoulders of the mayor.

'Poor old Wedlock!' one of the clerks was saying, wringing his hands, as we came in. But he seemed as upset by the confusion of the corporation's papers as by the dead body lying among them on the floor of the little room. I knew from my own many years as a Foreign Office clerk that he and his fellows would have the rough edge of everyone's tongue, whether they deserved it or not, poor devils.

The door to the small room had been forced open and hung askew on its hinges as we edged further in, to find a doctor crouching over the dead man. There was something faintly familiar about the broad set of the doctor's shoulders and the way he moved his large paws gently about the dead body, a familiarity explained when he turned around to look at us.

'Good God, Piggy!' I said.

I almost began to wonder if this whole episode was some kind of elaborate dream in which all those I had formerly loved and hated were to appear to me one by one, like the faces of the dead. But the doctor's own face, which had always put me in mind of a benign St Bernard, was staring back at me with an equal astonishment that did not seem at all dreamlike. Then, recovering from his surprise, he smiled with happy recognition, and I remembered to be more polite.

'Pythagoras, my dear fellow, I didn't know you were in Helston. Mr Philpott, sir, this is my cousin on my father's side, Dr Pythagoras Jago.'

Piggy was a year or two older than I was, a shambling Newfoundland of a man with a look of general good humour that perfectly reflected the benevolent heart within his stout breast. I had always liked him a great deal. Philpott took him in with a swift, observant glance and touched his hat in greeting, seeming satisfied with what he saw.

'William Philpott of the *Weekly Cannon* at your service, Dr Jago. But saving the pleasantries for later, what can you tell us about this poor old creature here?'

'Only that he is certainly dead,' Piggy answered, turning his doggy gaze back down to the body. 'He has been a trifle unwell this past week, and under my care, but why he was here, and what he was doing, I can't possibly say. Perhaps the clerks can tell us more.'

The clerks duly twittered together for a minute until one of them was pushed forward. He was the best informed, having raised the alarm himself.

'I heard a lot of thumpin' and shoutin' coming from

inside the room,' he told us. 'But the door was locked and I couldn't get in. I asked what the blazes he was doin' and he shouted out that he was damned if anyone would vote and was determined to burn the poll book. I told him the book warn't in there but he wouldn't listen.'

The clerk had the poll book in his hand and gave it to me. When I opened the marbled leather covers all the elections of recent years were there, the names of the dwindling band of voters written down in neat copper-plate hand with a record of who they had voted for in a column beside the names. At the last election there had been only two electors' names remaining, Thomas Wedlock and John Scorn, but the list for this one had sprouted to add the thirty-two new electors Glynn had mentioned. The column beside this longer list of names was as yet blank, waiting to be filled in at the hustings on polling day, when each man would climb the steps to the platform, announce his choice before the whole town, and that vote be noted down in the book.

'A very rash proceeding.' Piggy was turning the body over to reveal another gnarled old face very like that of the irascible old voter on the coach with the duke. If Piggy was a St Bernard, the dead man was an aged and extremely bad-tempered Scottish terrier, having a fine beard with bushy eyebrows and grey hairs curling out of his ears. He had been lying on his stomach when we came in, hands arrested in the act of scrabbling among the papers that were scattered all around him. A large puddle of burnt documents in the corner attested both to the source of the fire and to its speedy extinction with water. To all appearances, frustrated of the poll book, Wedlock had been throwing other papers at random into the blaze.

'I tried to dash down the door, but couldn't budge it,' the clerk was going on. 'So I ran to fetch the others. When we did finally get it open, a lerrupin' puff of smoke come out which near choked us, then the flames got up and we went to fetch water.'

'Fire likes a current of air,' Philpott said knowledgeably. 'Any man knows that.'

'Then I incline to think he has choked on the smoke, that's all,' Piggy said, examining the body again and lifting arms and legs by turns. 'There is no sign of any other injury. Of course, if he was in such a rage as you say then he could have collapsed from other causes – an apoplexy, for instance, or a stroke to the heart.'

Even as he spoke he was feeling again for the old man's pulse. Though Thomas Wedlock was clearly dead, no doctor wishes to bury a man alive and must scrupulously observe the formalities to the last, a custom of which I must say I heartily approve. But no one could have survived the smoke produced by the blaze in that tiny room for long. I took in the scene again. The dead body on the floor. The papers, the mess, the puddle. Something caught my eye among the scattered sheets and I bent to retrieve a small wooden tinderbox carved with some kind of design. When I opened it to show the others, the contents were all present – tinder, striking steel and flint.

'Well, he had to start the blaze somehow,' Philpott said. 'But I suppose you should keep hold of it, my boy.'

I put it in my pocket as the undertakers came in. Piggy stood up, relieved of his professional responsibilities, and shook my hand warmly. 'Your mother told me you were in America.'

'So I was.' I followed him out of the cupboard room. 'But Mr Philpott started a feud in Philadelphia and we were obliged to leave in a hurry.'

'You will find the whole story excessively interesting, being a medical man yourself,' Philpott told him as we began to descend the stone steps to the market yard. 'I shall tell you the whole tale the moment we are at leisure.'

Piggy looked innocently pleased at this, not being yet acquainted with Philpott's various assertions that his enemy Dr Benjamin Rush had bled his patients to death and received twenty dollars from the coffin makers for each corpse. I did not think Piggy would much like to hear a doctor maligned as the slayer of thousands, nor relish Philpott's customary reference to the gentleman as *that bleeder*. Dr Rush had certainly not liked it and his action for criminal libel had led to our hurried flight from America. The subsequent catastrophe attendant on that flight still left me furious with Philpott.

Dusk had fallen while we were indoors, and the market yard was now suddenly empty. The news had filtered out to the crowd that the poll book had not been in the room and the election was therefore not in danger. The crowd had accordingly followed the body away, and the four streets which met here at the Market House were almost deserted. Only the veil of dust raised by the general commotion was evidence that a great multitude had just passed.

'And you, Piggy?' I asked him. 'What the blazes are you doing here?'

He rubbed his eyes against the dust, a gesture which made him look rather like a tired child. 'I was just returned home to Penzance when this appointment came up. The town's usual surgeon, Dr Johns, had fallen very ill and was obliged to go to Bath for the water cure. I am appointed to hold the fort until he returns in the winter.'

'A very nice position for you,' I said. 'And how long have you been here?'

'Two months or so, since Easter.' Piggy smiled at me, the tired look vanishing. 'I must say I like Helston very well, Laurence, and as you will imagine I was particularly glad to get away from Penzance.'

I knew what he meant. Piggy's father, like my own, was a difficult man. A self-made merchant with a small fleet of ships operating out of Newlyn harbour, he had ambitions for his family that had outstripped even my own father's hopes for me. To that end, my uncle had fancied to give his children classical names thus pretending to an education he himself had not had. Unfortunately, the only Greek names he knew were gleaned from his rudimentary mathematics. Euclid had renamed himself Eustace in adult life. Isosceles was scarcely a name at all, only a triangle, and the poor girl called herself Izzy whenever practicable. But Pythagoras was a dutiful son and as far as I knew, had not yet rechristened himself. Still, it had been indiscreet of me to call him Piggy in front of all the clerks.

'Well, and what now?' Philpott asked, more taken up with the death than our cousinly gossip. 'I suppose the coroner will be obliged to examine the poor old man?'

Piggy turned to him, remembering to be a doctor again. 'Yes, certainly, as in any unusual death. And there ought to be a dissection, but I don't suppose his family will consent.' He glanced across the street to the Angel, the large, handsome coaching inn where we should have disembarked if the coach hadn't been held up by the earlier mob. 'And I suppose I must tell the duke what's happened to his voter. His Grace is staying at the Angel. He has the whole first floor for himself and his retinue.'

'Sir James Burges,' I said. 'I know him.'

'Yes, indeed, along with Sir James's six-year-old son and a governess of sorts. Then there is also the duke's own wife and son. His other candidate, Charles Abbot, didn't trouble to make the journey, expecting to be elected quietly without all this fuss.'

I found I couldn't ask about Anne, especially not in

36

front of Philpott who knew all my history with her. Piggy was looking glum. 'The duke will be dreadfully displeased about Wedlock, of course.'

Philpott had been turning his eyes from one to the other of us, and now, struck by inspiration, grinned his rather wolfish grin. 'But this is splendid! Laurence, you must go with him.'

'Go with him?' I was startled. 'What does any of this have to do with me?'

'Nothing at all at present, which, as a journalist, I see is a problem to be remedied. Sir James will remember you. Go and make yourself reacquainted and offer your services if necessary. Good God, my boy, I thought we was merely to report on a case of a shocking old rotten borough, but now it is far more interesting. I can even see the headline: *Blue Helston now a Scarlet Town*. And you acquainted with half the persons involved! Yes, yes, 'tis heaven sent, my boy.'

I dare say he expected me to refuse, having been so surly an apprentice since our departure from America, but my heart fairly choked me at the chance of seeing Anne again so soon. Was it possible I could go to her now? How would she look when she saw me for the first time? And what if I found out she was truly married to George Canning and altogether lost to me? These thoughts ran through my mind in a confusion of hope and despair. 'But I parted from Sir James in highly unpleasant circumstances,' I said.

'Then get your revenge by making use of him, as he once used you.'

It would be better, after all, to know the worst. Better to cut off my hopes before they could grow too tall. And, I confess, quite apart from meeting Anne, I knew it would vex Sir James exceedingly to be talked of in the press, and for that alone the idea was agreeable. Perhaps to Philpott's surprise I nodded my head meekly.

He looked about him at the darkening street. 'Meanwhile, I suppose I must collect my family and find us some accommodations in the town.'

'You will fail in that,' Piggy said. 'With the election there's not a room to be had, except for Dr Johns' empty bedchamber, which is very small and will not accommodate a family, I'm afraid – though you can have it, if you'd like it, Laurence.'

'There's a good moon.' I glanced at that orb now rising above the rooftops. 'Hire a cart from the Red Lion, Philpott, and go to the farm. Give my mother a kiss from me.'

Philpott looked rather put out to be banished, but he could hardly leave his family to sleep on the streets and he reluctantly agreed. He promised to have the cart drop my luggage at Dr Johns' house, which Piggy pointed out, a shabby but conveniently placed dwelling on Church Street just across the road from the Market House and Guildhall. Then we parted, and with the blood pounding a little louder than usual in my ears, I followed Piggy across the wide sweep of Coinagehall Street and through the archway into the courtyard of the Angel Inn.

The courtyard was lit by lamplight from the inn's back windows, and the knee-high well lurking uncovered in the centre of the yard was only faintly visible. We carefully skirted this black hole to perdition and climbed the flight of back steps to the inn. The duke and his party had quit the streets while we had been examining Thomas Wedlock's body, and when we arrived on the first-floor landing, we were met by a hubbub of voices. Loud female interchange and deeper male conversation, punctuated by shrill infant screams, all conducted at once, all emanating from the same room, and all apparently oblivious of each other's competing claims, except in a generally rising volume.

It was the sound of fashionable society, which I knew so well from my former London days, and I glanced down with sudden doubt at my travel-creased clothes. But it was too late now, for there being no one to announce us, Piggy was already scratching at the door as a dog might. His knock being far too apologetic to be heard, and the hope that Anne was sitting just on the other side of that door being a torture to my nerves, I lost patience and took my own knuckles to the door with a will. The conversation inside subsiding at the very same moment, my hammering fell into the silence like that of a bailiff come to confiscate the silver.

'Good God, how discourteous,' the duke's voice honked

from inside. 'Well, well, come in, whoever you are; come in, I say.'

THE OPENING DOOR revealed a very large, very comfortable room, which stretched the whole length of the inn and had fine sash windows looking down on lamplit Coinagehall Street below. There was a crib in the corner, with a boy of about six years old leaning over the occupant, at present only to be glimpsed as a writhing set of blankets. Every face in the room turned at our entrance. The plump, beribboned woman I had seen earlier in the street was doubtless the duchess. Dressed in the same sumptuous blue silk gown, she was perhaps five and twenty and very handsome, her fine bosom projecting like that of a figurehead on one of my uncle's merchant ships.

Anne was sitting beside her. She looked hardly older – it was, after all, only eighteen months since we had parted – but she looked wearier, somehow, and very thin. Her dark hair was caught up to reveal the slender neck I had once kissed. Her dress was a good deal plainer than the duchess's. Naturally Her Grace must always be pre-eminent, but would George Canning's wife be allowed to look so drab? My eyes moved to her hands, but they were clasped together so tightly I could not see if she wore a wedding ring. Her knuckles were white. At last, gathering my courage, I looked into the huge, dark eyes that stained her pale face. She was staring at me as if I too were some kind of ghost or dream, but whether come upon her happily or unhappily I couldn't tell. The only certain thing was that she had not lost the old intensity of her stare, which had always made me feel as much a specimen for examination as a man to be loved.

Piggy had made his bow – as I suppose I had also done without noticing – and he was now advancing on Sir James and the duke by the unlit fire grate at the other end of the room. I fancied Sir James's moon face also turned a little pale at the sight of me, an unwelcome apparition from the past sprung on him without warning.

'Yes, yes,' the duke said in his squawking voice, and beckoned Piggy over. 'Tell us everything. Wedlock is dead, we hear, dead as a doorknob?'

'I'm afraid so, Your Grace.'

If Anne was deadly pale, Piggy had turned a little pink. He adopted a dignified manner that might have made me laugh in any other circumstances as he padded over to stand before the duke obediently. 'It appears Wedlock had decided to burn the poll book, Your Grace, and after setting the blaze he collapsed from the inhalation of smoke. He had unwisely locked himself inside the room and soon succumbed to the fumes.'

I found I dared not risk another look at Anne until my heart had slowed, so instead I fixed my eyes on the duke as he calmly tapped his snuffbox. 'And the poll book?'

This did not seem to me to be the main concern, but Piggy assured him that it was safe.

'Hmm.' The duke took a pinch of snuff and scowled. 'Well, I am one elector the lighter, it seems. Fortunately, John Scorn will stick to me, come what may. Mrs Bellingham insisted we bring the old creature back here, after the meeting. He looked so shocked she thought he might die too, which would have been highly inconvenient. Highly inconvenient, I say. But we fed him brandy and instructed him on his duty. No harm is done, I suppose, no great harm at all.'

'Except to Thomas Wedlock,' Piggy ventured gently, but apparently, having let down the duke by getting himself killed, the old man was not to be mourned. The duke was exactly as I remembered him from long ago: ill-tempered and remarkably callous.

'I have been advising you for weeks to woo the mayor's thirty-two new voters,' the duchess said, and I allowed my eyes to turn back towards her – and to Anne at her side. Anne's colour had returned. She was flushed now and had unclasped her hands. She was smoothing her skirts in a nervous gesture and I saw she wore no rings at all. Again my heart thumped into my throat. I thought I was probably deliriously happy, though it seemed probable I might die of the feeling before I could properly enjoy it.

'And now see!' the duchess was going on. 'Even if Parliament decides for you and Scorn this time, there is only one of him and he is so very old. This will certainly be his last poll, and then where will you be?'

The duke didn't answer. The duchess frowned at him and then startled violently as the infant in the crib emitted a sudden piercing shriek. She shook her curls and her bosom in a comprehensive quiver and turned her fine eyes to Piggy. 'Sidney has been squealing like this all day, Dr Jago, and there's no settling him. And yet he has no fever. No coming teeth. And Mrs Bellingham has been walking him up and down and maintains there's no griping either. I wish you would look at him while you are here.'

'Gladly, Your Grace.'

Piggy crossed the lofty room to the crib. After a moment's hesitation, Anne followed him, and then with far less hesitation I followed her. When we came up, Piggy had bent to exchange looks with the infant in the cradle. It seemed pleased enough at the novelty of a new face and smiled up at him gummily. Piggy put out a stout finger which it grasped with affable goodwill. The six-year-old child who had been keeping the infant company retired to a small distance and watched us.

The duke had gone to the window and was now looking down into the dark street. 'Camping like God-damned gypsies, all crowded together, that's what does it, Kate. How can *anyone* settle, crowded together as we are? How can *anyone* find repose, I say, camping like God-damned gypsies?' I had forgotten the duke's habit

43

of saying everything twice, as if it made his observations twice as true. He was doubtless too great to have had anyone disabuse him of the notion. 'Lushington is better accommodated, I expect,' he added with some venom. 'Far better accommodated than we are, I don't doubt.'

Sir James answered in his smooth, soothing voice that brought the quiet confines of the Foreign Office back to my mind in a tumble of memories. Old tapestry, snuff, the smoking fire in the kitchen where we clerks had made cups of tea. 'Lushington *is* in comfort, up with Glynn at The Willows, your Grace, but only because he is sick and in need of attention.'

'Damn them both.' The duke sat himself down again and began to bite his fingernails. 'Damn them both to hell, I say.'

Meanwhile, the infant patient had transferred Piggy's finger to its mouth and was chewing experimentally, its blue eyes ruminative and unfocused. Piggy ran his free hand gently across the downy head and the infant smiled again and squirmed like a caterpillar.

'I never thought to see you here,' I said to Anne quietly. We were so close that I could see fine frowning lines between her eyebrows that I did not remember from former times.

'Nor I you.' Her voice was scarcely more than a whisper, as if she feared to be overheard. In all our previous acquaintance she had been utterly self-possessed, to the point that I had sometimes doubted she owned a human heart. Tonight she seemed more real, more flesh and blood. I had certainly never known her so discomposed. She had gone pale again.

'You are here with the duchess?' I asked. When I left England she had still been living with her mother and stepfather, old Aust, the Permanent Under-Secretary to the Foreign Office. I supposed she must have met the duchess through Aust's connections in the Ministry.

But she shook her head briefly. 'With Sir James. His wife is confined, and I offered to come as a kind of governess to his little boy.' At my look she shook her head again, as if she did not presently want to tell me more. 'It is complicated, Laurence.'

There was a jaundiced tinge to her complexion that put me horribly in mind of the Yellow Fever we had left in America. 'You look ill,' I said.

'And you look grubby.' She was vexed. 'Your face is dirty and your horrible old eyeglasses are smeared. I dare say if you took them off the world would look a deal more wholesome.'

I did as I was bid, and realised she was right. The green lenses had combined with the yellow lamplight to make everything look bilious. 'You still look tired,' I said.

'And you still excel at gallantry, it appears.'

I looked away at the duke who was still droning on. 'Abbot should have shown his face here,' he was saying. 'Shown his face, I say, it being his first election as my candidate. I would have had him explain the *felicific calculus* to those tomfool electors.'

Sir James looked mildly enquiring. 'The *feli*— what, Your Grace?'

'His brother's theory, his stepbrother Bentham, the philosopher, you know. A most cunning *algorithm* to decide all political questions.'

'An algorithm?' Sir James now looked something between amused and interested. 'From the Latin, *algorismus*, I suppose? But that is a mathematical term, not a philosophical one, is it not, Your Grace?'

'Quite so.' The duke looked a little more cheerful. 'Bentham thinks the greatest happiness of the greatest number is the only consideration, and to be decided coolly in a mathematical spirit by answering a number of essential questions.'

Sir James took out his snuffbox and concealed his astonishment at this democratical notion with a raised eyebrow. 'And how do you apply his method to our present crisis? If it is a mere matter of figures then thirty-two is certainly a far larger number than two – or should I now say, after Wedlock's death, *one* – and we are therefore defeated.'

'Oh – but that is too simple. They ought to consider the wider reputation of the franchise, which they seek to throw into all confusion by challenging my patronage. Not to mention the good of the country, surely to be best served by men of rank like ourselves, Sir James, not that merchant adventurer Lushington.'

Sir James nodded dutifully at this cunning interpretation of Bentham's cool mathematical method, but a quiet yelp at my elbow made me turn to discover that a youth of about fifteen had appeared among us unseen and was now dealing the six-year-old child in the corner a discreet clout about the head.

'It's this little brute you're after,' he announced. 'He's been pinching Sidney all day when nobody's looking. Hence the tiresome squawks.'

3

THE YOUTH BORE A striking resemblance to the duke, and I surmised him probably the son and heir as he grasped the six-year-old child by the ear and presented him for our inspection. We all bent our eyes on the party thus accused who, when released, rubbed his ear and looked thoughtful. He seemed desirous of sloping off to Anne's protection, but Piggy detained him with his large paw. 'Remind me of your name, young man.'

'Charles,' the child muttered with a cautious set to his mouth. 'Charles Burges.'

'Charles Burges, *sir*,' Anne prompted, but the child ignored her.

'And you have been poking young Sidney here, for your own amusement?' Piggy asked.

Charles Burges maintained a veritable politician's silence and Piggy glanced up at the youth who looked ready to clout him again. 'Can you not entertain the child, somehow? Can you not take him out about the town for amusement?'

'I am hardly his nursemaid – poor Mrs Bellingham takes on that task, God help her. And I am quite as bored as he is.' The youth grimaced at the child. 'Perhaps I'll torment *you*, Charles. See how you like it.'

I glanced at Anne, pretty much unable to imagine the name *nursemaid* ever attached to her. She was not soft or motherly, and never had been. She was all intellect and beauty, despite the tired pallor I had been tactless enough to mention.

'How long does your father intend to stay in town?' Piggy was asking the youth.

'Until Tuesday when the election is over. Then back to London, thank God.'

I looked at Anne again. Was she also to disappear after only three days? I was evidently forgiven for my earlier discourteous remarks, since she nodded at me cordially and this time when she spoke it was in the old cool, clear tone I remembered.

'Yes, we will certainly all go. Sir James will be required back in the Department whether he succeeds in the vote or not. Any replacement must be groomed for office, you know.' Her confident acquaintance with Ministry matters had not deserted her whatever else might have changed.

Meanwhile, the youth had finally noticed me. 'You have not introduced me to your friend, Dr Jago.'

'Forgive me, sir. Let me present my cousin, Mr Laurence Jago, formerly of the Foreign Office.'

The youth regarded me with a look of new, dawning interest. 'Are you another emissary sent down to mind my father? Make sure he behaves himself?'

'No, sir,' I said, but knowing the duke as we all did, I couldn't help smiling. 'In fact, I only arrived from America this evening, and bumped into Pi— uh, Pythagoras, quite by chance. I came with him here to remember myself to Mrs Bellingham and to Sir James, of course, who was formerly my superior.'

I thought Sir James was listening, even though his face was turned to the duke. The youth looked even more interested than before. 'Well, I am George Osborne, the duke's son, and have been dragged to this godforsaken place for the sake of this absurd election.'

'I have gathered it is more contentious than usual,' I said.

'And therefore of great general interest in the town, as I expect you have noticed. Are you a gambling man, Mr Jago?'

'No, sir, I am not.' At least, I added silently, not with money, only far too many times with my life and reputation.

'What a pity. The whole town is convulsed in an orgy of betting on the outcome. If you venture down to the Blue Anchor, they have a chalkboard with all the current odds displayed.'

We had all taken our eyes off young Charles Burges for a moment, and the infant Sidney split the air with another horrible shriek. The child was clearly immune to Piggy's moral reproaches, or to George Osborne's threats, and if Anne was supposed to be minding him she had been too interested in our conversation to remember it. I fished in my pocket and produced a farthing, which I held out to the child's gaze so close he went cross-eyed. 'If you desist from this obnoxious practice, Master Burges, I will give you this farthing tomorrow, a sum which, spent wisely at the confectioner's, will be enough to make you sick. Is it a bargain?'

The child looked from me to Piggy to Anne, and then to George Osborne, as if calculating how this arrangement was to be policed, and if he could have his farthing and torment the infant anyway, an outcome probably the most satisfactory to his mind.

'I will watch you,' George said, with a hideous grimace. 'I will be eyes and ears for Mr Jago.'

Just then the duchess looked up at us where we clustered around the crib. 'Well, Doctor, have you made a diagnosis?'

Piggy recurred at once to his former, dignified tone, so promptly that I wondered if they taught it at the hospital. 'Only that your own was quite correct, Your Grace. I can find nothing amiss with little Sidney. Perhaps he merely wishes to make his presence remembered to the company with these repeated ejaculations.'

At this juncture there was another knock at the door, brisk and businesslike this time, and the coroner came in. I knew him vaguely from former days, and he remembered me, too, his eye pausing upon me as he took us all in. He gave me the briefest nod of recognition.

'Well, Roskruge,' the duke said, 'is it all settled? Have you made your report?'

'No, Your Grace.' The coroner was apologetic. 'In fact, I am here in search of Dr Jago, to come with me for another look at the corpse. The Wedlock family tell me the old man had been under Dr Jago's care this past week and I'd have him explain all the possible causes of death, and which one seems most likely, for me to set out in my statement.'

'Take him and welcome,' the duke said carelessly. 'I'm sure he's no use to me.'

'And is that Mr Laurence Jago I see with the doctor?' Roskruge turned a little less official and a little more friendly. 'Dear me, sir, it must be ten years since I last saw you.'

'Ten years or more,' I answered. 'I am here to remember myself to Sir James, whom I used to serve in the Foreign Office.'

The duke cast me the merest glance, but I was rather too much of an insect for his taste. Sir James, meeting my eye for the first time since that initial, embarrassed look we had exchanged on my first entry, appeared to have reconciled himself to my presence and to have decided to make use of me as Philpott had hoped. 'Being peculiarly interested in the matter, I suppose it will be in order for His Grace to send a representative. Perhaps Mr Jago could go with you.'

'Certainly,' the coroner said. Anne looked at me and, for the first time since I came in, the ghost of a smile hovered about her mouth. Perhaps she was thinking as I was, that miles of ocean and months of separation were as nothing to the Ministry, which – supposing it found me useful – would likely pick me up as if it had never dropped me. Or perhaps she was merely pleased to see me restored in some wise to Sir James's favour. Whatever it was, I clung to that ghostly smile, and at that moment I would probably have jumped into the sea off Nare Head if Sir James had directed me to do it.

THOMAS WEDLOCK HAD lived at the bottom of Coinagehall Street, opposite the Coinage Hall itself, where the miners brought their heavy ingots of tin into town, each quarter day, to be assayed by the Duchy's commissioners and to pay the duty on the quantity of good metal stamped.

When we came in to Wedlock's house, his small family had gathered. They already knew Piggy and the coroner very well and showed us into the best parlour, where the old man had been laid out on the table and his terrier hair and whiskers combed into an unnatural sleekness. He still looked rather fierce, but the trait did not seem to have extended to his successors. His son, Thomas Wedlock the younger, was a man of about sixty, a faded and more tousled version of the same terrier type. The dead man's grandson, William, was a long-haired fidgety young man with a pink, questing face that put me in mind of a newborn puppy. The puppy was dressed in clerical black and introduced himself as the curate at the parish church. His mother, old Wedlock's daughter-in-law, wept into his shoulder throughout our whole interview.

Piggy bent over the dead body with gentle courtesy, removing the pennies from the eyelids to lift them and examine the dead eyes beneath. He looked for a long moment and then closed them again, replacing the coins. 'No sign of apoplexy in his gaze,' he said and Roskruge made a note. Next Piggy held the lamp up to the dead face, paying close attention to the hairs that curled from the unmoving nostrils. 'They are a little scorched,' he said to the coroner, 'which suggests he breathed in some smoke. But whether enough to asphyxiate him, I cannot say without an internal examination. Nor can I diagnose *angina pectoris* without a dissection.' He turned to the watching family, his face apologetically mournful. 'I know you will not like it, but if Mr Roskruge is to do his duty, we really ought to open the body and examine the heart and the lungs. Without doing so, I cannot say for certain exactly how he died and whether it had anything to do with his indisposition this past week, which I was treating.'

'What does it signify?' Thomas Wedlock the younger looked weary. 'He's dead, and with this spring warmth, he won't last long. They undertake to bury him tomorrow afternoon, if the grave be dug quick enough, for the whole house will soon stink if we tarry.'

At this the weeping woman's shoulders heaved even more convulsively.

'It need not delay the funeral,' Piggy said, scratching the back of his neck awkwardly but looking kind. 'I could undertake the business at once, you know, and still bury him tomorrow. It would be a kindness to me if you would permit it, for I feel some anxiety that I may have missed something, even though his health seemed better when I was with him this afternoon.'

The weeping woman gave a kind of strangled cry. 'Ye'll not slice him up for your own diversion.'

'Be reasonable, Mother.' The curate's pink face squirmed anxiously. 'Do you not want to know how Grandfer died?'

'What's the use?' the woman asked, wiping her eyes and clutching hold of the curate's hand. 'For the Lord's sake, he was eighty-four.'

Her husband nodded his agreement and the curate looked at us apologetically from under the curtain of long hair that hung across his forehead. The matter seeming to be closed, I remembered the tinderbox I had found among the papers and fished it out from my pocket. I handed it to the curate. 'This was his, I think. I am so sorry for your grief.'

The young man looked at the tinderbox rather blankly, and then handed it to his father. 'This ain't Grandfer's, is it?'

His father gave it the merest glance. 'Never seed it afore.'

It was at that moment, I suppose, that the case subtly shifted in my mind to something more curious than it had first appeared, but no one else seemed particularly struck and I took the thing back from Wedlock's son and put it in my pocket.

Roskruge was now in consultation with Piggy. The family were quite within their rights to object to a dissection, and his official mind had already moved smoothly on. 'I suppose we might look into old Wedlock's movements today,' he said. 'Find out why he wanted to burn the poll book at all.' He looked at Wedlock's faded son. 'I don't suppose he told you of his intention to do it, or you would have stopped him?'

'I hadn't the first notion,' the man said in the same defeated tone as before. 'But he always had his foolish quignogs.'

Roskruge frowned. 'And I am run off my feet,' he said, 'while the sheriff and his men are too busy going about the county supervising the election to look into this.'

'I could make inquiry,' I offered. 'You know my family,

sir, and I have done similar work for the Government, as Sir James will tell you if you ask him.'

The coroner frowned again but looked a fraction more cheerful at the prospect of getting out of the trouble himself. 'I dare say that will do,' he said. 'Where will you begin?'

'Perhaps with this tinderbox.' I showed it to him again. 'It likely started the fire but seems not to have belonged to Wedlock after all. Therefore someone else may have lent it to him, or they may know something about it.'

Roskruge nodded. 'Keep it, sir, and show it about the town. Any other witness would be very useful – if such a one exists.'

And then, at length, and by now dog-tired, Piggy and I were permitted to trudge back up Coinagehall Street past the Angel to the Market House and Piggy's surgery. In my eagerness I would have gone in to report at once, but the duke's windows were in darkness and I would have to wait until tomorrow before I could see Anne again.

A large sign had been pinned to the wall of the Market House, and the bold letters were easy to pick out, even by lamplight.

Toby, *The Celebrated Sapient Hog*

Will Perform for the Town Of Helston
at the Generous Expense of
His Grace, The Duke Of Leeds.

There will be an Evening Entertainment in
the Angel Inn's Assembly Room on
Saturday 28 May
(Entry: Half A Crown)
And a Noon Performance Open to All on
Monday 30 May in Coinagehall Street.

Toby has Performed throughout Europe
and Recently Attended at Windsor for the
Entertainment of the Entire Royal Family.

So that was what the duke had meant by superior entertainments for election day. They had heard of the Sapient Hog even in Philadelphia.

Piggy crossed the street, unlocked the surgery door, and led me into a dim hall that smelled distinctly medicinal. The dispensing room lay to our right and Piggy turned in for a moment to lay down his bag on a bench beneath shelves and shelves of physic jars. From where I loitered in the doorway I could see laudanum on the shelf, that most sovereign remedy for pain. But I had fought that demon in America, and won, and could now look on the large bottle almost with equanimity.

After that, Piggy led me into a rather dismal masculine parlour with bulging, yellow-papered walls and a dark brown ceiling stained by years of pipe smoke. He turned up the lamp and his shadow blossomed across the ceiling as he went to the decanter and poured us both a brandy. It was very welcome after such a long day and I would have settled forthwith in the armchair by the empty fire grate except that I had not eaten anything since leaving Falmouth and was ravenously hungry. I thought of the Philpotts by now arrived at the farm and of all the repast Mother would set forth for her prodigal son when I finally followed them home. But for now I found my way to Piggy's kitchen, a neat and tidy apartment built on to the back of the cottage, where the fire was slumbering but still hot enough to toast a plate of saffron buns I found in the pantry. I lathered them with soft butter, turned slightly rancid from the warmth, and took the plate back through to the parlour.

4

EVENING, VERY LATE

I HAD BEEN GONE perhaps twenty minutes and, when I came back in, Piggy was already half asleep on an extremely ugly horsehair sofa. He roused himself to take a glistening bun from the generous pile on the plate I offered him. Then the door creaked open and a black cat walked in. For the merest moment I expected it to be Mr Gibbs, my old dog, and when it wasn't I felt the usual pang of grief and worry I had been feeling every hour since we had left him behind in Philadelphia.

Since Philpott had left him behind.

It was the one thing I had bid him be sure of, when we made our hurried flight to the ship. I had been out in the town when Philpott sent word of our imminent arrest and I sent word back to him at our house on the corner of Market and Ninth Street to be sure to bring Mr Gibbs and his old leather leash from where it hung behind the door. Philpott had brought the leash but forgotten the dog, a fact I only discovered when the ship had slipped anchor and we were halfway down Delaware Bay. Philpott still maintained, all these weeks later, that six children and a wife had been enough on his mind, but I had not yet forgiven him. And if my desperate letter and bag of coin sent back with the first ship we crossed did not bring Mr Gibbs to me, I never would.

The cat jumped on the mantelpiece and looked down at us. I held out my finger, coated in butter, and it scratched me.

'Bitterweed,' Piggy said through a mouthful of saffron bun, as if that explained everything. 'She belongs to the doctor and I suppose she misses him.'

Bitterweed began vigorously licking at her flank.

'I have had many cats,' Piggy remarked apropos of not much. 'Demelza, when I was a young lad.'

'I remember her.' As a child I had often visited Piggy's family in their tall house on Market Jew Street in Penzance. His older brother had thought tormenting a small half-French weakling like myself an amusing pastime. Piggy had always stood up for me, God bless him.

'I think I chose to be a doctor the day she was run down,' he said. 'I was dreadfully sad but fascinated with her injuries, nonetheless. The glimpse inside her broken body, you know.'

'No, I don't know,' I said, munching on a bun, the warm butter running through my fingers. 'I have seen a good many injuries myself in recent years and have never felt the slightest inclination to poke about inside them.'

Piggy smiled at me in the dim lamplight. 'You were always squeamish. Remember when Euclid put that spider in your shoe?'

I certainly remembered my own shameful screams that had made Euclid chortle. Piggy had dried my tears and put the monstrous spider carefully outside under a plant pot.

'My father forbade all animals after that,' Piggy went on, still thinking about his infernal cats. But then, as I had just been brooding on Mr Gibbs I supposed I was no better. 'Father was right,' he went on, 'our street was far too busy, so after that I had to make do with the schoolmaster's cat, Mordecai. He would greet me every morning, and then go and sit in a cupboard for the rest of the lesson.'

'A hermit?' I suggested, absentmindedly licking a drop of errant butter from my wrist.

'Possibly. Or as bored with the Greek as I was.' Piggy poured us both another brandy, which agreed surprisingly well with the sweet bread. Either that, or I was very hungry.

'And then there was Mrs Tompkins, in London,' he added. 'My landlady's cat while I studied at the hospital. A harlot, if ever there was one, but the kittens were very sweet.'

'And you are just lately returned from London?' I asked him. 'Is this appointment your first?'

He nodded. 'My first in sole practice. I have worked under several medical men throughout my studies, of course. But I feared I was to kick my heels in Penzance, waiting for a position, so I was very glad to take this opportunity when it presented itself.' He looked at me over the rim of his brandy glass. 'And you, Laurence? Did I hear you left London in some trouble?'

'I'd tell you the whole story,' I answered, 'except it would take all night. Suffice it to say, I found out some things about my masters best left undiscovered, and they got rid of me. I went to America with Philpott and am now returned.'

That was all I wanted to say about the past and Piggy did not press me further. 'And now?' he asked. 'What are your plans? Do you mean to be a journalist like Philpott?'

'No one could be like him,' I said. 'And being Philpott's apprentice has turned out to be a bruising, madcap existence.' Alone at sea without Mr Gibbs, I had discovered an aching emptiness within me, at my long, homeless existence first in London and then in America, which I realised the dog had always filled with his unquestioning persuasion that we belonged together. 'But in fact,' I said slowly, thinking aloud, 'I rather wonder if the Ministry might take me back? You saw Sir James bid me act for him tonight as if I had never been away.'

'I did see,' Piggy said. 'I also saw you obeyed him. You are minded to let bygones be bygones, then, and return to them?'

'I would not have said so. Not until tonight. But that lady with the duchess – Anne Bellingham …'

He was watching me, quizzically. 'There is some history there?'

'A long one. Twelve years and more. She never thought me good enough for her. But she said she was acting as governess to Sir James's boy. Something has changed in her life.'

'And you'd have her, even though she would not have you until now?'

'Yes,' I said. 'She knows everything about me, Piggy. More than I wish she did. And if, knowing all that, she still wanted me—' I broke off. Tonight she had chided and smiled at me by turns, just as she always had. In previous times I had hoped she scolded me because she loved me. Perhaps now she scolded me because she didn't. More than a year had passed since we had parted and so much had happened to me she did not know. In the same period she had clearly lost her eminent admirer, Canning, and who knew what else might have changed? I was getting ahead of myself.

'But tell me about Helston,' I said. 'I recognised a good many faces, but things have certainly changed, not least with all this new election fever.'

Piggy had been watching me with kind attention, but now looked glum again, and I remembered how he had always hated arguments, always been the peacemaker among us boys. 'The fuss will die down after the polls

65

close on Monday,' he said. 'Or at least, I hope it will. The whole place has split down the middle between Mohawks and Cherokees – the mayor, and the duke. I've never known such bad blood, and why most of the town should care at all is beyond me. But they have all picked sides and won't be reasoned with.'

'The old way is indefensible, surely,' I said. 'The idea the duke pays two ancient old men to vote as he wishes.'

'Yet common enough.'

'And therefore all the more scandalous – especially now he is reduced to only one elector. The whole idea is laughable.'

'I would agree, except that the mayor is such an unpleasant man,' Piggy answered. He hesitated for a moment as if on the verge of a confidence, but then only said, 'For all Glynn's pious talk about corruption, the duke is right, I am sure. The mayor merely wants the duke's power for himself. He's no democrat either, and his choice of candidate—' He broke off and then shrugged. 'Well, suffice it to say the chairman of the East India Company is just as useless to the town as Sir James Burges or the duke's dogsbody at school. For Lushington himself it is merely a stepping stone to Parliament. They none of them care a fig for Helston or its people.' He emptied his glass. 'Poor old Wedlock. However he died – by suffocation or his heart giving out – it was ridiculous rage about this vote that finished him either way.'

I took the tinderbox from my pocket and looked at

it again. It had a dragon carved into the lid – quite a common design for an article meant to make fire – but this dragon looked as bad tempered as the duke's old men. 'John Scorn seemed as fierce as the devil,' I said, 'and even dead, I shouldn't have liked to cross Thomas Wedlock.'

'Cornwall used to be a lawless place.' Piggy rubbed his eyes again. 'It bred such men.'

'You don't think …' I showed him the tinderbox. 'If this didn't belong to Wedlock …' I hesitated again. 'And with so much bad blood, as you say …'

He shook his head at me as he caught my drift. 'Wild talk surely, young Laurence. You are quite as fanciful as Miss Glynn.'

'Miss Glynn?'

'The mayor's niece.' A sudden bashful colour in his cheeks made me smile.

'Oh yes? Do I surmise the excessively fanciful Miss Glynn is also very beautiful?'

'You probably saw her,' he said, still blushing. 'She was at the meeting, dressed in red.'

I did remember the vivid black-haired girl and looked at Piggy with new respect. 'Good Lord. And is she …?'

I was going to say, *your intended*, but he thought I meant something else. 'Yes, yes, she is Glynn's niece; so you see though I dislike the man, I must appease him. And so it goes across the board. The town is divided, but tendrils run through it like fungus, connecting us all one

67

to the other in deeper ways.' He nodded at the tinder-box. 'So to talk of violence against Thomas Wedlock is as unlikely as it is reckless.'

I wasn't sure I agreed with him, having witnessed more than one man resort to unlikely violence. I was still turning the tinderbox in my fingers and Piggy's eyes were still fixed on it.

'It probably fell out of a clerk's pocket when they were dousing the fire,' he said. 'There is no need to look for trouble, Laurence, or make this unpleasant division in the town any worse than it already is. We shall bury the old man decently tomorrow and the whole unfortunate business will be closed.'

I could have argued further but in truth I was suddenly worn out by our long weeks at sea and all these subsequent excitements since landing. Piggy propelled me to the absent doctor's room, a rather cramped chamber with scarcely space for a bed and therefore, as Piggy had said, quite unfit for Philpott's numerous family. I hoped they had arrived safely at my mother's farm. And then I wondered what Anne would say to me tomorrow, when I took my report of tonight's business to Sir James.

How extraordinary was the fact of her appearance here in Helston! And could she really be reduced to the rank of a governess, though her mother had previously married a Murray of Dunmore, and only a year ago she herself had almost married a rising politician? How could it have happened? Had her stepfather, old Aust, gone bankrupt, or had some other calamity befallen them? Whether it was some wretched change that had left her looking tired and rather sallow – whatever she tried to blame on my eyeglasses – was a question only she could answer.

SATURDAY
28 MAY 1796

He turnd his face unto the wall,
As deadlye pangs he fell in

5

MORNING

WE HAD SCARCELY broken our fast before Philpott was at the door. His eagerness for the political story would have brought him back early enough from the farm, but my mother had brought him even earlier. She was delighted to see me and furiously angry all at the same time as she came in and shook her grey-streaked curls free of her bonnet. Mrs Philpott followed in behind her, as quiet and stoic as ever, but looking about at Dr Johns' damp cottage with a good deal of dismay.

Mother embraced me and then stood back. I might have been a small weakly child when Piggy's brother tormented me, but I had shot up like a bean plant over subsequent years and now the top of her head only came to my chin. '*Mon Dieu*,' she said. 'I have been in such terror all night, thinking you dead in a ditch with a broken neck from riding home in the dark.'

My mother had a habit of imagining all possible mishaps to those she loved, and I feared my peripatetic life across oceans had provided her with ample material for such alarms. I thought I must have inherited the tendency myself, for since losing Mr Gibbs, I had indulged in similarly lurid fears on his behalf. Was he still locked in the house on Market and Ninth? Had he starved to death? And, if not, was anyone attending to his rheumatism?

Mother was still frowning up at me. 'Mr Philpott said you would stay in town, but I did not believe him. Why do you listen to him like such a meek little lamb?'

I said I didn't quite take her meaning.

'Why did you not come home, instead of sleeping on your cousin's floor? It is a nonsense.'

I remarked that given her anxieties for my neck riding in the dark, I had in fact shown remarkable prudence and that, moreover, Piggy had provided me with a very comfortable bed.

'But your sister longs to see you, and the boys, too. When are you coming home?'

'I have promised the coroner to look into a death,' I said. 'And Sir James, my old superior from Whitehall, has also bid me represent the duke in the matter. Moreover, it will furnish Mr Philpott with a good story for his paper. There is the funeral this afternoon and I must ask questions around the town. When all that is finished—'

'You mean to work again for those monsters? Those

scoundrels who drove you away to America? You will come back at the click of their fingers like a little dog?'

I wasn't sure if it was worse to be a little dog or a little lamb. I had hoped for the fatted calf, but it did not look likely to be forthcoming from my mother so long as I did the bidding of other folks than her. But it had been partly on her account that everything had gone so badly against me in London, since I had foolishly concealed my French blood and consequent fluency in that language. It had not seemed to matter until war broke out between our nations. Afterwards, it had been too late to confess; for by then my French sympathies had led me into other, more serious indiscretions than merely reading a message or two I decoded at my stool in the Downing Street garret.

'I have been thinking about it all night,' she said, 'and I remembered an advertisement in the *First and Last* this week, for an opening at Wallis's Bank on Cross Street. It is but a clerkship, Laurence, but of course a well-qualified man would soon rise to a senior position.'

I was purposefully obtuse. 'You are thinking of it for Anthony?' Last time I had seen my youngest brother he had been all elbows and knees, a raw sixteen.

'Anthony, nonsense,' Mother said. 'Don't be provoking. You know quite well what I am thinking.'

'And is this the bank that was refusing your mortgage two years ago, on account of your nationality?'

She tutted at me. 'No indeed. That was Mr Grylls, who

knows nothing about anything and was most disagree-able. I took my business to Mr Wallis directly, and he has been very kind. I pay him scarcely above five per cents.'

I didn't think this sum much less than Mr Grylls had been demanding in the weeks before I left England. But I held my peace and instead for the merest moment let myself imagine how it would be to play banker in the town. You would know everyone's business, and hold their chances of success both in commerce and in family life in your hands. You could encourage the deserving and punish the wicked – or at least, just so long as the withdrawal of their deposits didn't bring down the bank. If I hadn't seen Anne, I might have been tempted.

'You should go to see Mr Wallis on Monday when the bank opens and find out about it,' Mother said. 'It would do no harm, you know. You need not take the position if you do not like it. But I have always thought Cross Street the finest part of town, with some very nice rooms.'

I smiled at her scheming face and kissed her cheek. 'I'll think about it.'

Piggy's housemaid was now coming in with another plate of edibles. Tirza Ivey was a middle-aged woman in wooden clogs who had battered about the house all morning like a trapped bumblebee. She had remarked with some meaning on the missing plate of saffron buns at breakfast and Piggy, with rather a dereliction of the benevolence I remembered, had lost no time in blaming me for their disappearance. Mother sat down and poured herself the last cup of tea in the pot before handing it back to Tirza. Mrs Philpott was still loitering in the doorway as if she feared the damp might get into her bones if she came further in.

But it turned out that this new provision of edibles was only an excuse for Tirza to get a look at Philpott, whose paper was famous even in Helston. 'Eh, that poor Thomas Wedlock,' she said to him after she had set down the plate on the table. 'If you want to know anything about that old man for your paper, just you come to me, sir. Known him since I were three-year-old and had to bat him off since I were fifteen. 'E were sweet on me, see, and eager to wed me. Yes, yes, I know all about him.'

Philpott looked at me over Tirza's head with a raised eyebrow, but though recent events might have reconciled me to coming home from America, I was still resolved to be angry with him about everything else.

'And t'other old elector, John Scorn,' Tirza was adding, 'he was sweet on me too, but I thought both of 'em far too old and told 'em I could do better. They warn't best pleased, but they loved me too well to turment me.'

'And did you?' Mrs Philpott asked in her gruff voice, finally venturing into the cramped and hideous parlour. 'Did you do better than them?'

Tirza smiled, revealing a very considerable lack of teeth. 'John Ivey was a good man, God rest him. But I don't believe I shall consent to wed again.' She poked

Philpott in the chest. 'But just you mind, I do know all about both those old buggers. Bless me, I feared they would lock horns, so I did, being both so set on having me.'

We all looked at Tirza, our collective imaginations probably defeated by this picture. 'But I would never have had either of 'em,' she added. 'Fierce as stags, they were, and han't the first idea o' fun.'

'And have they argued since?' Philpott asked.

'Argued!' Tirza looked blank. 'I've given them no cause these thirty year. Always made a point of treating both of them just the same.'

'About anything else?' Philpott was uncharacteristically patient. 'Might they have argued about other things than yourself, madam?'

'How the blazes should I know that?' Tirza hugged the teapot to her chest and looked wise. 'They were dreadful quarrelsome men, all of 'em in those days, and Scorn the worst. Used to call him Helston's old Satan and he didn't mind it at all – took it quite as his watchword in the town.'

'Mistress Ivey is referring to the Hell Stone,' I said, seeing Philpott's puzzled face. 'Where the town supposedly gets its name.'

At this Philpott looked delighted. He was always collecting lists of information – breeds of cattle arranged by size, sailors' superstitions, the business interests of members of parliament – and this was exactly the sort of useless thing he liked. He got out his notebook, licked his pencil and looked at me expectantly.

'Once, long ago, the Archangel Michael had a tremendous fight with Satan in the skies above Helston. The devil availed himself of a huge boulder and hurled it down, meaning to destroy the town, but St Michael diverted its course and the Hell Stone fell harmlessly to earth. You can still see it, smashed up in the courtyard of the Angel Inn. The inn sign shows a very lively depiction of the battle, and the church is named for St Michael, the town's saviour.'

Philpott looked up from his scribbling with gleaming eyes. 'I must go to view the stone directly.'

'Then mind the well,' I said, remembering skirting it with Piggy in the dark the previous evening. 'It's only knee-high but it's forty feet deep, and the ostlers have a shocking habit of leaving the cover off.'

At this Tirza Ivey unexpectedly moaned and clutched the teapot more tightly to her bosom. 'By Golles,' she said, looking as if she might faint, clogs and all, which would certainly have made a notable thump. 'Mr Jago, you'll make my heart go nickety-knock, so you will, talkin' of that gashly story.'

I looked at her in some surprise, not being aware there was any particular story to be told.

'You recollect,' she said, 'that poor devil what fell down it, must be five and twenty year ago, God save him.'

'Which, in fact, God did not do,' Mother said

79

unexpectedly from the table. 'Tirza, you do always be harping on that same string, and you know fine well it was an accident. The coroner said so.'

I hadn't thought Tirza had suggested anything different, but she batted out of the room in a sudden temper.

'That woman must always be the centre of the story,' Mother said. 'I remember that poor man dyin'. He was a farmer from Illogan, in town for market day, and hard drinking in the Angel till past dark. When he left the inn to get his horse and wagon from the yard, he mistook his way and fell down the well. His body was slammed off the walls and being knocked out, he drowned as soon as he hit the water. But Tirza caused a great deal of trouble, saying it was on account of another lovers' feud.' Mother looked so disgusted I couldn't help laughing.

But though I loved her and was as delighted to see her face as she mine, I was still more eager to be gone to the duke's rooms to see Anne again. I was making some excuse, preparatory to passing Mrs Philpott, who was now running a fingernail down the bulging yellow wallpaper with a look of extreme sorrow, when Piggy came in from the hall.

'I have been called to Glynn's house,' he announced. 'The coroner has sent a message. I am summoned to give my deposition about Wedlock's death to the High Sheriff, who is apparently just arrived there.'

'The High Sheriff? I thought the coroner said he was busy elsewhere about the county?'

'It seems Glynn sent for him last night,' Piggy answered. 'But why, I don't know.'

'Splendid,' Philpott said. 'Laurence, go with him. The duke will certainly require an account of what is said. Find out all you can, my boy, and meanwhile, I shall console your mother for the loss of your company with an introduction to the Sapient Hog.'

I remarked that she would probably find this an acceptable substitution.

'The creature is set on calling at every house in town, I gather, collecting alms for the poor in exchange for charming little nosegays, delivered by his very own snout. Whimsical, I dare say, but a remarkably effective way to advertise himself and secure the best audience at the Angel Assembly Room tonight.'

I thought my mother, being a good farmer's wife, would be more interested in the Sapient Hog's hams than his intellects. As for myself, if I went with Piggy my visit to Anne would be delayed again, but on the other hand I would have far more to tell, making myself more useful to Sir James and therefore, God willing, more than ever welcome in the duke's rooms.

THE MAYOR'S HOUSE, The Willows, stood a few yards down from the church, on a junction with the elegant Cross Street which my mother so fancied for me, haunt of the town's lawyers and moneymen.

The Willows was a rather ugly house, quite new, and unsoftened by any flowers or the green embrace of ivy. The bay windows stood out like the fortifications of a medieval castle, angular half-hexagons, and the servant's attics seemed to have been glued down above them like an ill-fitting afterthought. I couldn't see any sign of willow trees. They had probably been felled to make way for the house.

Inside, the mayor was entertaining guests in his large drawing room. There was quite a crowd and, as at the Angel last night, a hush fell over all the other persons present as we came in. I suppose a newcomer is always of interest and despite my connection with the town I was a stranger to most of them. But it was mainly Piggy they were looking at, being the medical authority come to pronounce on Thomas Wedlock's dramatic death. Glynn made his way over, smiling and beckoning a servant with a tray of drinks to where we were loitering by the door. 'Will you have a bite to eat?' The mayor beckoned another servant, bearing a plate of devilled kidneys. 'The sheriff is arranging his papers in my study and we only await the arrival of the curate. I felt obliged to ask him to be here, being a relative of Wedlock, you know.'

I took a devilled kidney and sipped at the wine, trying not to stare too brazenly over its rim at the tableau of glossy wealth before me. Lushington, the East India man, was holding court in the window seat. His heavy corpulence gave him no pomp or grandeur, and as I had noticed the night before, his cheeks were red and hectic.

Meanwhile, a bevy of young women with hair elaborately dressed stood in an animated conclave, which our entrance had interrupted, their pretty faces – and others not pretty but very well tended, which went some way to make up for it – all turned towards us. One broke away from the group and came over, with a rustle of brocade and lace. It was Glynn's raven-haired niece and she was holding a pug in her arms, a very matronly creature apparently in imminent expectation of puppies. I glanced at Piggy and was amused to see he had blushed quite as scarlet as the dress she had worn the night before.

'Ah, Sarah,' Glynn said. 'Here is Dr Jago for you.' His eyes turned to me. 'And you are …?'

'Laurence Jago,' I said.

'My cousin,' Piggy added.

I wondered if I should explain I was there to represent the duke but decided against it. Glynn was far more likely to be unguarded if he thought me merely Piggy's relative, and he was well mannered enough not to question why I had seen fit to intrude myself into his drawing room without an invitation.

'Well, I must go to the sheriff,' he said. 'Sarah will entertain you better than I can while we wait for the curate. Heaven knows where he has got himself to. Probably waylaid by old ladies expressing their condolences about his loss. It would be too much to hope he has gone for a haircut.'

He strode away through the guests, who had now turned back to their former occupations. Only Sarah remained, and in the ensuing pause the pug in her arms snorted irritably. I wondered if Piggy had noticed that with its short muzzle and shallow wrinkles around the mouth it bore a striking resemblance to our mutual grandmother. I stroked the velvet muzzle and the dog's small tongue peeped out. 'Your little dog is expecting?'

'Yes, at any moment.' Sarah Glynn turned the pug towards her to kiss its snout, upon which it sneezed. 'I have been p-persuading Dr Jago to have one of the p-puppies.'

Piggy turned pink with pleasure to be thus singled out. 'But as I have told you, Miss Glynn, I'm afraid my habits wouldn't suit. I am out and about all day, visiting patients, and would wear its little legs quite out.'

'And yet how very grave it would look in a doctor's b-black suit and hat.' She smiled at the idea and kissed the pug again, who looked about as pleased with this fuss as our grandmother might have done in the same circumstances. Piggy watched with a look that told me he would die of delight if she kissed him on the nose in like manner. 'Of course, carrying its doctor's b-bag might prove a difficulty.' A little hesitation came and went in the girl's speech on the plosive sounds and the effort it took to say them made a rather attractive frown come between her eyebrows.

'I suppose it would wear it about its neck,' Piggy ventured with an air of great daring.

'So it would.' She laughed at him and he smiled back, blissfully. I looked from one to the other of them and thought I had never seen a man more delightfully in love, or a woman better pleased to know it.

'I hope you will be at the Assembly Room tonight,' she said to him. 'There is bound to be dancing, you know, after the Sapient Hog has done his tricks.'

'I will try to come,' Piggy said. 'If my patients don't keep me away from such happiness.'

I wondered if Anne would be there. It being the duke's treat I thought she must be, and if she was, I might dance with her, too, and under the cover of the music ask her all the questions I had turned over in my mind last night before sleeping.

Sarah was now looking at me with the same cheerful raillery she had bestowed on Piggy. 'And you are Dr Jago's cousin, are you? I must say you are the most dissimilar cousins I ever saw.'

'We take after our mothers.' It was true enough. I was pale and Gallic, while Piggy was as ruddily English-looking as any man could be. Our common grandmother had not, I hoped, passed on any pugginess to either of us.

'I have p-praised the Lord for your cousin's arrival here,' Sarah went on, with what seemed like remarkable lover-like candour until she added, 'the former doctor was very disagreeable. He p-positively ran away when he saw me coming.'

I made a noise indicative of polite surprise and disbelief.

'No, it is true. I teased him too much for information.'
She lowered her voice and leaned closer to both of us so
we had to bend our heads politely. 'To be frank, I fear
he was too ignorant to answer my questions and was
ashamed. Are you a lover of the Gothic, Mr Jago?'

'The Gothic?' I was caught rather off beam by this
sudden swerve in subject matter. 'I am certainly fond of
an arch.'

'No, no. Gothic novels, I mean. Have you read *The
Castle of Otranto* or *The Mysteries of Udolpho*?'

'I regret—'

'Oh, I suppose you'll say you are too b-busy and far too
solemn. A p-pity, for your own sake, for they are sublime.
But at any rate, I am writing one myself and have an
inordinate need for murders.'

I began to discern the logic of the conversation again.

'Miss Glynn tells me that a Gothic heroine's life is a
very precarious one,' Piggy explained earnestly, looking
at Sarah as if she were a marvel of nature.

She cast him a wry, confederate glance. 'Quite so. And
one cannot be always stabbing and strangling, you know.
It b-becomes mundane. Or so Claudia tells me.' She
kissed the pug for a third time and it once more endured
the caress with stoicism. 'Dr Jago has been kind enough
to suggest more unusual methods.'

Before I could ask for enlightenment – or observe that
I had myself encountered a number of singular deaths if
they might be of service to her – Sarah's eye had been

caught by a movement at the door. 'Ah, here is the curate at last. I shall take you to my uncle.'

Lushington had also seen the curate's arrival from his place in the window seat. He rose stiffly to his feet, seeming bent on joining the conclave, and Piggy hastened over to help him limp towards the door. Lushington had no better right to attend than Sir James would have done, and I was glad I had come along to represent His Grace even if no one had exactly ordered me to do it.

6

NOON

THE OFFICE OF HIGH SHERIFF circulated among the Cornish wealthy at the pleasure of the Prince of Wales. At present, the incumbent was a self-made gentleman named Hitchens from St Ives. He had one eye very much larger and more protuberant than the other, which in repose gave him rather the look of a quizzical flatfish.

Hitchens was already seated behind the desk in Glynn's study. Glynn and Lushington and Reverend Wedlock sat themselves down in the arched bay window that looked out on to the quiet street. Piggy went to stand with the coroner before the desk, ready to be questioned, and I leaned on the door, trying to avoid Glynn's puzzled eye – no doubt wondering again at my audacity in joining them.

'I have been called in by the mayor to investigate this

unfortunate affair yesterday in the Guildhall,' the sheriff began, in a voice that jangled like an ill-tuned harpsichord. You did not have to be a doctor to tell that his lungs were in a state of ruinous decay, but he managed to wheeze out a question. 'You were at the scene, Dr Jago, and examined the body?' Piggy nodded. Hitchens bulged his eye at him. 'And your findings?'

'I judged it likely to be a death by asphyxiation from the fumes of the fire. But, as I told Mr Roskruge, the coroner, without a dissection I cannot be absolutely certain. The old man was apparently in a passion and it is not impossible his heart gave out before the smoke killed him. There were no signs of other injury, and he had locked himself inside the room, so that the smoke would have been very thick once the papers caught fire. The clerks confirmed that was so when they broke down the door.'

'Hmm.' The sheriff jangled to himself quietly and seemed to turn his strange eye inward in contemplation. 'The mayor tells me he intended to burn the polling book. Do we know why?' But he did not wait for Piggy's answer, instead turning to Glynn and Lushington in the window. 'You have heard a little more about it, I gather?'

'A mere rumour.' Glynn looked very smooth. 'A suggestion only, that perhaps...' he hesitated. 'Perhaps Wedlock had quarrelled with the duke.'

The curate looked astonished at this, and Hitchens boggled his eye at Piggy again. 'Dr Jago, you visited the duke last night, I think?'

'Yes, sir.'

'Did His Grace say anything that might suggest such a quarrel?'

'Not at all.' But Piggy hesitated, evidently feeling obliged to be as precise in his description of the duke as he had been about Thomas Wedlock's death. 'He did not express much sympathy with the poor old man, however.'

'Hmm. And how was his manner?'

Piggy hesitated again. 'Irritated.'

I did not much like the direction the conversation was taking. I knew too much of political intrigue to doubt that Glynn was hoping to spread this rumour of a quarrel – indeed, was probably the author of it – in order to smear the duke in the election.

'The duke is always irritated,' I broke in. 'I worked for His Grace at the Foreign Office a number of years ago and can vouch for his general bad temper.'

Glynn looked up at me swiftly, not very pleased with this intervention. I remembered Piggy say he was an unpleasant man. 'But is it not very strange?' he asked. 'Why did Wedlock not unlock the door and leave, when he began to suffer from the fumes?'

'What in God's name are you suggesting?' I was rather taken aback. I didn't like the duke either, but it was going too far to suggest he'd knocked his own elector on the head. Why should he? After all, if anyone would benefit from Wedlock's death it would be Glynn himself. But even then, so long as John Scorn made his vote the duke's position was not materially altered, as His Grace had himself observed the previous evening. More than anything I thought it very bad taste to make political capital out of the affair in front of Wedlock's poor grandson.

'Perhaps he lost his bearings in the thick smoke,' Piggy said. 'Perhaps his hand was too weak to turn the key. It is a heavy old door and he was a feeble man and very aged. Or perhaps, as I have already suggested, his heart gave out before the flames took hold, and he never even tried to leave at all.'

Glynn seized on Piggy's first words. 'Old and feeble! Indeed he was, and so is Scorn. Thank God, when he is also dead all this nonsense of division and party will finally be at an end and Helston much the better for it.'

The curate looked offended at such callousness towards his grandfather and even the sheriff looked a little disgusted. 'I dare say it will,' he said, his chest jangling more vigorously, 'but as you well know, Mr Glynn, it is not for us to judge between your new electors and the old man. That decision belongs to Parliament and I, for one, am glad it is their responsibility and not mine.'

Lushington had been listening to all this quite calmly and now changed the subject. 'John Scorn was in a dreadful passion at the political meeting last night, we all saw it. Ten to one he knows something.'

'Which is why I have called him here.' Hitchens raised his eyes to me. 'Will you go and fetch him, Mr …?'

'Jago, sir.'

The sheriff looked mildly perplexed at this multiplication of Jagos but flicked his fingers at me just as if I were a lowly clerk again. I obeyed him and found Scorn outside in the hall, sitting on a bench, and looking just as aged and tremulous as he had done last night on the coach. His ancient face was a mass of frowning, baggy wrinkles as he munched stolidly through a plate of devilled kidneys, which must have been fetched to him by the footman. He rejected the offer of my arm and shuffled behind me into Glynn's study wheezing almost as heavily as the sheriff, his old hands trembling in fists at his sides.

'Mr Scorn, as you know we are gathered to investigate the death of Thomas Wedlock, your old friend and colleague,' the sheriff said, as I brought up a chair for Scorn to sit in. He chose not to avail himself of it and only stared at the sheriff with an absolute lack of deference that was really rather admirable. Under his fierce gaze, Hitchens tapped his knuckles on the desk uncomfortably. 'Can you tell us aught of Wedlock's state of mind these past days? We have heard he was angry.'

'And why not?' Scorn's voice was rough. 'We was both vexed when we saw what Mr Glynn meant to do at this election.' Though he was well spoken, his accent put me in mind of Wedlock's faded son, and Tirza Ivey too, the old Cornish intonation very strong. Perhaps it is ever thus, that with each passing generation the character of a particular place is diluted by incomers and time.

Again, I remembered Glynn's desire that Helston should change – should turn its face to the globe. No wonder an old man, born and bred under the old system of guilds Glynn despised, should be so passionately averse to find the world slipping away from him.

'I told Wedlock and shall tell 'ee, 'tis a struggle for the town's soul,' John Scorn said, 'and so long as I live I'll see the old ways do. The electors of the borough used to be shoemakers, craftsmen, and merchants like myself. Now they're churchmen and lawyers. What do they care for Helston? Look at this candidate, here, chairman of the East India Company. What does he care for young Skues, the maltster, or Benedict Jane, the stay maker, though they have been fool enough to go over to the new corporation? Nuthin' at all, and they should know better. That's what I told Wedlock.'

'You told him? He did not agree?'

The old man's eyes flickered to the curate, whose pink face was working with distress at all this anger. 'I have disagreed with Thomas Wedlock these sixty year, and his grandson can tell you so. 'Tis no wonder we still argue now and then.'

'Did you know he had gone to the Guildhall last night?'

'I did not.'

'Do you know why he meant to burn the poll book?'

'I do not.'

So far the sheriff had done the questioning, but now

94

Glynn put his oar in. 'Did you ever think the duke wanted rid of Wedlock, Scorn?'

'For God's sake,' I said. Glynn was verging on slander. 'Either leave off these ridiculous hints against the duke or cut up the old man and be done with it.'

Glynn wound his neck in abruptly and looked bland. A dissection would not serve his purpose, which was certainly only to raise groundless suspicion in the hope it would get to the ear of Parliament and help his case against the duke.

I fished in my pocket and laid the tinderbox on the desk. 'I found this last night,' I said. 'I supposed it belonged to old Wedlock but, as the curate will confirm, his family don't know it. I will ask the clerks if one of them dropped it while they fought the fire, but if not, it may point to another unknown witness whom the sheriff may also wish to examine.'

Hitchens picked up the tinderbox, gave it a cursory glance and then handed it to Glynn. Glynn scarcely troubled to examine it at all but passed it straight on to Lushington. Lushington's hand was trembling as he took it, probably from whatever illness afflicted him. But he only shook his head and offered it to the curate who waved it away mildly. 'I have already seen it,' he said, 'and as Mr Jago tells you, we none of us knew it.'

That only left John Scorn who frowned over it so fiercely I thought it might burst into flames under his scorching gaze. He thrust it back at me roughly, not meeting my eye. But I didn't take his manner person-ally: he did not know of my connection with the duke and that I was, in actuality, a potential ally among these unfriendly faces. Besides, I remembered Tirza Ivey say his nickname had been *Satan* when he was a young man, and there was indeed a terrible air of general ill will hanging about him, infecting the room like a prickly miasma. One thing was certain: I should not have consented to marry him myself, and I thought Tirza Ivey had been very wise to refuse him all those years ago.

WHILE WE HAD BEEN with the sheriff, the party in Glynn's drawing room had dispersed. John Scorn and the curate left together, and I would have followed them directly out into the street except that Piggy had his romance to consider and instead trailed after Lushington into the drawing room. Though above everything I wanted to go back to Anne, it was still pleasant enough to see Sarah Glynn's sunny face again, and Claudia's wrinkled one. The pug was in no wise similar to Mr Gibbs, that old shaggy fellow with his wolfish gait, but she was at least a dog – and, at present, one very set on building a nest among the cushions on the chaise longue. Sarah turned up her face to Piggy as we came in and let him take hold of her fingers.

'I saw that p-preposterous old man go into my uncle's

study,' she said to him. 'Was he shockingly rude to the sheriff?'

'Not rude at all,' Piggy answered, leaving go of her hand with obvious reluctance and perching beside her on the chaise longue. They looked into each other's eyes, labouring under the amiable misapprehension that their feelings were decorously hidden. 'But he is a bad-tempered old fellow in general, I think.'

'P-Poor Eleanor's life is a terrible trial to her, cooped up with him.' Sarah swept Claudia up into her arms just as the little dog seemed finally to have arranged the cushions to its satisfaction, and it squawked a feeble objection. 'If there was ever a cruel guardian, liable to lock up a girl in a nunnery, John Scorn is the very man to do it.'

'Who is Eleanor?' I asked.

'His granddaughter, who is obliged to live with the old ogre after the death of her p-parents. Her aunt had made a b-bad marriage which drove her grandfather quite as mad as an Italian count in a castle full of ghosts. I have known Eleanor all my life and living with that disagreeable old man and being b-bent to his wishes is a fate I shouldn't relish.'

'Nor is it a fate you would tolerate for a half-hour,' Mr Glynn said, coming in to the drawing room and closing the door behind him. 'You would either stick him with the stiletto blade hidden up your sleeve or escape down a secret passage with the gallant hero. Or both, one after the other, no doubt.'

I was surprised to find John Scorn had a granddaughter of any description, for a granddaughter must mean he had eventually found a woman brave or reckless enough to marry him. 'What kind of a man is Scorn, really?' I asked. 'And why is he so angry?'

'Oh – he is only an old merchant,' Glynn answered, coming to sit down beside Lushington in the window. 'He did well enough in the clothier business once, but he didn't change with the times and over the years his trade dwindled away to nothing. He still keeps a good house next door to the Rodney on Meneage Street, but he has little else to speak of. He'll be dead in a year or two and the duke is a fool to stick to him. His Grace would do far better to win our electors to his side.'

'The duchess said the same last night,' Piggy observed absently, still feasting his eyes on the object of his affections in such a guileless way that I might have laughed aloud, if I hadn't thought his words rather indiscreet – a judgement confirmed as Glynn looked suddenly interested.

'Did she? Well, she has more sense than her husband then. But the duke's too damned stingy to spend the money. John Scorn's is a cheaper vote.'

The pug delivered herself from the girl's arms with a convulsive heave and scuttled back to her nest of cushions. Sarah dragged her eyes away from the charms of Piggy's visage which, I confess, had until now rather escaped me beyond its general doggy goodwill. She showed the pug a cushion ripped by its over-eager little claws. 'What is the matter with you, Claudia? Look! You are turning vandal.'

'I think she wants a comfortable place to have her pups,' I said, and at this Sarah glanced at me with a shade more interest than before and looked remorseful.

'Poor Claudia.' She kissed the pug's nose. 'But she can certainly not do the deed on the chaise longue. I shall go directly to find her a box.'

Piggy's interest in the party at The Willows evaporated with her departure and he would have left, except that Lushington asked him for a medical consultation and Piggy obligingly agreed. I left alone and walked back down Church Street, calling in at the Guildhall on my way. It was humming with activity, and I was able to show the tinderbox to every clerk and establish beyond reasonable doubt that not only did it not belong to any of them but, like the Wedlocks, they had never seen it before in their lives. Piggy had hoped Wedlock's death at worst a foolish misadventure. But for myself I confess I should now be a little disappointed, not least because my usefulness to the duke would be diminished and my excuse to call at his rooms much reduced.

'It's a curious thing, howsumever,' one of the clerks said as I took my leave. 'We dashed down the door because it was locked. But we have never yet discovered the key inside. Will you ask the curate if he has it, sir? I dare say it was in his grandfer's pocket, and 'twould be convenient for us to have it back.'

The Market House clock tolled one as I came out and crossed the road to the surgery. I was now very impatient to go to the Angel and see Anne, having been thwarted all morning, but the Philpotts and my mother were waiting in Piggy's parlour and I was foiled again.

'How was the Sapient Hog?' I kissed my mother's cheek and sat down beside her on the lumpy horsehair sofa. The contrast with the silk chaise longue Claudia had just been destroying was rather marked. 'Did he read your fortune for you?'

Mother frowned at me in mock annoyance. 'Not at all. He is *keeping his powder dry* for tonight, he said.'

'Discourteous of him.'

She stroked my sleeve, pretending to find some speck or crumb. 'I thought so, too, especially as I told him I must go home to the farm before milking.'

I thought she might have made an exception in the circumstances but, of course, the farm had its inexorable routines that took up all their time. If she frolicked about in Helston, who would milk the cows, churn the butter or clot the cream? If I wanted to see my brothers and sister Grace, I would have to go to them, not expect them here. The farm had seemed like a dream since I left England and, still hindered from going home, it remained almost entirely theoretical to my mind.

'But seriously, Laurence,' Mother said, 'The pig is a swindler. He is going from door to door demanding money.'

'Only money for the poor,' Philpott objected. One look at his glowing face told me he was already highly taken with the creature.

But Mrs Philpott was also needed by her children, she said, whom she had left in the care of my sister – a torment I thought poor Grace had hardly deserved. Mother would be back in Helston with her wares for the market, the pig, and the election on Monday, she said, but Philpott announced his intention of remaining in town for the day. If his children impaled themselves on hayforks or drowned in the pond, Mrs Philpott would manage their funerals admirably without him.

'I'll come home as soon as I can,' I promised, as Mother did up her cloak, climbed up into the small cart beside Mrs Philpott and took up old Olive's reins with a practised hand. I envied them the drive home through the green lanes: at this time of year the hedgerows would be purple with foxgloves, fragrant with twining briar roses, and the farm's muddy track a tunnel of lambent young green leaves overhead.

When I came back into the parlour, Philpott asked me about the meeting with the sheriff.

'It's damnable,' I said. 'The mayor is trying to start a rumour of some ill-doing on the part of the duke; some ill will towards the dead man. Preposterous, of course – what good would it do His Grace to nobble his own voter?'

'None at all, on the face of it,' Philpott answered, looking first mildly surprised and then thoughtful. 'But there must be something in it.'

'Why must there?'

But, in fact, I knew why. It was because he was a newspaper man, and any whiff of news must be true until absolutely proved otherwise, especially if the news was discreditable to well-known persons.

'The duke is a dreadful man,' Philpott said. 'We all know that. So dreadful his first wife ran off with Mad Jack Byron.'

'Ran off? I thought His Grace found them together in the marital bed and threw her out?'

Philpott waved a hand at such quibbling. 'Ten to one that son ain't his at all.'

I remembered George Osborne from the previous evening. 'He is the spitting image of his father.'

Philpott ignored me. 'Quarrelled with Pitt, too. Pitt was having trouble with the Cabinet, and the duke presented himself uninvited at Number 10, offering to relieve him of the office of Prime Minister. Said he was willing to make the great sacrifice of assuming the labour himself. Pitt, being on his third pint of port, was entirely incapable of polite pretence and fell on the carpet laughing. Who knows whether he will allow Parliament to favour the duke's electors?'

'But they would certainly have favoured two more than one,' I said impatiently. 'It's nonsense to blame the duke, Philpott, and you know it.'

WHEN I FINALLY came into the Angel, the duke was not at home and his family party wore an air of quiet contentment without him. The duchess was sitting with Anne at the dining table, surrounded by piles of papers, while Sir James was reading the news in an armchair by the fireplace. Young George Osborne was playing solitaire at the other end of the table from the women, turning over the playing cards fastidiously with long, pale fingers, while the delinquent Charles Burges was keeping a very commendable distance from little Sidney in the crib.

Anne only spared me one searching glance before going back to her papers, but the colour had risen in her cheeks again which made me glad, and the duchess greeted me cheerfully.

'The proverbial cat is away,' she said, 'and we are making mischief as a consequence.' She waved me to a seat opposite them at the table and I sat down. 'My husband won't countenance talking to the new corporation's electors himself, so we are reduced to secrecy and intrigue every minute we can snatch.'

'You are making the overtures yourself?' I looked at the letters scattered across the table, and the half-written paper under Anne's hand. 'You have already begun?'

'Yes, indeed, and very enlightening the whole business turns out to be. Mr Abbot's philosopher brother Bentham has the matter entirely on its head. It is not the happiness of the *greatest number* that drives everything, but the interests of the individual. They are almost all of them to be bought, even – or I might say especially – the clergymen. Who would have thought it when they always act so pious?'

'And what is their price?'

The duchess shook her beribboned curls at me. 'Reverend Pasmore has a fine living at St Just in the Roseland, but would very much like another, to which he can farm out a curate and take the income for himself. And so say all the churchmen with greater or lesser frankness. The lawyers want business in London, of course. The few remaining old merchants are rather less worldly in their demands, bless them. An organist for the church, and a promise that Mr Lushington will not swamp the town with his East India wares, which I fear is like Canute standing out against the tide.' She shuffled her papers. 'Sir James will cost their demands and then we shall present them to the duke. But since, in truth, I have very little hope of my husband parting with another farthing, I am also turning my mind to the Sapient Hog.'

'He is certainly a wealthy gentleman, I gather. But I don't suppose he will stretch to purchasing the livings for you.'

It was a poor stab at wit, but while Anne only smiled the duchess snorted an appreciative laugh. 'Very droll, Mr Jago. I rather think to have him nudge Glynn's electors in the right direction by appealing to their superstitious sides, of which there are many, especially among the old merchants.'

'Won't the churchmen be immune to that?'

The duchess waggled her head at me. 'As much as they are to money, *the root of all evil?*'

'But what exactly does the pig do?' I asked after another moment. 'I have read about it, but never seen it perform.'

'I saw it once,' Anne said, passing her sheet of paper to the duchess. 'It is a remarkable piece of conjuring. It can do arithmetic with numbered cards and spell out words using the letters of the alphabet. It tells fortunes and advises those who have lost things where they can be found.'

I looked at her hungrily. I wanted to know so much about her present life and her present feelings. It was a joy to hear her voice, and her old sensible judgement of affairs, but it was torment to sit so close and be prevented from asking what I really wanted to know by the presence of all the others.

'You call it conjuring?' was all I said.

Anne shrugged, looking every inch as shrewd as I remembered. 'Is not everything? The physician in his black suit, the lawyer in his gown and wig, the priest in his cassock.' She shot a look at the duchess. 'And we ladies, in our silks. Everything is show, everything is imposture.'

I wondered if she had expected Canning to offer marriage, as I had done, and was feeling bitter. But I was a little offended on Piggy's behalf, nonetheless. 'I wouldn't call my cousin an imposter. He doesn't pretend to amputate a man's leg.'

The duchess was still thinking about the election. 'At any event, I am determined to drop a hint to the pig's owner, Mr Nicholson, that it might pay him well if the Sapient Hog expresses some doubts as to Mr Glynn's character or his candidate's – or some special approval of my husband and his men. I have a little pin money of my own and I am sure the thing can be perfectly easily managed. George is to arrange it all with Mr Nicholson, being rather less on his dignity than his father. He is quite his mother's child in that regard.'

George looked up from his cards. 'I think my father would prefer you to enumerate the ways in which I resemble *him*, Your Grace, not my mother.' But there was no need. From the top of his elegant head to the tip of his well-made boots – the youth was certainly a languid Osborne, not a disreputable Byron.

Sir James had been beckoning to me for some time, and I reluctantly stood up and went over to where he was sitting.

'Well?' He turned his pale moon face up to me. 'What have you discovered?'

'Nothing very good,' I said, leaning on the mantelpiece, from which vantage point I could admire the careful arrangement of Sir James's hair. He seemed to have grown one side very long, so he could comb it across the top of his head and thereby conceal his bald patch. Necessity being the mother of invention, I supposed many such cunning stratagems were now in contemplation across the newly wigless nation. 'No one knows why Wedlock was in the Guildhall making fires,' I said, 'and the only rumoured answer reflects badly on the duke.'

I told him what Glynn had hinted, and Sir James shifted irritably in his chair. 'Damned mischief maker. He may be a wealthy man but he has not the dignity suitable to his office.'

I studied Sir James's face and for a moment allowed myself to take Glynn's hints and Philpott's poor opinion of the duke seriously. I had certainly seen enough of Sir James in the Foreign Office to know that despite his mild-mannered face he would stop at nothing to get the Ministry's way. I took the tinderbox out of my pocket and held it under his nose. 'This was at the scene of the fire. I thought it belonged to the old man but evidently not. Nor was it innocently dropped by one of the clerks. Someone else could therefore have lit the blaze.'

He batted the tinderbox away. 'I need not point out to you that you should be guarded in your questioning of witnesses, and until you are certain, I would counsel you strongly against sharing these fanciful surmises with the duke.'

George had been listening and now laughed. 'And so would I, unless you want something thrown at your head. My father is known as a pin in Whitehall, and Sir

James as his pincushion. It is very noble of Sir James to put up with my father at all.'

Sir James went back to his newspaper. 'I am only grateful to His Grace for affording me this opportunity to cross from the ranks of the civil service to those of Parliament's elected representatives.'

George tutted at such cant. 'But you could still have stayed at home, safely out of the way like his other candidate.'

'Lushington also chooses to be here,' I said.

George screwed up his face at me. 'Only because Glynn wants to dangle the man's mighty patronage in front of his crew of voters, and from what Sarah Glynn tells me, Lushington likes a scrap. Glynn's other voter, Elliot, is as absent as Charles Abbot, probably off philosophising, too, for all I know.'

'You know Glynn's niece?'

'Certainly, being the only wealthy young people in town. We shall all meet tonight downstairs in the Assembly Room and I shall dance the first dance with her, I fancy.'

I hoped this wouldn't interfere with Piggy's romantic ambitions, but the mention of the Assembly Room made me glance at Anne. Her eyes had brightened and I surmised she would also be there, for after all, the Assembly Room was built on to the back of the inn, scarcely a step away. Again I hoped that under the noise of the pig show and the music I would find out exactly what had brought her here and what her own feelings about our unexpected reunion might really be.

'But before that is poor Wedlock's funeral,' she said now. 'I thought we should go, but Sir James believes it unnecessary.'

This was very plain speaking for someone supposedly a governess, but Sir James answered her just as he might have done in her stepfather's Kensington drawing room. 'The common people won't expect it, Mrs Bellingham. They will be happier without us. And in any case, ladies should not attend funerals, you know. It is not done.'

Anne's previous husband had been lost at sea and there had been no funeral for him at all. As I left, I bent over Anne's hand. The duchess and George had started on some good-natured argument, and I spoke quietly under their noise. 'Will you give me the first dance tonight, Anne?'

Last night she had smiled at me only faintly; now her old good-humoured candour seemed quite restored – as if all the intervening trouble had been forgotten and we were back in our old comfortable, bantering relations. 'Oh, I suppose I might, if the Prince of Wales or the King doesn't ask me first.'

7

Thomas wedlock's funeral was set for one o'clock. When Philpott and Piggy and I came into the churchyard a half-hour beforehand, the grave was still being excavated under the supervision of a gnarled old sexton leaning on a cane and barking out irritable orders. A few yards away, another group of old men, and one young one, were sitting on the gravestones, smoking pipes.

'That's the choir,' Piggy said, exchanging amicable nods with the group. 'Or some of them, at least.' The gnarled old root had by now finished haranguing the workmen and was coming over to the rest of the choir, who shambled to their feet at his approach. 'And that's the choirmaster, Jeb Nettle,' Piggy said. 'Sexton at St Michael's for fifty years, they say, and very possessive of his graves.' The youngest chorister was just at this moment tapping his pipe out on the gravestone, and the old bog-oak proved Piggy's point by rapping the lad's ankles with his cane.

'Mind yer manners, boy. That's my great-great-uncle John you're befoulin' with your filthy baccy.'

'Old Wedlock was in the choir,' Piggy volunteered. 'They are a very venerable body of men, from all walks of life in the town. I joined them soon after I came to Helston and I suppose they'll want me to sing today.'

'Then after we've spoken to the curate I'll talk to them, too.'

'They won't all be here, it not being Sunday,' Piggy added as we walked on towards the church. 'Cyrus Best will be off at work or carousing as usual.'

'Then God bless Cyrus Best, whoever he is.' Philpott thought working men should enjoy themselves as often and as energetically as possible, their revels preferably ending up in a fight or a riot or, in the best of all possible worlds, both.

St Michael's Church is a handsome, modern building, with a plaque on the wall declaring it the gift of the Duke of Leeds after the conflagration of the previous structure, Helston thus seeming a town disturbingly careless of fire. We found Reverend William Wedlock in the vestry, making his preparations for the ceremony, and I pitied him for being obliged to conduct his own grandfather's funeral. He looked up as we came in and squirmed pinkly under our collective gaze.

'Forgive us for intruding,' I said. 'As you know, the coroner has charged me with further investigation into your grandfather's death, and I am come to ask a few more questions.'

The curate dropped his gaze to his hands, smoothing out a black funeral stole. 'I hardly know what you could think to ask me.'

'Chiefly about his movements yesterday,' I said. 'And his general views on the election.'

The curate draped the stole carefully around his shoulders and adjusted it to make sure both falling bands were equal. 'As for his movements, I'm afraid I can't say. I was out all day visiting dying children, as Dr Jago will tell you.' He looked up at Piggy. 'How is little Jane Landeryou now?'

'Very bad. The fever has turned putrid, as I feared.'

William Wedlock shook his head at this gloomy news.

'The town is suffering dreadfully from the scarlatina,' Piggy explained. 'Dr Johns' books show it carried off thirty children between Christmas and Easter. It seems to have been lurking and biding its time, for there are three new cases I've seen this week.' He turned back to the curate. 'And did I see you visiting old Julian earlier today? How was he?'

'Also very bad. He is too unwell to visit church, so I said some prayers with him and offered Communion.'

Again Piggy explained. 'Poor Julian, a grocer on Coinagehall Street, has a tumour that will kill him before the summer is out.'

William Wedlock nodded at this and then turned to me. 'As for politics, Mr Jago, I did my best to avoid discussing it with Grandfer. He was always in a passion about something and wore us all quite down to the nub.'

'Dr Jago's housemaid said your grandfather and John Scorn fought for her favours once. Has there been any recent bad blood between them on her account?'

'Bad blood? Over Tirza!' Only the curate's very rigid, clerical dignity prevented him hooting an unsuitable boyish laugh. 'But it's true Grandfer and Scorn fought like hyenas when they were young men. They were both elected freemen and argued about everything at Guildhall meetings, too. It's a strange joke that they have found themselves the last two men left. Lately they have had a deal more to do with each other than they liked, being the duke's only remaining voters.'

'A rare trio, then, the duke being as angry a man as any,' Philpott observed.

'My grandfather and John Scorn are Helston men of the old type, Mr Philpott. When Dr Wesley began his preaching tours of Cornwall, he durst not come to Helston at all and it was twenty years before he could ride in without stones thrown at him. He called the town a place of rebels and persecutors and they did indeed disrupt his meetings. The old town was riven with discord among the guilds, the merchants and the poor. Grandfer's feuds and quarrels have done nothing but weary my father and mother, and shame me in my profession. But thank the Lord the world has changed and Helston is now a far more Godly place.'

From the riotous evidence of last night it seemed to me that in fact nothing much had changed at all, even if there was now a Wesleyan meeting in the town each Sunday. But the curate's father had indeed looked down-trodden and having such a cantankerous parent must have been tiresome.

'And what do you think of the mayor?' I asked. The curate paused and raised his puppyish head.

'Mr Glynn is a forceful character and now rules every-thing in Helston, except in the matter of the election and the duke's patronage. It is no wonder he seeks to challenge His Grace.'

'Have you met his new candidate? The chairman of the East India Company?'

'I dined with the mayor and Mr Lushington on Thursday night. The rector and I were both invited. I thought Lushington was a decent man if a little over-bearing like the mayor. But in his case, it is not to be wondered at, since he is so very powerful, even if so poorly.'

'It is gout,' Piggy said. 'And no—' He looked at us admonishingly. 'Don't smile. It is a wretched condi-tion, even if often enflamed by too rich a diet and too much port. When I examined him this morning I asked him about his symptoms, and he answered remarkably candidly. "Ate too much at last night's dinner," he said.

"Drank far too much brandy. I am my own worst enemy and you can't reproach me more than I do myself. But it is so God-damned hard to be virtuous in a wealthy man's house with a good chef." He had a fine silver nutmeg grater hanging from his pocket on a chain – a nonsense piece of ostentation which I have often seen in London, and which betrayed him more than anything as a bon vivant. I chided him for over spicing his food with the thing and he took it meekly. In fact, his manner impressed me, as did his knowledge of his disease. He knew all the common symptoms. Copious, pale-coloured urine. The bowels obstinately costive. "Yes, yes," he said. "I know it all well enough. Knew what I was in for when I over-indulged last night. But the excitement of the meeting and the elector's death made me forget to be careful."

'I asked him what his London physician prescribed and he rattled it all off. Portland powder, hot flannels, blisters. *Eau Medicinale. Colchicum Autumnale.* There was really nothing more I could do for him except recommend the abstinence he already knew was the best remedy. But he was unhappy and in pain, so I examined the swelling in his foot and applied a soothing tincture. "Good God," he said to me. "My own physician has not touched me in fifteen years. Thinks it below his dignity and merely studies my shit and prescribes treatment from a safe distance by the door."'

'You will find yourself appointed his private doctor at this rate,' I said with a smile, 'and end up Physician

Extraordinary to the King.' For what everyone knew was that Lushington held vast, transforming patronage in his painful hands, and Piggy's father would doubtless have been delighted to see his son there in such intimate conclave with the great man.

Piggy laughed but coloured a little. 'He did seem to take an interest in me after that. Asked me why I had left London. "You don't miss it?" he asked me, with quite a scrutinising look. "This seems a strange place for an educated man like you." I don't know why, but I found myself eager to show him I was ambitious. And that I was not particularly a supporter of the duke and his ridiculous old electors, begging your pardon, William.'

The curate had been listening to this tale and waved a deprecatory hand. I got the impression he and Piggy were well acquainted and liked each other, ministering as they did to the bodily and spiritual needs of the town between them.

'And what do you really think of John Scorn?' I asked. 'We hear so much against him, but I gather he has a granddaughter. He must have found a lady would marry him once.'

William Wedlock's pink face snapped shut abruptly like a clam shell. 'Poor woman,' he said. 'And poor Eleanor.'

'You know his granddaughter?'

'Since we were children. I studied Greek with her brother.'

'And where is her brother, now?'

'Moved away to Camborne the minute he could contrive it.'

It appeared from the curate's face that in John Scorn's case he could summon little Christian charity. But, in truth, we had so far met no one with a good word to say about him.

Above our heads the bell began to toll – eighty-four chimes for Thomas Wedlock's eighty-four years. The bell-ringers would be briefer for the poor children dead of scarlet fever, I thought, and the sexton's workmen far less wearied by digging their tiny graves.

'And by the by,' I said as we turned to go, 'the clerks at the Guildhall have not yet found the key to the room your grandfather died in. Was it in his pocket, do you know? They are anxious for its return.'

William Wedlock looked blank. 'I don't think I have seen it, but I imagine it will have been a big old thing, for that massy door. I shall ask my mother.'

We left him, then, to say his prayers in preparation for the service, and followed the last of the mourners into the body of the church. They looked remarkably pious and genteel, and not at all as if they had been rioting the previous evening, but they were also rather few.

The choir were coming in, going up a broad staircase to the gallery above. Piggy plodded away to join them. The bell had stopped tolling and before we could find a seat the choir had struck up an anthem and Reverend

Wedlock was coming up the aisle behind us. He brushed past my elbow, followed by the clerk and the church-warden in procession.

I turned to look up to the gallery and the singers, who were a motley crew of men, all heights and girths. There were no accompanying instruments, only the voices singing in four parts, and they made a fine fist of it for a provincial choir. I could see Piggy at the back, mouth flapping lustily, which made me smile.

Philpott nudged me. 'Curious, ain't it, this business with the wigs?'

It was indeed of particular note in church, since every man had naturally removed his hat, and we gazed out over a sprinkling of bare heads, some bald, some thatched, some curly, some brushed flat to the scalp and all shades of yellow, brown and ginger. 'I made enquiry o' your brothers,' Philpott went on, 'and it seems they went out of fashion overnight on the fifth of May last year, when Pitt put a hefty tax on the powder. What a pity we cannot tax wickedness and be done with it just as easily, my boy.' He creased his eyes up at me in his usual cheerful way, but he would not succeed in placating me merely by making me smile.

'We are gathered together to bury our brother, Thomas Wedlock,' the curate said when the singing had died away and the congregation's murmured conversation fell quiet. 'A good old man, though a sinner like us all.' His voice caught a little and I thought it must be strange to be pastor to your own grandfather and be required to take a parson's view of him.

'The unfortunate man had no time to take the holy sacrament or receive the blessings of repentance at the point of death, so I have agreed with the rector that today we shall take the Holy Communion in his memory. The bishop complains that the Church neglects the ceremony and it is regrettably true that we have not taken bread and wine at St Michael's since Easter.' He pursed his lips with pious professional disapproval. 'Though I hear the church at Wendron has not held Communion for over a year, God save them. But, in any case, this quarrelsome week of all weeks we do well to repent our sins and remember what the Bible says. *Whosoever shall say, Thou fool, shall be in danger of hellfire.*'

His young face turned suddenly severe and he rather glared at us from under the long hair that hung across his face. 'Yet think carefully before coming forward for the holy sacrament. We must all tremble at partaking in the mystery of Communion and remember the great peril of the unworthy receiving thereof. As the prayer book says, "Search and examine your own consciences that ye may come holy and clean to such a heavenly feast." Remember that to take the body and blood of Christ in a state of mortal sin leads only to hell. "Repent you of your sins," the book says, "or else come not to that holy Table; lest the devil enter into you and bring you to destruction both of body and soul."'

I hoped he had not terrified the poor old grocer with this alarming prospect when he offered him Communion earlier in the day. But now the burial service began, with its many readings and psalms which all contrive to assure the departed's kin that he will be waiting for them on the other side of the river in white raiment and eternal bliss. In Thomas Wedlock's case, it seemed more than usually doubtful he would relish such an existence and wouldn't start disputes among the angels out of sheer mischief. But we sat, dutifully pious, and at length it came to the act of Communion, if we dared drink and eat of that sacred meal. For myself, I decided I didn't, and remained in the pew watching as Philpott and Piggy went up to join the small line of mourners sufficiently confident of their own virtue to partake.

John Scorn was the last of them, behind Philpott in the queue, on the arm of a sturdy woman of about my own age, whom I thought must be his long-suffering granddaughter, Eleanor. When Philpott stepped aside, and Scorn went to the rail, William Wedlock looked at him from under his long hair with what seemed almost like surprise, doubt and perhaps even some timid fear. Scorn knelt, piously enough, but he kept his eyes fixed on the poor young curate belligerently, as if daring him to object to his presence. I thought that John Scorn was probably the kind of man who would take the curate's warnings as a challenge whatever the consequences to his immortal soul. He was quivering all over, as he had done that morning at The Willows, and looked, quite frankly, at death's door. Anne had feared the same the previous evening, I remembered, and had taken him to the Angel after the political meeting to ply him with the duke's brandy.

But there again, apart from being as argumentative as Thomas Wedlock, who was apparently with the angels nonetheless, there was no real reason Scorn should not take the sacrament, and – who knew? – it might even be a welcome sign of his desire to reconcile with his old enemy beyond the grave. The curate put his hand to the common Communion dish and produced the wafer. 'The body of Christ which was given for you,' I heard him say quietly to Scorn. As the old man closed his mouth on the wafer, he looked for the first time as if he doubted himself. He flushed, his eyes still bent on the curate, but I thought with some new anxiety.

After a somewhat pregnant pause Scorn took a deep, shuddering gasp and burst out into a sudden and alarming fit of coughing. William Wedlock, looking startled, proffered him the chalice of common wine, but the mouthful left in the cup was apparently no remedy, and Scorn's coughs redoubled with every whooping inward breath. Still looking somewhat perplexed, the curate went to the altar to refill the cup, while Philpott thumped the old man between the shoulder blades in a cheerful manner that rather undermined the solemnity of the whole occasion. Scorn was still in a paroxysm of choking when William Wedlock returned with the replenished Communion chalice and put it into his hands. Whereupon, to the curate's apparent consternation, Scorn lifted it to his lips and downed the whole cupful in one.

'The blood of Christ which was given for you,' William Wedlock murmured in a reproving tone. The old man, having certainly drunk more of Christ's metaphorical blood than was absolutely proper, said 'Amen' in a hoarse voice and returned unsteadily to his seat in the pews. He had been trembling enough as he bent his miasma of ill will on the curate, but the shocking coughing fit now appeared to have spent him entirely. Perhaps Glynn had been right and the world would be a better place when all these wicked old men were dead.

Afterwards we went to the grave and watched the old man's coffin lowered down into the deep hole. William Wedlock's parents threw in their clods of earth, as did the curate in his capacity as both priest and mourner. The clods, baked half to brick by the hot spring sunshine, tapped off the coffin tinnily. Then the congregation dispersed. The sexton remained by the grave to instruct his men on refilling the hole, while Philpott had some final words with William Wedlock. But the curate looked rather distracted and was peering about at the small knots of mourners standing around the graveyard. When I followed his gaze, it had fixed on old Scorn and Eleanor who, from the expression on her face, was quite as irritable as her grandfather. Near them the gravediggers were refilling the grave. Behind that was the church wall, and beyond that again were green fields falling away down towards the sea, which glittered blue on the far horizon.

The choir was now loitering together in a low-voiced conclave by the older graves and I detached Philpott from the curate and led him over to speak to them. There had not been many mourners, and even fewer now remained. 'A poor showing for such an elder of the town,' I observed to Piggy as I came up.

Jeb Nettle, the sexton, was arriving behind us, his cane tapping. 'The Mohawks will stay away, Thomas Wedlock having been chief among the Cherokees; and he has outlived everyone else, save me and John Scorn.' Nettle sucked what stumps of teeth remained in his ancient jaws and looked smug. '*I* mind 'em both as childern. Will you guess my age now, sirs?'

But he spared us the ill manners of guessing either too high or too low. 'Ninety-six. That's my age, if you'll credit it. Born on the dot of the new century and have lived through four monarchs and nine wars since.'

'And none the wiser for any on it,' said another chorister, a stripling of about seventy who seemed to have heard this boast one time too many over the years. 'Nettle, boy, you know nuthin' 'bout nuthin' save litany and skelingtons and pigeons.'

The old man bared his stumps. 'But unlike some, I do

take notice of what I 'ear. What do 'ee know about the present war, fer an instance? You tell me that.'

The other man looked shifty and cast his eyes about at the gravestones for inspiration. 'I know the French king has gone mazed and been put in a 'sylum.'

Nettle opened his mouth to argue, but then a shade of doubt crossed his own fossilised face. 'Aye facks, now you say it, I *'ave* heard something about a mad king, I do confess.'

The younger chorister who had offended earlier by showering Nettle's great-great-uncle with his pipe leavings snorted. 'Ye're both cakey. The mad one's ours. The Frenchies have chopped off their own king's head like a top o' cabbage. *That's* why we're gone to war.'

I interrupted this exchange of great minds. 'And what can you tell me about old Wedlock? Any reason he might have run antic himself and burned those papers?'

'Oh, I do know all about that,' Nettle answered, before the sensible young chap (of whom I frankly had more hope) could even open his mouth. 'I seed Wedlock huddling with the mayor's electors last week, and when I axed him what the blazes he was up to, he said he fancied to change his vote.'

'Change his vote?' I echoed and Philpott harrumphed in gratified surprise.

Nettle nodded sagely. "Ess, 'ess, that's what he told me. Confidential, mind. Fed up with the old duke, he was, and meant to lick the mayor's boots for a change.'

'Are you sure of this?'

'Sure as I stand 'ere. He thought the whole vote a non-sense and that he and Scorn would look like fools when they were dashed down in Parliament, as he thought they must be.'

Philpott's mind had moved faster than my own. 'But if he meant to vote for the mayor, why burn the poll book?'

Nettle looked at him pityingly. 'You didn't know him, sir. You may as well ask a dog why it rolls in shit.'

I had thought John Scorn generally disliked, but the old root had nothing good to say about Wedlock either. I felt some renewed sympathy with Glynn and his modernising impulses, whatever his own interests in the matter might be. But could any of this be true? As the sexton hobbled away, I turned to Piggy. 'What do you know about Nettle? Is he as ignorant about local matters as he is about the war?'

Piggy shook his head, perplexed. 'He knows a great deal about church music, Laurence, but for the rest …'

'Skelingtons and pigeons, I know.'

John Scorn was now coming past with his grand-daughter, looking worse than ever, and Piggy volunteered his services to help the old man home. Scorn was extremely ungracious about it, but from what we had heard of his character that was hardly a surprise.

'God damn me, though,' Philpott said once they had shuffled off. 'You see what this means, my boy? If that knobbly old turnip is right, and Wedlock meant to change his vote, it would have been disaster for the duke – split his vote clean in half. In the absence of a third deciding voice, Parliament would have had no choice but to turn to Glynn's electors. Two to one in favour of the mayor, and old Scorn and the duke left high and dry.'

'So, there was some sense to Glynn's hints after all,' I said. 'If Nettle's right, it would certainly have turned the duke against Wedlock.'

Was it possible the duke had been fool enough to be somehow involved in Wedlock's unfortunate end? A fool might act rashly and leave others to clear up the mess behind him, and Sir James had certainly looked chary when he warned me to be discreet. But I remembered the duke's complete lack of sympathy with the dead man. In the preposterous event His Grace was really somehow involved in Wedlock's death, surely he would have had the sense to at least pretend to a sorrow he did not feel?

'Give me another look at that tinderbox, will you, Laurence?' Philpott asked. It was still in my pocket and I handed it to him. He showed me the carving of the dragon on the lid. 'Have you not noticed the resemblance of this to something in town?'

I looked at it more carefully than before. 'The Angel sign,' I said.

Philpott nodded. 'The dragon on the inn sign is the very spit of this. I wonder if the tinderbox belongs to the inn? 'Tis just the kind of nonsense waste o' money a landlord might fancy.'

127

I could see his mind working to fit this fact to his suspicions of the duke. 'Just because it came from the Angel does not mean the duke set the fire,' I said. 'It is nonsense to say so.'

'Of course it is,' Philpott agreed. 'He would not do it himself. But he could have given the article to whoever did, to act on his behalf. And if his lackey was fool enough to drop the thing at the scene of the crime, God damn me, the duke will be livid.'

Again I remembered Sir James's look of disgust when I showed the tinderbox to him. But then, Sir James always looked disgusted.

'And that was a strange moment, at Communion,' Philpott said musingly. 'The curate said the devil would steal the soul of any man who took the sacrament in a state of sin, and then John Scorn almost gagged on his wafer with a terrible look of guilt.'

'From what we've heard, Scorn is always in a state of sin,' I objected. 'And besides, he wasn't at the Guildhall when the fire started. We saw him at the political meeting with the duke when the news came.'

Philpott shook his head. 'But where had he been before? We know nothing of when the blaze started.'

'It could hardly have been long before the alarm was raised. That old building would have burned down in minutes if a fire had really caught hold, and the room was full of papers, perfect kindling.'

'Yet the clerks said the flames only got up after they

opened the door and let in air. Before that it was only smoke, they said.'

I was impatient. 'Very well then. Accepting your ridiculous fantasy for a moment, can you truly think John Scorn was the duke's tame assassin?'

Philpott looked cagey. 'He seems a fellow worth quizzing, that's all. One way or another, I fancy he must know something.'

'You are building a story out of nothing,' I said, though in truth, after the sexton's tale it was not so very ridiculous as before. 'God damn it, Philpott, you ought to have learned from what happened in America. If you libel the duke he will have you arrested, just as Dr Rush tried to do in Philadelphia.'

'In which he failed.' Philpott looked smug.

'Only because we ran.'

'A strategic retreat, my boy. And, I congratulate myself, one excessively well executed, I must say.'

I stared at him. 'Excessively well executed?' I began to tremble with impotent rage. '*Excessively well executed* when you forgot the one thing I asked you to bring? The only thing in America I cared for at all? Who may be now ill, or mistreated, or dead, and for whom I cannot go in search because due to your idiocy I will be arrested if I set foot in America ever again?'

8

MENEAGE STREET WAS always busy, but there was a special *frisson* of something in the air as we drew near to the Rodney Inn, source of last night's trouble. I feared it might be the men with red faces up to no good again, but in fact the commotion was caused by the presence of the Sapient Hog. Helston was a town of two thousand souls, and to give each a posy, and demand of each a coin, would probably fill the pig's days to overflowing between now and his final performance on Monday.

I had imagined an immense old boar like my mother's, with strange dangling wattles and a bristly chin, but when Toby was finally presented to our view he was rather dapper. Black haired and very sleek, he was a gleaming porcine aristocrat. He was also quite young – younger than I had supposed – and I wondered if the famous Sapient Hog was really a succession of beasts taught their tricks and presented to society for a couple of years before the unbecoming wattles and bristles inevitably made their appearance.

Just now, he was knocking at the door of a fine townhouse next door to the Rodney – or at least Mr Nicholson his manager was – an extraordinary-looking man in a striped waistcoat and preposterously tall hat shaped like a stovepipe.

'I think that's John Scorn's house,' I said to Philpott. 'Glynn said it was a big old place next to the inn.'

'His wealth never extended to a genteeler street, then,' Philpott observed as we drew closer. 'Or perhaps he likes all the bustle and noise outside his windows, just as I do.'

The door to Scorn's house was opening, and a pretty young maidservant appeared, wiping her hands on her shabby apron before accepting the flowers and disappearing inside a moment, presumably for the requested coin.

'No footman to open the door,' Philpott observed. 'Only a maid of all work from the look of her hands. Scorn is certainly fallen on hard times, just as Glynn told you.'

Philpott was right. Even from a little distance I could see that the paint on the window shutters was peeling. The maidservant returned, rather pink, and spoke low to the pig's owner. After a moment's altercation the girl fetched the nosegay from inside and returned it to the pig who took it politely by the stems, the flowers contriving a rather fetching ornament by his pricked ear.

'John Scorn refuses to pay,' Philpott chuckled. 'God damn me, we should have guessed he would.'

The door shut and the striped man and pig moved on to the next house. We skirted the knot of merry figures who had nothing better to do on a Saturday afternoon than follow the pig's progress and knocked on Scorn's door in our turn. The brass knob was dull, another hint of a shortage of servants, confirmed by the same girl opening the door again with a look of harried vexation that turned to surprise at the sight of two more strangers. She had not mastered the art of doorkeeper and only gawped at us.

'We're here to see Mr Scorn, if he can spare us a moment,' Philpott said. 'This is Dr Jago's cousin.'

The girl did not seem quite to grasp his meaning. 'You do want the master?'

'If he is at home,' I said politely. On the way from church I had reluctantly conceded that there were certain aspects of Philpott's theory that held some water. John Scorn had certainly looked shifty when he was called up before the sheriff that morning, and the sight of the tinderbox had brought him up short, though the actual meaning of the fury on his face at the sight of it had been obscure.

The maid went to the first door on the left and rapped timidly. The old man's voice answered, and she stuck her head in a moment before re-emerging. 'What do you want with him, he says? He's tremendous busy.'

'The sheriff requires answers to a few more questions and has sent me to ask them,' I said. This wasn't exactly true but at least it had the desired effect. Another muttered consultation around the door ended in the maid holding it open for us to pass through.

Even if the place was shabby now – even if the passageway smelled of day-old fish – the house had certainly once been a prosperous one. The front room we entered was high-ceilinged and airy and, perhaps on account of the old man's legs being now too feeble to attempt the stairs, served as his bedchamber as well as his study. There was a heavy, old-fashioned curtained bed against one wall, while a large desk stood under the sash window, scattered with ledgers and papers. Facing the door was a fine fireplace with a jumble of ornaments on the mantelpiece above it, including a carved wooden tobacco jar and a particularly ghastly toby jug. There was the muffled din of passing pedestrians and carts outside the window and John Scorn was sitting in his desk chair with a cup of tea at his elbow, his back turned to the lively outdoor scene.

'I have not the time for this,' he wheezed before we had even given our names. 'I am a man of business with many a call on my time.'

The shabby room and the newspaper belied him, so we ventured closer, pulling up chairs to sit down across the desk from him. He picked up his cup of tea and gulped noisily. He looked worried, his hand was shaking, and some of the tea spilled down his waistcoat.

'I am Laurence Jago, employed by the coroner and the duke to look into Mr Wedlock's death,' I said. 'We have just heard he meant to change his vote. Do you know if that is true?'

Scorn slurped at his cup again and when he set it down on the desk it was empty. 'So he told me, sir.'

'Told you? When?'

'Some days ago. I cannot exactly remember.' Scorn seemed vague, distracted, and a strange sweat had broken out on his forehead. He glanced at me, and then over my shoulder. I thought he was looking at Philpott, but when I followed his gaze he was staring at an empty space by the fireplace with a kind of fixed fascination.

I tried to draw his gaze back to me. 'And what did you say when he told you of his intention?'

Scorn's fingers began a curious dance on the arms of his chair. 'Same as I said to the sheriff. He was a fool to think Glynn and Lushington cared for him or the town.'

'And then there was this.' I took the tinderbox from my pocket and put it on the desk in front of him. 'I think you knew it, sir, when I showed it to you this morning. Do you know what happened at the Guildhall? Do you know who else might have been there?'

He didn't answer, only stared at the tinderbox with the same look of incandescent fury he had worn earlier, but now overlaid with an excessive trembling that made his head weave above it like a snake rising from a charmer's basket, while his fingers gambolled oddly on the chair arm.

'You *do* know it, sir,' I said.

He still didn't answer. He only cast a look back towards that vacant spot by the fireplace, as if he hoped some help would come to him from that unlikely quarter. ''Twas come-by-chance what happened to Wedlock,' he said at last, as if talking to the unseen phantom behind my shoulder. 'I was with the duke. He can vouch for me.'

That was true, and it was also true that the clerks had not seen John Scorn at the Guildhall. It had been only Wedlock's voice they had heard through the massy oak door. But now Scorn's hands were dancing more than ever. He looked hunted. Haunted. He stared through me, not at me. I got the strange impression that he now hardly knew we were there at all. The sweat was suddenly pouring off him, and I thought I could see a pulse racing in his scrawny neck. 'God damn me, I never should have done it,' he moaned suddenly, looking either terrified or mad, or both at once.

'Done what?' Philpott's eyes were popping at the old man's peculiar frenzy, but Scorn was talking on, rapidly, to himself or to that unseen presence behind me.

'The curate was right, God damn it. I should never have done it.'

'The curate?' I clutched at something I thought I understood. 'What should you not have done, sir? Taken the sacrament? You were somehow guilty and should have stayed away?'

But then, all at once, John Scorn's agitation ceased.

A veil fell across his expression, until now so full of passion and fear. A strange glassy look. He had been flushed scarlet but now he was waxy pale. I reached out and took hold of his bony wrist.

'Are you unwell, sir?'

His pulse was frantic, but at my touch he came to himself and shook me off with surprising force. 'Get out of this house.' His voice was rough and pained. 'I have no more to say to you.' His eyes turned to the fire. 'Or to you, God damn it.'

I glanced at Philpott and saw alarm on his face that matched my own. We hastened out, telling the maid to mind the old man, who seemed to be suddenly very ill. Outside the house we stopped and looked at one another.

'He was deadly frightened of our questioning.'

Philpott nodded. 'God damn me, I thought his heart might give out before our very eyes. But he was there when the fire at the Guildhall was set, Laurence, I assure 'ee – or he knows who was.'

'I'll go to the Angel,' I said. 'Scorn must be questioned under oath and Sir James can contrive it. But I think you had better go for Piggy and tell him to hurry to Scorn, for he looked dreadful.'

AT THE ANGEL THE duke and duchess were engaged in a spirited argument. There was a broken lamp on the carpet and Sir James was crawling about the duke's feet collecting up the shards of glass and putting them in the coal scuttle. The careful lock of hair he had cultivated to hide his bald patch in the absence of a wig was standing up like the crest of a cockatoo.

Amid all this bad temper, Anne had wisely elected to conceal her faded dress among the faded window curtains, rather in imitation of a chameleon, and there was no sign of the baby Sidney, the child Charles Burges or George Osborne at all.

'It is no use, Kate.' The duke's hand was still quivering from his destructive exertions. 'You do not understand the matter in the slightest degree. Not in the slightest degree, I say.'

'Well then, I'm sure Sir James does.' Her Grace appealed to the under-secretary who looked up uneasily from his hands and knees, wiped a smear of coal dust from the scuttle across his cheek, and did not answer. 'What can a few country livings signify, to give to a few country vicars?'

'A vast sum, even supposing I could get hold of them,' the duke retorted. 'A vast sum, I say. They are not in my gift, Kate, and you must leave off persuading me as if it were any of your concern. By God, I shall give it up,' he added angrily. 'Whatever happens, I say I shall give the damn borough up, for there's no relying on anyone.'

It was at this juncture that I was obliged to begin my tale of the afternoon's events. For a moment I thought the duke was to take it all philosophically. 'I am rather displeased with Wedlock,' he said with remarkable calm. 'Rather displeased, I say. Choosing to throw in his lot with the other side and betray all my patronage of so many years. By God, if he had voted with the thirty-two, Glynn and Lushington would have claimed even *he* saw the justice of their case. And my vote would have been split, quite split down the middle, with no candidate to return to Parliament at all. To be frank,' he added with rather less cool detachment, 'I am damned glad he's dead.'

'I would recommend Your Grace refrains from such an observation in public,' Sir James said, sitting up on his heels and taking out his pocket handkerchief to wipe the coal dust from his fingers. 'If the story is true, Your Grace would be the apparent beneficiary of the man's death, and it would be tactless to point it out.'

'We are all quite used to my husband,' the duchess observed. 'There is no talking to him in this mood. And, Sir James, you had better go smooth your hair at the looking glass. You are quite nonsensical.'

Sir James got to his feet, put the coal scuttle back by the fire and did as he was bid. Meanwhile, the duke had begun gnawing his fingernails, looking thoughtful. I wondered what was passing in his mind. General resentment at Wedlock's treachery, of course, but surely, I thought again, he would not have been so unguarded in his outburst if he had really been involved?

'At any rate, Your Grace,' I said, 'I am certain John

Scorn knows more than he tells. He claims he was with you when the fire was set, but there are circumstances which make me think we must call the sheriff and arrange for his arrest. He recognised the tinderbox that started the fire, I am sure of it, and seemed discomposed. He was not very forthcoming with me just now, but he would be obliged to speak more frankly under Hitchens' formal questioning.'

At this the duke looked even more dismayed. 'But what of the vote? Will they allow him to cast his vote if he is detained by the sheriff? God damn me, Sir James, I'll not be robbed of both my electors.'

Sir James came back from the looking glass and examined me with some disfavour. 'It is very unfortunate, Your Grace, but I don't see how we can avoid it. I advised Jago to be discreet and not act rashly, but he has clearly disregarded my counsel and I am afraid the damage is done. Your Grace must be seen to be scrupulous if we are not to be implicated in this whole grubby affair.'

'Implicated – or defeated.' The duke took out his snuff and took a meditative pinch. 'One or the other it seems. Either I keep quiet and get Scorn's vote at the risk of being called an accessory to mischief or I deliver my voter to Hitchens and by doing so concede defeat forthwith.' He rose to his feet slowly and the duchess frowned.

'Implicated or defeated, by God!' he said. 'Christ in heaven, what have I ever done to deserve such injustice?' He threw his snuffbox with some energetic force at the fire grate. It missed its target, smashed a vase on the mantelpiece, and, the clasp of the box breaking open, filled the sunlight shafting through the windows with a cloud of floating snuff. No one dared remonstrate except for the duchess, who said, '*Well, really!*' before sneezing violently.

At that moment there was a smart rap at the door and Philpott hurried in without waiting to be asked, looking hectic and excited. The duke glowered at the advent of his large, plebeian figure, and Sir James recoiled, as if Philpott's florid face had sparked a torrent of disagreeable memories just as mine had done last night.

Being too full of his news, Philpott didn't notice either man's reaction, or the snuff swirling in the sunlight, or still less Anne, who was now convulsing discreetly among the window curtains. 'Begging your pardon, Your Grace, but I am come from the doctor,' he said. He sneezed violently into his sleeve and looked puzzled. 'I sent him to John Scorn, the man having seemed out of sorts after our interview, and Dr Jago has just now sent me word that the old bugger is collapsed.'

At this point Philpott and I sneezed in unison, but the duke appeared immune to the contagion of swirling tobacco dust. 'Collapsed? What the devil do you mean by that?'

'Is he alive?' the duchess asked, holding her handkerchief to her nose.

'Five minutes ago, I believe he was, Your Grace. But what has happened since—'

Philpott was now sneezing too energetically to say anything intelligible and I turned to Sir James, who had remained admirably calm at the receipt of this news. 'Scorn was seized with a trembling when he saw the tinderbox,' I said. 'Perhaps the fear of discovery was too much of a shock for his heart.'

The duke was even less pleased with me than before. Having first suggested his one remaining voter should be arrested, it now seemed I had killed him outright. I wasn't sorry to be immediately banished along with Philpott to go and find out whether John Scorn was still breathing at all.

A LARGE CROWD HAD gathered around John Scorn's door as we came up. 'No interferin' now!' someone shouted out. 'Tell the doctor not to be meddlin' with the wager board.'

'God's will be done,' another voice agreed, and then there was a general ruckus as Scorn's supporters made known their displeasure at this mercenary spirit. For myself, I didn't think God would object to Piggy exercising his medical skill, whatever its effect on the bets at the Blue Anchor. Philpott waved an irritable hand at them, and I slammed the front door behind me in their eager faces. The maidservant led us into Scorn's chamber again, where we now found him lying on the carpet instead of sitting at his desk. His granddaughter was on her knees beside him, dressed in her outdoor clothes, and Piggy was bent to the old man's waistcoat, listening for his heart.

Eleanor sat up, taking off her bonnet to reveal fine raven hair like Sarah Glynn's, though far less richly arranged. 'T'old bugger's still breathin', Dr Jago.'

'He has the constitution of an ox, whatever else.' Piggy sat back on his heels and looked down at his patient with a frown.

'What exactly happened?' I asked.

Piggy looked up. 'As you know, Laurence, Philpott came to fetch me after you left him, worried about the old man's state. I was not a minute in the door before Scorn collapsed.' He shook his head. 'I brought him home earlier, after the funeral, while Miss Scorn went to fetch Miss Glynn for a walk. He was tired and shaken, but did not seem exactly ill, so having another appointment at The Willows I left him here alone with a cup of tea.' He looked at Eleanor. 'Did you call in at all before your walk?'

'I popped in to change my bonnet.'

'And how was he then?'

'Sour as a rig. I told him 'e was a nasty old knack-kneed tongue tab and went off for some rational conversation with Sarah.'

'You argue with him often?'

'Twice a day and ten times on a Sunday.'

Piggy shook his head. 'Then I'm afraid that was another

shock, among all his shocks today – shocks which may finally have killed him. But do not blame yourself.'

Eleanor folded her arms and glared at him, as if blaming herself had never yet occurred to her and would certainly not be entertained now. 'Killed 'im? He's still snortin' like a bleddy hog as best I see.'

John Scorn's breath was, indeed, coming in laboured stertorous grunts, and when I exchanged a glance with Philpott I could see he was thinking the same thing I was. Even if Scorn had been somehow involved in Wedlock's death there would likely be no need of proceedings against him now. He was quite unconscious and his crumpled form put me in mind of my own father's death years ago from a stroke of apoplectic palsy.

Piggy had begun quizzing Eleanor. 'Has your grandfather shown any confusion in recent days?'

'I wish he had.' Eleanor's eyes were like glossy pebbles and had about as much tenderness in them.

'Difficulty sleeping, then? Headaches?'

'He do never sleep well – always too busy nurturin' his grievances.'

'Please, Miss Scorn, for God's sake. Your grandfather is at death's door.'

'Is he?'

'You doubt it?'

'If you knew my grandfer, you'd be betting on his recovery down at the Blue like everyone else.'

'I understand he has always been a forceful man. But even strong men must die in the end.'

She threw up her head like an impatient horse. 'And thank God for it, else we should all be teased to death.'

Piggy seemed to despair of Eleanor's testimony and bent to the old man's mouth, sniffing his breath.

'What do you think ails him?' Philpott asked.

'I don't know. But there's some strange smell. What was he like when you visited him? Excited or stupefied?'

'Excited,' Philpott said.

'Pale and sweating and trembling,' I added, trying to be of more help than Eleanor, which wouldn't be hard. 'I almost thought he was seeing things. Some ghost behind my shoulder. Is it an apoplexy, do you think?'

Piggy raised Scorn's eyelids and then looked up at us, shaking his head in surprise.

'What is it?' Philpott asked.

Piggy looked back at the old man's face. 'It is certainly not an apoplexy. In that case the gaze would be deflected in the direction of the lesion in his brain.'

'Then is it his heart?' I asked.

Piggy felt the pulse. 'His heartbeat is very swift and skipping, yet strong.' He lifted Scorn's eyelid again. 'But I have never seen anything like this. His pupil is so dilated, I can scarcely see the iris at all.'

'And what does that mean?'

'Some kind of intoxication.' He looked at Eleanor. 'Was your grandfather drinking today, Miss Scorn?'

She returned his gaze as if he were quite mad. 'Grandfer don't touch a drop. Hasn't for years. The only thing he learned from that old bugger Wesley.'

'He was certainly not drunk when we saw him,' Philpott said.

Piggy shook his head. 'Nor when I walked him home from church.' He sniffed again at the old man's lips. 'And besides, this smell isn't alcohol.' He pulled himself to his feet, still looking puzzled. Scorn's breathing was growing more laboured by the minute, and his face had now suffused a deep and unnatural purple. 'Will one of you others smell his breath? Tell me what you think?'

Philpott and I looked at each other. I always expected him to be less squeamish than I was, and in this I was always wrong. I didn't much like it but, as Eleanor did not seem to be listening at all, it fell to me to do as Piggy bid.

I don't know what I expected. The horrible, noisome stench of an old man's bad teeth, perhaps. The visceral stink of death. In fact, the scent was more pungent than I had expected but not at all unpleasant. 'It is not spirits,' I said to Piggy. 'Nor wine, nor beer.' I sniffed again. 'But there is some hint of spice, isn't there? It almost puts me in mind of a Christmas punch.'

I wasn't sure if Piggy was listening, for he was frowning to himself. 'Firstly, he has suffered no apoplexy. Secondly, we all agree he was not drunk. Thirdly, if he had taken opium, his pupils would be pinpricks, not so strangely dilated. Fourthly, there is a scent on his breath

146

that speaks of something strange taken by mouth.'

He turned to the women. 'Can you tell me what Mr Scorn has eaten today?'

They exchanged a puzzled glance. 'Just his breakfast as usual,' Eleanor said. 'Then, when I come in from church Loveday was offering him a mutton chop.'

'He wouldn't take it,' Loveday said. 'He didn't fancy nuthin' after the kidneys he'd had at The Willows, he said. He just had a cup o' tea instead.'

Philpott swelled with excitement. 'He was glugging away at it when we came in,' he said. 'Swallowed it down like a desperate man. But I dare say they poisoned him elsewhere and he was only thirsty as a consequence.'

'Poisoned? Nonsense,' I said, but Philpott was looking eagerly to the maid.

'But, so as we may be certain, where is the empty cup, girl?'

Her hand was at her mouth, her eyes wide and uncomprehending.

'The cup of tea he was drinking after church,' Philpott urged her. 'Where is it?'

She went wordlessly to the kitchen while my mind raced. Was it really possible there had been some mischief against John Scorn as well as Wedlock? Was the man I had begun to think involved in Wedlock's death now another victim? The maid was coming back with a collection of broken china in her hands. 'I threw the cup in the dunny heap, sir, for it got smashed when he fell.

But there were nuthin' in it. He had drunk it all down to the very last drop.'

'Devilled kidneys,' Piggy was saying. 'The devilling signifies spice, does it not? You had one, Laurence. Could this scent have come from the seasoned meat?'

'I don't know,' I said. 'I thought of vinegar and mustard, not punch.'

Piggy sighed. 'And in any case, until I identify the substance that has struck him down, I cannot say how long ago he took it. For instance, a misadventure with mushrooms is a slow affair. Twelve hours or more before it takes its fatal effect, while other harmful substances are much quicker acting.'

Eleanor had been watching and listening to all this with a horrible frown. Afterwards I thought it strange that she did not shriek, or faint, or even protest at all these surmises. She only said, 'You do truly think he may die?'

Piggy patted her hand. 'It is too soon to tell, my dear. We do not know enough. He may rally yet.'

'I must send for Cyrus,' she said, almost to herself. But then she looked at us with a new accession of alarm. 'And what the blazes will become of the vote?'

'My dear,' Piggy said, 'I very much doubt your grandfather will ever vote again.'

Eleanor had *buggered* and *bleddyed* and it was clear she was made of the same hot-tempered stuff as Scorn. I now reckoned, in her misplaced worry about the vote, she was also quite as callous as the duke.

9

THE DINNER HOUR

THE DUKE HIMSELF retained his preternatural calm for the few moments it took Piggy to recount his assessment of John Scorn's case. The old man's symptoms, the scent on his breath. What might have so badly disagreed with him was as yet unclear, Piggy explained as he had previously explained to us. But he had evidently been thinking more about it between Scorn's house and the Angel. The scent was reminiscent of spice, he said, and therefore he would examine his dispensary shelves for a match, since the old man might have injured himself by too great a dose of a tonic flavoured with cinnamon or some such, which though a medicine in moderation might possibly be a toxin if taken to excess. '*Sola dosis facit venenum*,' he ended. 'As Paracelsus says, only the dose makes the poison.'

The Latin phrase fell into a perplexed silence in which

the duke stared at Piggy, who now sat down uninvited on a nearby, very low chair, looking suddenly exhausted. If his guess was right, it must be a terrible shock to him as one trained to save lives with physic, to find that, if abused, it could do exactly the reverse. I looked at Anne, who had been sitting with the duchess, sewing quietly, when we came in. She had now laid down her work in her lap and was staring at my cousin.

The duke's tranquillity proved predictably short lived and his imagination quite as fevered as Philpott's, even if his suspicions flew in a precisely contrary direction. 'Those bare-faced scoundrels,' he said. 'Those bare-faced scoundrels, Glynn and Lushington, I say. Sir James, should I call them out?'

George had arrived home during our absence and was now sitting with his long legs folded over the arm of a chair. 'Oh, do, Father,' he said. 'Line them up and take potshots at them. That would be a vastly dignified proceeding.'

Anne hid a smile, while Sir James was quietly discouraging. 'I imagine Lushington is quite handy with a pistol, Your Grace. I do not know about Glynn; but if you killed him it would only cause a regrettable scene.'

'And so instead I must sit here and grin, must I?' The duke bared his teeth in what he seemed to imagine was an example of such forbearing. 'Sit here and grin, I say, with the damned polls closing on Monday night, one elector dead, the other knocked insensible, and Lushington and

Glynn lurking in The Willows, parcelling out poisoned kidneys?'

Piggy shifted uneasily on his too-small hard-backed chair. 'I have blamed no one.'

The duke looked down at him with displeasure. Piggy being the bearer of bad tidings he was bound to be the poor proverbial scapegoat. 'Don't squirm, Dr Jago. You tell me my elector has been poisoned and there are men with a good motive to destroy me in town. I'd like to see you put another complexion on it.'

The fact that this destruction had been visited on his unfortunate puppets rather than on himself seemed temporarily to escape the duke. But it was undeniable that both his voters had now been eliminated only days before the contest, and the only possible beneficiaries of that were Glynn, the mayor, and Lushington, his candidate.

'Without proof, such an accusation would be slander,' Sir James said, as mildly as before. 'And besides, Your Grace, it would be rather startling in men of Glynn and Lushington's standing. I do not think poison has been the political weapon of choice since the Borgias.'

The duke ignored him, his mind skipping on. 'And what of the election? What are we to do about that? I suppose if John Scorn lives, we can carry him down to the hustings to make his vote. There is no law says an elector must be on his feet.'

Though he didn't exactly say so, I now saw His Grace

was going to use this new development to gloss over the questions I had raised, and conveniently forget my suggestion that the old man ought to be arrested and questioned.

'But I think he must be conscious, Your Grace,' Piggy said. 'Scorn is at present in a deep stupor, what we physicians call *coma*. If he persists in that state he will not be able to declare his choice of candidate even if you can get him to the hustings.'

The duchess spoke up. 'And again, I tell you, Francis, that the whole matter is in your own hands. Instead of skulking here, weeping into your snuff, you should be canvassing the new corporation's electors and persuading them to accept your patronage and vote for your candidates. They will like the Sapient Hog as much as anyone, I should think. Glynn could never have procured such a marvellous entertainment for Helston and you should tell them so.'

No one answered her. The duke took out his snuffbox again, looking thoughtful. Every set of eyes fixed anxiously upon it, fearing another explosion, but at length he seemed to come to a conclusion, tapped it with a decisive finger, and then, to general relief, put it back in his pocket.

'Sir James, call for the sexton. We must dig Wedlock up again.'

Sir James maintained his invincible air of calm. 'Dig him up, Your Grace?'

'Yes, yes, is it not obvious? We must see if he was poisoned too.'

For the first and perhaps last time in our acquaintance I thought the duke was on to something. At the very least, it was a possibility I had not yet considered in the hurry of recent events. But Piggy ran a weary hand through his hair and shifted his large frame on the small chair. 'Thomas Wedlock was certainly not suffering from poison earlier that day, for I saw him. Besides, Your Grace, too much time has elapsed since death, and the deleterious effects of the grave—'

The duke picked up a particularly fine vase from a side table and began passing it meditatively from hand to hand like a cricket ball, his eyes fixed on Piggy's uncooperative face.

'Dignity, Your Grace,' Sir James said with a soothing gesture and removed the vase from his hand, setting it down carefully on the mantelpiece. But the duke's expression did not change. He frowned at Piggy with a new and I thought very underserved loathing. 'You, sir, will establish exactly what substance has been used to attack my voter, for if it should get abroad that you have failed in so vital a diagnosis, no one will ever seek your expertise again. For the sake of your career, you have two days in which you must diagnose and rouse him, Dr Jago.'

'How intriguing,' George said, unfolding his long legs from the arm of his chair and getting to his feet. 'This will be yet another cause for excitement in the Anchor when it gets out. Another question to bet on. *Will Dr Jago succeed before the hustings close?* I must go directly and place my wager.'

The duke now turned his eyes on me. I was certainly an insect but, like the ant or bee, my industry might yet prove useful to him. 'You, sir, will investigate all the circumstances. Glynn and Lushington will have betrayed themselves somehow, for Glynn is only a country mayor and Lushington a novice in politics. Yes, yes, they will undoubtedly have made some mistake, I say, which any half-decent clerk will be able to discover. If you find them out, I dare say I will recommend you for a promotion in Whitehall.'

He didn't seem to have grasped that I was no longer in the Government's employ. Or was I? And if by some strange new development I actually was, how did I feel about it?

I T WAS ALMOST SEVEN o'clock before we returned to Church Street, to eat our long-congealed mutton stew under Tirza's reproachful gaze, and thereafter dress ourselves for the Assembly Room, where the pig's performance was to commence at eight o'clock, according to a notice pinned to the Angel's door. I told Philpott what the duke had said, while Piggy brought down his medical textbooks and propped them one against the other as he shovelled the stew into his mouth abstractedly.

'What made you tell the duke you thought it could be a misused physic?' I asked him.

'Because that is what I think. The scent on Scorn's breath put you strongly in mind of punch, and I thought so too. What spices are in punch?'

I thought about my mother's Christmas kitchen. 'Cinnamon? Mace?'

He nodded. 'Both of which are very commonly prescribed as tonics, usually suspended in brandy.'

'The brandy being the tonic, and the so-called remedy merely flavouring,' Philpott observed with unusual scepticism.

Piggy disregarded him. 'But I do not recollect that either of those spices has a toxic character.' He gestured. 'Which is why I am consulting my books.'

'And you are certain it is not laudanum?' I asked, my mind going back to the only other thing I knew was capable of flooring a man like brandy.

'As certain as I can be.' Piggy closed one book and opened another. 'Not merely from the wide dilation of the man's pupils, which, as I told you, is the reverse of an opium trance, but from the scent, too. Perhaps you aren't much acquainted with the stuff, Laurence, being young and healthy, but laudanum has a very particular pungent smell of its own.'

I avoided Philpott's eye as I meekly accepted this lecture.

'Moreover,' Piggy added, 'laudanum also uses brandy as its medium, and we would therefore have smelled alcohol.' He shook his head and looked at his pile of textbooks in some despair. 'Ten to one the answer, if there is one, will be in the bottom-most book in the pile. Meanwhile, we must attend this confounded Assembly and then I must certainly go back to see old Scorn later.'

I was remembering John Scorn's small household – the pretty but awkward maidservant, his irritable grand-daughter Eleanor, and the passionate old man himself, whose anger, according to the curate, had driven Eleanor's brother away to Camborne. Without the old man, Eleanor would be left high and dry and that might well account for her bad temper. Perhaps, under all her noise, she was actually frightened. And if she was, no wonder, since her own future was surely thrown into doubt by this turn of events. It all depended on what money remained to Scorn and what provision he had chosen to make for Eleanor in his will. His death might bring her some peaceful independence or, on the other hand, it might leave her penniless and obliged to remove to a relative's house – perhaps even to her brother in Camborne, far from all her friends. A young woman cannot come and go to please herself, and even the few miles that separated the towns might as well be an ocean. Did she have a sweetheart?

It was then that I remembered her say 'I must call for Cyrus', almost under her breath, as she gazed down at her insensible grandfather. The name rang a bell in my mind. I had certainly heard it somewhere before, but amid all the events of the day I couldn't now remember when.

IT MADE ME SMILE despite everything to hear Piggy say he *must* attend the Assembly. No doubt the compulsion was the desire to dance with Sarah Glynn, but I was no less eager and could hardly blame him. I had expected a tremendous crowd but, of course, the half-crown entrance fee deterred all but the well-to-do, while the poor would have their chance to see the pig perform in the street at noon on Monday. Tonight was a select gathering of the town's gentry and the visiting politicians. Anne was already there on George Osborne's arm. She blushed when she saw me come in, but she turned back politely to whatever nonsense George was spouting in her ear.

The duke was, as yet, absent, but Glynn was there with Sarah. She was dressed in the red silk again, which blazed brightly beside her uncle's sober suit. Behind her, I could see the curate in his clerical black. I was surprised to see him there, when he had just buried his grand-father, but he hurried over when he saw us. 'How is the old man? I have only just heard and am come to find you before I visit him.'

'He is very ill,' Piggy said. 'But I don't yet despair.

Having lived through the first throes of his malady there must be hope for him.'

'And the cause?' The curate looked like a frightened rabbit now instead of a puppy. 'I have been hearing some dreadful rumours—'

'I don't know,' Piggy said frankly. 'I am trying to find it out.'

The curate hesitated. 'Then ...' He looked like he was summoning his courage. 'Will you come with me into the courtyard for a moment? I may have something useful to tell you.'

'You know of someone with a motive to hurt John Scorn?' Philpott asked eagerly.

Reverend William Wedlock gave a distinctly unclerical snort. 'You'd do better to look for someone who hasn't.' But then the flash of everyday humanity evaporated and he remembered his vocation. How tiresome to be required to be always holy, I thought, as I reluctantly followed the others outside and left Anne with George.

We all sat down on the low coping of the well. The curate absently picked up a pebble from between the cobbles and dropped it into the well's mouth like the boy he really was beneath his sober churchman's dress.

'You know all about the Scorn family by now, I suppose?' he asked, looking up at us from under his long hair.

'We are only slightly acquainted with them,' I said. From inside the Assembly Room came a patter of gratified applause. The Sapient Hog must be beginning his performance and we were missing it. 'We were with old Scorn before he collapsed,' I went on. 'Since then we have met Eleanor, of course, and her maid—'

'Loveday.' William Wedlock nodded.

'And we have heard of a man – an admirer, perhaps – named Cyrus, I think, but we know no more of him than that.'

The curate's whole body squirmed. 'Yes, yes, it is Cyrus Best I must speak of. I know him well, you see, for he's a member of the choir and certainly the best singer St Michael's has ever had.'

That was where I had heard the name before. Piggy had said Cyrus would not sing at the funeral being more given to carousing, an observation the curate now confirmed. 'Cyrus Best is a man quite without religion. The duke pays the choristers' wages and he would not sing if he weren't well paid. As it is, he gambles it all away on some foolish wager or another at the Blue Anchor. He is merely a housepainter and makes a very poor living.'

Eleanor was rather a fool to fancy him, then. But the curate's disapproval had sent Philpott's mind scampering off in defence of Cyrus again. 'And why shouldn't a fellow take pleasure at the tavern if he can afford it?'

The curate's squirming was now more in the way of vexation than anything else. 'Because Cyrus is a scoundrel who has already tried his hand against another man. That man fortunately escaped with his life, so no one was willing to listen to me.' A crimson tide was now rising up his cheeks as warm as the candlelight flooding from the windows of the Assembly Room behind us. 'John Scorn is certainly not the first man Cyrus has sought to harm.'

'You are telling us you believe this man Cyrus Best has poisoned Scorn?' Philpott was incredulous. I knew he was bent on the affair being political and any other explanation would not suit him at all. But the curate did not know this and looked aggrieved at Philpott's tone.

'I do, and if you'll only listen to me, I will tell you why.'

Piggy spoke kindly out of the shadows. 'Go on, William,' he said. 'We are listening.'

Philpott shrugged and picked up a pebble of his own to drop into the well. I listened for a splash, but none came. The water must be very low.

'Eleanor is set on having Cyrus to husband, but her grandfather refuses to accept him,' William Wedlock said. 'Her aunt made a bad marriage to a poor roper who drank away all his wages. Scorn cast them off and now he fears Eleanor is about to do the same. He and Eleanor have been going at it hammer and tongs these six months, and the more he tells her nay the more set she is on having the man.'

From the little I had seen of Eleanor, I could well believe it. 'But even if her aunt's husband was a scoundrel, Cyrus Best may not be. Not enough to murder a man, surely?'

The curate hesitated. 'I shall have to tell you the whole story.'

An outbreak of delighted laughter from the Assembly Room made me hope the curate's *whole story* would not take too long. But his careful hesitation before he began his tale did not bode well for much enjoyment of the Sapient Hog tonight.

'As I told you,' he began, 'a position in the choir brings a financial reward any man would relish – and that's the only reason Cyrus sings.' He paused, marshalling his words carefully, for fear of maligning anyone unjustly, I thought, or inadvertently telling an untruth. It was all very becoming in a clergyman, but I wished he would just get on with it.

'There's a mason in Helston, named Beaglehole, who has a fine and thriving family down among the workshops on Lower Green, past the bowling ground. He has a very handy way with slate and can split it so cleanly there's not a scrap of waste on any roof he cuts. Consequently, he is sought after, and well set in money matters, but he has the finest tenor voice you ever heard – save Best's, of course – and considers the gift God-given.

'When the previous chorister left town for a position in Truro, he and Best were both up for the vacancy. I arranged for them to sing for Jeb Nettle, the choirmaster, after practice one Tuesday night. Well, when the day came, Cyrus invited Beaglehole for a friendly drink in the Rodney before the trial. And between the Rodney and the church, Beaglehole lost his voice.'

'Lost it?' I said. 'How?'

'Dreadful pain in his throat. Later that night he bled from the mouth.'

'And, so, Beaglehole had a sore throat and Cyrus got the position.' Philpott was unimpressed. 'Folks come down with the sore throat every day, I assure 'ee.'

The curate looked impatient. 'After their drink, the landlady of the Rodney found green powder in the bottom of Beaglehole's pint pot. Powdered glass, she thought it was. I told Dr Johns, but he was eager to dismiss me. He said that powdered glass would not harm the throat but the belly. That if I was right, Beaglehole would bleed from the anus, not the mouth. In truth, he disliked the whole story. If Beaglehole was coming down with a putrid throat, quite independent of any malpractice, it would be a very injurious rumour to spread, he told me. Suppose in the course of a week or two, Beaglehole died of it? Then the story would take on another colour most injurious to Cyrus Best and the poor landlady would be called upon to testify to murder.'

'And was it the putrid throat?' I asked. 'Did Beaglehole recover?'

'He did.' William Wedlock frowned. 'But now I fear Cyrus escaped accusation then, only for us to see another man poisoned – a man who is thwarting Cyrus's hopes of marrying his granddaughter. And whose present incapacity will also be a very nice windfall on Cyrus's guinea wager at the Anchor.'

'Guinea wager?'

He nodded at my surprise. 'I told you he was a hard-gambling man. Second to George Osborne's bet, it is the largest wager placed by any man in town. And it is against John Scorn. He has bet a guinea that Glynn and Lushington's candidates will be returned.'

We were all silent for a moment. Now I hardly noticed the happy crowd inside the inn for I was thinking hard. The duke was sure Lushington and Glynn were the culprits we sought in the case of John Scorn's poisoning, but the members of Scorn's own household would certainly have had far more opportunity to feed poison to the poor old devil, however unlikely it seemed.

'So is Best's motive love or money?' Philpott asked. He did not sound much more persuaded than before.

'Perhaps both,' the curate answered, 'though I don't believe he really loves anyone. As I told you, he does not thrive in his profession and gambles heavily. Eleanor's grandfather may look shabby, but he was rich once, and there might still be money enough in the estate to please a poor man if he can only get hold of it.'

'You think he meant to kill Scorn to bring about the marriage?'

The curate spread his hands. 'All the present obstacles to the union will melt away if the old man dies.'

If the curate's tale was true, there might be more to John Scorn's steadfast rejection of Cyrus than mere pride of position or the fear that Eleanor would be unhappy like her aunt. With this added whiff of rumour – for the curate could surely not be alone in his suspicions about Beaglehole's curious illness – there would be quite enough amiss with Cyrus to turn any loving grandfather against him.

'But why do it now?' I asked. 'If you are right, what pushed Cyrus to act on such a hazard this week?'

William Wedlock had an answer for that, too. 'A perfect time, in a way, with all the election excitement and the old man wrought to such a pitch. Dr Jago might easily have called it an apoplexy, in the same way Dr Johns dismissed Beaglehole's case.'

There was something to that, I thought. And even if foul play was suspected, with the Mohawks and Cherokees at each other's throats the authorities would probably look to politics – as we had done – instead of a much more personal motive. A cunning man might hope his own benefit from the death would slip below everyone's notice.

But Philpott was not to be persuaded. 'Well,' he said, pressing his hands on his knees preparatory to rising from the low wall, 'that is a very interesting tale, Reverend Wedlock. But I'm afraid there is a fine line between the pleasure of speculation and pure fantasy. For there is also your own grandfather to consider. Could Cyrus Best have killed him, too?'

William Wedlock looked astonished. 'Cyrus kill Grandfer! Why the devil should he want to?'

'Exactly,' Philpott said. 'And therefore I am inclined to think your accusations unfounded.'

'But there was no hint of murder in my granfer's death,' Wedlock objected. 'The doctor said so. If you are fools enough to think his death suspicious too, then don't you see that is yet another very convenient circumstance for Cyrus? Who knows, perhaps that's another reason he decided to act now, hoping John Scorn's death would be confounded with Granfer's and all the circumstances muddled. Which,' he added, with some unexpected severity for such a puppy, 'is exactly what you are doing.' He stood up. 'I beg you to listen to me. If you don't, I fear you'll be sorry later. In the meantime, I shall go to Scorn and say a prayer for him.'

After he was gone, Philpott got to his feet. 'Stuff and nonsense,' he said. 'The man's cakey, as I believe they say in these parts.'

I shook my head. 'Perhaps. But he knows the town better than we do. And he is a man of the cloth, and surely wouldn't lie. Besides, why should he?'

Philpott answered this question with another one. 'And so we are to believe that Cyrus Best, house-painter, availed himself of a poison so uncommon your cousin cannot find it out, and fed it to John Scorn at his own house? *Never mind the fact you hate me, sir, let me offer you food or drink of doubtful taste and strange appearance.*'

'Someone might have helped him,' I said.

'Who? Eleanor? Loveday the maid?'

Piggy looked pained. 'God preserve us, I hope not.'

There was more laughter and more applause coming from inside. 'Come on,' I said. 'I suppose if all else fails we can ask the pig what he thinks.'

10

EVENING

As WE CAME IN, the Sapient Hog was concluding his performance by kindly acquainting an old lady with the fact that her missing spectacles were hanging around her neck. George had attached himself to Sarah Glynn, the only members of the two rival parties willing to cross the yawning political divide. I went straight to Anne, who was now standing alone.

'You missed the performance,' she said, arching her neck and looking at me rather sternly.

'Forgive me, governess,' I said. 'But the curate was full of suspicions and determined to share them with us.'

She had frowned at my feeble joke but now looked more interested. 'Was he? What exactly did he say?'

I shrugged. 'He blames a local man with a grudge against John Scorn. But Philpott doesn't believe any of it. He wants the duke to be guilty.'

'The duke?' She raised her eyebrows. 'On what possible grounds?'

'I'll tell you if you'll dance with me.'

The fiddlers were starting up an allemande in the music gallery. She nodded and held out her hands. When I took them, I forgot all about John Scorn, Reverend William Wedlock and Philpott's wild theories. 'I never thought I'd see you again,' I said. 'Or if I did, that you'd be married to Canning by now.'

I thanked God it was an allemande and not a cotillion square of dancers that would have suppressed all chance of private talk. The steps took us away from each other but then together again, sometimes our arms entwining as we turned, sometimes our hands clasping. Her arms and shoulders were bare above her long gloves, and an ill-pinned lock of hair fell from her chignon. Her usual cool composure was slipping into something more joyful and more sensual. But instead of enjoying this moment of freedom, and with my usual talent for ruining everything, I promptly embarked on the questions that had troubled me ever since I saw her first in Helston.

'Tell me what happened to you,' I said the next time the steps brought us together. She frowned as we retreated one from the other again like the tide. 'If you will,' I added, as we converged again. 'I know I have no special right—'

'Don't be absurd, Laurence. I should think you have

every right to know why I am not Mrs Canning, since I threw you over for the man.'

We turned; our arms linked.

'I am not proud of myself, not least for my own stupidity,' she said. 'George Canning is Pitt's particular pet and will make sure to fall in love with an heiress when the time is right.'

The man certainly had no money to speak of, I remembered that much. 'He did not ask for you?'

'Nary a word. He was merely dallying. And interested only in the flesh.'

That would be a cardinal sin for one who was, I thought, almost entirely intellect. 'I must confess to an interest in that line myself—'

'Yes, yes, of course. You men cannot help it. But unfortunately my flesh was not even alluring enough to make him forget his ambition.' Our arms embraced again. 'I had too little money or influence then and have even less now.'

'But even so, why are you a governess? Aust is not gone broke?'

She laughed at that, and any onlooker would probably have thought us flirting, not talking of politics and money. 'No, no. God forbid. But he has retired now, Laurence, and we live very quietly. We have nothing to do with Whitehall at all and are therefore of no use to anyone.'

To imagine her banished from all political excitements

was both terrible and at the same time more promising to my old hopes than any other picture she could possibly have painted. 'You don't see anybody?'

'No one of any interest,' she answered. 'Mr Erskine still visits and brings his dreadful Whig friends with him. Mr Fox is tolerable, but Mr Sheridan is all hands.'

Mr Sheridan was the most flamboyant man in Parliament and Fox was a former Cabinet Minister and leader of what little opposition remained to Pitt in the House of Commons. But not being in power, she had as little use for them as Canning had had for her.

'Why exactly are you here?' I asked. 'You seemed more like a companion to the duchess this afternoon, if anything.'

'I am quite their maid of all work,' she said, 'and governess seems certainly not to be the worst of all possible slaveries. But I was bored to death at home in Kensington, Laurence, and when I heard that Sir James was coming here – and that his wife could not accompany him though he wished to take little Charles to see his first election – I eagerly offered to go with them.'

'But why as governess?'

'Oh – merely to prevent talk. You know there has been much scandal in the duke's household. He would not tolerate Sir James in company with an unmarried woman, and I didn't know the duchess very well then. Now it is all explained and we are quite as comfortable together as living with the duke can possibly allow.'

It was deflating to see she didn't really need my pity. All I could think to say was, 'It has turned out a far more interesting expedition than you might have expected.' I meant the death and the poisoning but she took my hand for a moment as we turned and squeezed my fingers.

'I want you to forgive me.'

'Forgive you?'

'I never understood you. Not really.'

'How could you, when I kept so many secrets?'

'Mr Aust has explained it all to me. The Foreign Office is full of mysteries and schemes, he told me, just like your hidden French mother. And he told me you had gone to America on their orders.'

I frowned at that. 'They certainly gave me money and a task to do. But I'm not sure I'm still in their employ.'

She raised her dark eyebrows at me as we drew close. 'Are you not? See how Sir James favours you.'

If anything, Sir James had been remarkably tetchy. But perhaps I was to be a pincushion of his very own. 'I have been apprenticed to Philpott for over a year and Mother wants me to stay in Helston and join the bank.'

She studied me as we parted again with her old incisive gaze. I had always thought her mind as sharp as a needle, her intentions adamantine as diamonds. I had once thought that if she decided to love me she would bind her own interests to mine, not as clinging ivy but as the slender, unshakeable column on which it grows. She had abandoned me for Canning only because I had proved less stalwart and more perplexing than herself. Before the disasters that had driven me from England we had kissed, and the possibility of marriage had been understood between us, though the words themselves had never been exactly spoken.

Whatever I had expected her to say next, it was not what she did say.

'Your mother's farm is close, I believe?'

'Four miles. An hour's easy ride, no more.'

She quirked her mouth. 'It is easy to deal with Mr Philpott – I dare say you will be as valuable to him in government as a novice writer. But your mother should understand that within a six month you will be quite restored in Whitehall – nay, even promoted, if the duke is true to his word – and it would be a shocking waste for you to leave London for a country bank.'

The music was ending. We bowed and curtsied. And then, before I could ask her who exactly was to explain the matter to my mother – or even wonder that anyone cared about me enough to think such an explanation important – Sarah Glynn was upon us. 'Your horrid cousin has insisted on going b-back to that dreadful old man,' she said to me. 'Are all doctors so disagreeable?'

I introduced her to Anne, though as they had been cooped up together in the coach last evening, it was hardly necessary. In this good-humoured atmosphere they examined each other with far less repugnance and far more curiosity. They bobbed perfunctory curtsies one to the other. Then the music started again and George was coming over, his eyes bent on Anne. 'You are about to be honoured with the hand of a dukeling,' I said.

Anne rolled her eyes, but not unkindly, as he drew near. 'He is a very amusing boy, but endless jokes grow irksome in the end. The only thing he ever takes seriously is his gambling.'

George led her off to make up a square at the cotillion. A squat, elderly man was bearing down on Sarah, who took prompt evasive action by pleading thirst, and leading me off to fetch her a drink. Away from the dancers she held the glass in a gloved hand and looked at me over the rim.

'It has come to Uncle's ears that you are acting for the duke. It's very tiresome, for it will put him off Pythagoras, b-being your cousin. Is it true that the duke thinks Uncle has been p-poisoning old John Scorn?'

There were evidently no secrets in the town, and no point in trying to keep them if there were. 'His Grace is inclined to think so, yes, it being his own voters that have suffered. But it is my task to find out the truth.'

She looked sceptical. 'Even if the truth would displease him?'

'Of course,' I said. 'I would hardly be of use to him otherwise.'

'Then you had b-better quiz me at once, and I shall tell you all the facts I know.'

I had not thought of such a thing, and whether she

would answer honestly I couldn't guess, but under her cheerful gaze I obediently asked her where her uncle and Lushington had spent the afternoon.

'Uncle was at home all day.'

And Mr Lushington?'

'Oh, he never goes out, without it causing a terrible stir of servants, you know, being unable to do as he p-pleases, poor man.'

'And were there any visitors at The Willows today?'

'There are always p-people coming and going. Some of the aldermen came, I believe, and I saw Mr Nicholson and the Sapient Hog at the b-back door, collecting alms for posies.' She glanced up at me and blushed. 'And of course, Pythagoras visited Mr Lushington twice, once after the meeting with the sheriff this morning, as you know, and then again this afternoon. I was out walking with Eleanor the second time and he was there when I came b-back; but before we could be comfortable he was called away to nasty old Scorn, and you know all the rest.'

'And yesterday, before the political meeting?' I asked, remembering the fire. 'Where were your uncle and Lushington then?'

'At home again all day, I think, the same as today. We walked up to the Rodney just as the crowds were b-beginning to gather. Uncle was cross with Lushington that we had not come sooner, as we were a little jostled about. But he need not have troubled himself for I found it all quite amusing.'

'Did you see the duke and John Scorn at the Rodney before the meeting?'

She frowned. 'They came even later. But they were not even invited, you know.'

'And how did Scorn seem to you then?'

'Quite his usual self. Ready to p-punch someone if he only had the strength in his arm to do it.' She followed my gaze to where George and Anne were still dancing. 'But it is all a most remarkable story, is it not? A better p-plot than my own, I confess. Fires, death and p-poisoning. And a handsome young doctor to save the day.'

Handsome? She really was as far gone in love as Piggy, who, moreover, had shown no sign of saving anything as yet. He hadn't even identified the supposed toxin at issue, and it occurred to me for the first time to wonder if it was possible his diagnosis was mistaken. 'Perhaps there is no poison at all and Scorn's collapse quite natural.'

'Oh no, it must be a p-poisoning.' She was still thinking of her book. 'It would hardly be worth the trouble of a novel if the whole b-business had only been a muddle.'

'And who would be the villain of the piece? Your uncle, so eager to supplant the duke in the town? Or Mr Lushington, with his desire for a seat in Parliament?'

She wasn't offended at these questions, but she tutted at me. 'No, no. In a novel, you know, there would certainly be some hitherto quite unsuspected p-person who, it transpired, had contrived everything from start to finish.'

Piggy returned to the Assembly Room from John Scorn's house not long after, and at length we younger set found ourselves sitting together at supper, under Mr Glynn's disapproving eye. But Sarah Glynn did not seem to care for her uncle's disapprobation, and as His Grace had not yet appeared the rest of us were spared the duke's censorious gaze. I don't suppose George would have changed his behaviour even if his father had been there, while Anne seemed to think herself quite above the conflict, which indeed she was. And, as the town's doctor, Piggy must naturally also be neutral.

'I suppose old Scorn was poisoned with arsenic,' George asked Piggy carelessly over his supper plate. 'The Old Bailey trials are forever full of arsenic poisoning.'

Piggy shook his head. He looked almost peevish, but perhaps he was only tired. It had been a long day. 'It was very far from my intention to call it poison at all. I only called it something toxic taken by mouth. It is everyone else that calls it poison.'

He looked pointedly at Philpott who had joined us with a large glass of canary wine and was boggling at Sarah Glynn rather too admiringly for good manners. To be fair to him, he had not had a good look at her since becoming aware of Piggy's romantic hopes. He had exchanged one look with Anne, glanced at me with ill-disguised aston-ishment, and then bowed to her with excessive politeness. He knew I had loved her, and I fancied he looked rather offended that I had omitted to tell him she was in town.

'So not arsenic, then?' George looked grieved to be disappointed in this happy idea. Piggy shook his head again.

'Arsenic is very widely available, of course, especially as mouse poison, but its effects are violent vomiting and stomach pain, neither of which symptoms were evident in this case – and if they had, Mr Scorn would be dead by now.'

'Then what of *strychnos*?' Sarah asked from his other side. She was nibbling on a pastry and looking at him with eager eyes. 'That's the other p-poison of choice at the Bailey, isn't it?'

We could hardly be surprised at her acquaintance with murders, this being, after all, the present requirements of her art. 'Yes, indeed,' Piggy said, 'but a victim of *strychnos* poisoning would suffer spasms and seizures, again followed shortly by death. Whatever this is, it has so far exhibited a much milder effect. John Scorn is insensible, but not yet dead.' He paused, looking down at his plate unseeing, in a sudden reverie. 'You know, it is possible that even if he *was* attacked, his attacker only meant to stop him voting, not kill him.'

On first sight this was a cheering supposition, but if true, it did tend to support a political view of the affair. Killing a man to win an election would certainly be going too far but getting an elector dead drunk had always been a common way to swing a tight election. Such tricks were notorious, and a million cartoons lampooned the practice. Scorn did not drink, but if Glynn had therefore availed himself of another substance equally intoxicating . . .

The duke was now coming in with some bustle, the crowd in the Assembly Room parting before him like the Red Sea, though I hope Moses presented a rather more inspiring figure than His Grace, who saw George first, checked for a moment at the sight of Sarah Glynn beside him, and then carried on towards us. We all stood up, but the duke only addressed his son with magnificent disregard for the rest of us mosquitoes, upon which we mosquitoes sat down again.

'I have been detained with the sheriff,' he said to George. 'Was the Hog satisfactory?'

'Very,' George answered. 'He was particularly complimentary to your many years of patronage. He was also taken with Sir James, whom he said put him in mind of a young Hercules.'

The duke looked mildly puzzled and I remembered he was not party to the duchess's bribery of the pig for a good report. 'Glad I missed it. As you should be doing, Dr Jago,' he added severely at the sight of Piggy's pink face turned up to him. 'Hitchens maintains the poll must go ahead, God damn him. He says that the vote would not be halted by the death or illness of one of the thirty-two new electors and the same must apply to the old. But I told him you would have proof of poisoning by morning, in which case he must surely halt the poll.'

Piggy began to stir obediently and Sarah looked put out. 'But, Pythagoras, we have danced scarcely half a dozen dances.'

'I must go home,' Piggy said to her apologetically. 'The duke is right, I must consult my books.'

'I have gained one concession,' the duke was going on, 'one concession, I say, which you may relay to your uncle, Miss Glynn, if you'll oblige me. Hitchens will not expect Scorn to be carried to the hustings but will instead call at his house once all the mayor's votes are in on Monday night.'

'He may call,' Piggy said, now on his feet and hat in hand. 'But whether Scorn will have a voice to speak in is quite another matter.'

'Indeed. So I have also persuaded the sheriff to give us a form of paper for the old man to set his hand to, in any interval of consciousness between now and then, whether Hitchens happens to be there or no.'

Philpott whistled. 'I have heard of such novelties before. Secret ballots, or beans dropped in boxes with the different candidates' names upon them, or pins stuck in a board under a candidate's name. But such outlandish things must be very closely monitored for fear of fraud. How will the sheriff know the paper is genuine?'

'It is to be witnessed by a competent person,' the duke said in an offhand manner. And then, seeming to think this quite enough intercourse with a journalist as uncouth as Philpott, he turned away towards the door to his private quarters. Piggy left shortly after, while George poured himself another glass of wine.

'Well, I think we should forge John Scorn's signature at once and be done with it. I am as competent as any, I suppose, and could also countersign the thing. The work of a moment and all father's problems solved.'

'Nonsense!' Philpott said with much astonished decision.

'Nonsense? Why?' George was very reasonable. 'For all anyone knows, Father has handed the thing to Scorn in the past half-hour and Scorn has obligingly woken and signed it.'

Philpott looked fractionally mollified by this logic but Anne shook her head at George. 'Impossible. If it was discovered, His Grace would go to gaol, and so would you.'

'Gaol!' George laughed at her. 'Preposterous!'

'Gaol or worse,' she persisted. 'Mr Osborne, being young you are probably unaware that fraud and forgery are now capital crimes. With the rise of trade, honesty in money dealings is everything, and the penalty is always enforced.'

'But this is not about money,' the boy objected. 'No one's financial interests would be harmed.'

'But a vote is a precious possession,' Anne answered. 'Scarcely one man in twenty has it, and no women at all.'

George looked impatient. 'And those that do routinely sell it to the highest bidder, in any case.'

'Of course you're right,' she said. 'The whole system is a disgrace, as we can see from this ridiculous election. But to sell a vote you yourself possess is one thing. To be found out in actual forgery of another man's signature is quite another – not to mention when coupled with an unexplained death and a poisoning. It would cause the biggest political scandal since Warren Hastings, and your father's career would certainly be over, even if you were fortunate enough to save your necks.'

She was right about it all. I remembered the last hanging I had seen at Newgate the summer before I left England. A ragged postman who had stolen his letters; a failed, frightened highway robber, and between them the well-dressed corpse of the forger thudding to the ground, his clothes argued over by the hangman and the widow. At the time I had thought myself likely to end up like him: an apparently respectable man come to the worst end.

'Please say no more about it,' Anne was saying, still very much the governess. 'Promise me, George, you'll not be such a fool.'

'Oh, very well then. Come, Miss Glynn, let us dance again and scandalise your uncle instead.'

Philpott, looking regretful, also got to his feet. 'And I had best go seek some lodgings before the innkeepers lock their doors. I shall see you tomorrow, my dear boy.' With a half-salute he pottered out and Anne and I were left alone.

'Will you dance again?'

She shook her head. 'The only use of a dance is a little private conversation, which we may have here as well as anywhere, I suppose.'

She looked tired again, but no longer jaded. She had been bored, she had said – and perhaps I was now of use, furnishing her with a new interest. I hoped so, having felt so superfluous living in the Philpotts' peculiar and yet contented household all these past months.

Since leaving England one lovely woman had deceived me, and I had seen no other I had cared for. Philpott had encouraged me to court the pretty daughters of his Quaker acquaintances in Philadelphia, he being very taken with their principled and outlandish honesty. (His admiration had been born the day he had invited one old Quaker to express an opinion of his new suit. The courteous old man had advised him to throw it in the fire as the ugliest article he had ever beheld.) Enchanted with these curious people, Philpott had often taken me along to their houses. Some of their daughters had indeed been pretty, and despite their rigid moral code, far freer within the confines of their homes than most women of their station. But it had dawned on me that if I turned Quaker I should be obliged to stop lying, a quite unthinkable proposition. Anne would certainly never expect such inhuman perfection from me. She had lived her life among an equally curious tribe whose political business could never have been carried on at all under Quakerish conditions.

Sir James had been circulating all evening, making

himself agreeable to the company: probably part of the duchess's scheme to unsettle the loyalties of the thirty-two. Most of them were here, I supposed, since, as John Scorn had bad-temperedly observed, Glynn's new electors were wealthier men than the old. But it seemed Sir James had finally grown weary. He was approaching us and, seeing his face, Anne got to her feet obediently. 'It seems Cinderella has overstayed her time. Will I see you tomorrow, Laurence?'

'At church, if it please you.'

The night air smelled of rain as I came out of the Angel courtyard into Coinagehall Street. I met Philpott also arriving at the surgery door, just as the Market House clock chimed midnight, Anne's fairy-tale curfew.

'The most extraordinary thing I ever saw in my life,' he said as he followed me into Piggy's cramped hall. 'The town is fuller than ever with the pig show, they tell me, and there is not a bed to be had at all. Not even a half-bed to share with another snoring fellow.' He began to chuckle. 'No room at the inn, Laurence! God bless me, I am exactly like the infant Jesus.'

He did look rather chubby and cherubic by the parlour lamplight, where Piggy was still hard at his books, and I couldn't stop a laugh finally coming – at which Philpott beamed so broadly I realised how much he had felt my studied disfavour all these past weeks.

'Then I would offer you the doctor's stable,' I said, 'but we can probably do better than that. Piggy, do you consent to the Christ child sleeping on your sofa?'

Sunday
29 May 1796

For death is printed on his face,
And ore his harte is stealin'

II

MORNING

Piggy was out by the time I woke the next morning, and Tirza in something of a fidget since Philpott was still snoring loudly on the parlour sofa with the cat on his head, and she had nowhere to put the breakfast. When I went in to open the curtains and shake his shoulder he sat up in a panting panic, dislodging the cat. 'Good God, my boy, I thought you was a constable come from *that bleeder* to take us away.' He shook his head vigorously like a dog, by which procedure he seemed effectually to clear out the dreams and settle his brain back into its proper place.

We had hardly sat down before Piggy came in. Driven by the duke's ire he had gone early to John Scorn's house and been sorry to find that though the old man's pupils had now lost that strange, fixed dilation, he was still deep in the same intoxicated stupor as before. Having gleaned nothing of much use from his books, Piggy had abandoned diagnosis and now only thought of a cure. He had prescribed the usual course of stimulation in the case of any *coma*: clanging pans, pinching and slapping, and pungent mustard poultices to the head.

He had scarcely sat down at the table when Tirza came in with two messages. The first that he must repair to the genteel residence of a comfortable widow to evacuate the accumulated wax from her old ears. The second that he was required back with the poorly child, Jane Landeryou, whose case he had discussed with the curate the day before.

'The old lady's ears can hardly be urgent,' he objected. 'I shall go first to the child. There was a cheesy smell about her breath I did not like.'

'Alice Hodge is a very profitable patient, and on no account is she to hear that you have kept her waiting for the sake of a butcher's sickly brat,' Tirza answered with asperity and then slammed out of the room.

'I do abhor an ear,' Piggy said gloomily. 'I am engaged to whip off an infected finger for a poor farmer this evening, and can do such a thing quite cheerfully, but there is something nightmarish to my mind about these strange whorled emissaries from the ear's interior. But perhaps Tirza is right. In truth, I have no eagerness to return to the little child either. Since her fever turned putrid, the common treatments will scarcely have any effect. Not to mention that every textbook has its own pet remedies and contradicts all the others.'

Philpott had paused to listen, his fork at his mouth. 'I thought you liked your profession, sir?'

'I do like it, Mr Philpott, but while surgery slowly improves by trial and error, physic has scarcely advanced since Paracelsus.' Piggy buttered himself a slice of bread. 'Physicians look down on surgeons as mere butchers, but their self-congratulation is misplaced. Who knows whether any of our remedies work and, if they do, which ones? If disease is spread by bad air, then why do some children escape infection while others succumb? Why is a parched summer, when the wells dry up and the ponds shrink, so much worse for fevers? Why does the miasma of a swamp cause malaria? It is all groping in the dark. Men die before me every day and I can do little to save them. Women die even more frequently from childbed matters. And, most of all, children die. In London more children die than live, and even in a country town like Helston I suppose a quarter are buried before they are two, and a third before they are ten.'

While Philpott rummaged in his pockets for his notebook in order to note down these dismal figures, I remembered the teeming streets of London, filled with the daily influx of new and hopeful arrivals, while a nearly equal number perished in the rookeries of St Giles and Holborn each day. The city grew, but from without, not within. And even the wealthy were afflicted by the dreadful diseases that swept through the city, seeping through every opening as relentlessly as leaking water: smallpox, diphtheria and typhus fever, as well as the commoner misfortunes of summer diarrhoea and the putrid throat.

'This business with the old men is bad enough,' Piggy went on, 'but the child's case is far worse. After all, Wedlock and Scorn have both lived full lives, been freemen of the town and electors to Parliament, not to mention marriage and children and grandchildren. Wedlock has gone to his maker at a ripe old age and even if John Scorn recovers, what is there for him now except increasing ill health and impending death? But this child—' He shook his head. 'Four years old and the darling of her family. I'd rather save little Jane Landeryou if I could.'

This did not sound much like Piggy, but in truth he looked exhausted. I was wondering if he had slept at all, when Tirza appeared at the door again and informed us it was gone nine and the church bell was calling parishioners to worship. Piggy stood up. 'The choir will have to do without me this morning,' he said. 'But look out for Cyrus Best. He will certainly be there today, being paid for his Sunday services, and you will soon see why Eleanor Scorn fancies him enough to defy her grandfather.'

WHEN PHILPOTT AND I took our seats towards the back of the nave, the church was fuller than it had been for the funeral. We could see the duke's party on the front left pew, while the mayor and his niece sat to the right, studiously ignoring the rival party across the aisle. There was no sign of Lushington, being too poorly to attend, I surmised. As Piggy had suggested, I turned to look up at the choir gallery as they began to sing. There were the same ill-assorted men as yesterday, but now they were all over-shadowed by one particularly handsome specimen with a shock of blond curls, who stood forward at the rail with his eyes devoutly raised to the barrel roof. This new addition must surely be Cyrus, and if so Piggy was right: I did indeed see why Eleanor fancied him. I nudged Philpott and he turned to gape at the golden creature amid lumpen mortals high above us in the roof. An angel, whom, nonetheless, the curate had called a would-be murderer.

After the service we waited dutifully in the pews to watch our betters process out. The duke was scowling horribly and didn't deign to notice us, but the duchess smiled and nodded. Small Charles Burges looked very uncomfortable in his Sunday suit but fixed me with an intense stare probably meant to remind me of his farthing. Behind, and in nominal charge of him, came Anne, but George was whispering in her ear and she did not see us.

After the mayor and his niece had followed the ducal party out into the daylight, we lesser parishioners funnelled after them, nodding to the curate at the church door and thereafter gathering in small knots about the churchyard. The sun was gone in behind clouds and a faint mist of warm rain hung not disagreeably in the spring air. The lush grasses and weeds in the corners of the graveyard looked to be almost visibly growing, and I thought at this rate Wedlock's grave would be green before the week was out.

But regardless of this May glory, and within only five minutes of forgiving other people's trespasses, the assembled crowd was already arguing again, quietly now, but persistently, and more than once I heard the names Wedlock and Scorn drift across the churchyard on the damp, flower-scented air.

Philpott and I loitered with the curate. 'We saw your Cyrus Best in the gallery,' Philpott said. 'The 'andsomest man I ever saw in my life, I should think. And very pious-looking, too.'

'Pious!' William Wedlock was disgusted. 'You will see him in his natural state at the Blue Anchor within half an hour, I don't doubt. They play skittles despite the Sabbath and Cyrus is an eager player.'

'Did you look for the Guildhall cupboard key among your grandfather's things?' I asked.

'I did, and so did my mother.' He shook his head. 'But it wasn't there, I'm afraid, Mr Jago. I am sorry not to be of more help.'

'Ah well, perhaps the clerks have found it, since. I shall ask them tomorrow when the Guildhall is open again.'

I left Philpott with the curate then, for I could see Anne standing with the duke's party on the other side of the churchyard, under the yews by the gate.

George hailed me as I approached. 'Charles Burges wishes me to report that he has left off pinching young Sidney and desires his reward.'

I dug in my pocket for the required sum and put the coin into the child's little hand, wondering why all infant fingers need be so infernally sticky. He examined it closely as if he suspected me a sharper.

'If you give it me, Charles, I shall make it a guinea before I'm done,' George offered. But the child put the farthing carefully in his pocket with a look that suggested he had been gulled that way before.

'You are betting?' I asked. 'At the Anchor, I suppose?'

George nodded. 'Thank God there are always skittles, not to mention the wager board, else a Sunday in this town would be quite insupportable. Being an unashamed Sabbath-breaker, I am going there directly. Will you come?'

Remembering Cyrus Best, I nodded, but Anne was beckoning me to where she stood with Sir James, slightly apart from the duke and his family, who were now leaving. 'I will follow you directly,' I said to George and with a nod he loitered off after his parents, hand in hand with the sticky child. He was a good lad, I thought, whatever his minor dissipations.

'Sir James was very surprised to hear you think yourself dismissed,' Anne said to me as I came up. 'I have talked to him about it this morning, and he fully expects your return to Whitehall.'

I looked at Sir James in some surprise, wondering how far this could be true and how far merely the result of Anne's good offices. But Sir James looked bland enough. 'Mr Jago is not entirely a stranger to us,' he said, looking at her, not me. 'He undertook a small duty for us aboard the ship to America last year, and the Foreign Secretary would, I am sure, be interested to discuss his future in the Department, if he presents himself with all due humility for consideration. In the meantime, his help in this curious matter of Wedlock and Scorn may also demonstrate his goodwill to myself and the duke.'

It was strange to hear myself talked of in the third person when there were only three of us in the conversation. 'He is doing his best,' I said. 'He intends to be thorough and to pursue every possible avenue in search of the truth.'

Sir James looked displeased, but whether at my flippancy or my proposed thoroughness wasn't immediately clear. 'You must do as you see fit,' he said coldly, and then hesitated.

'Must I? Forgive me, I sense a *but* is imminent.'

He disregarded the question and only answered with another. 'What other *avenues* do you propose to explore?'

'I have heard bad things said of one of the choristers,' I replied, 'who has a particular relation to John Scorn that might have made bad blood. Such a solution to Scorn's poisoning would more or less discount any political malfeasance in Wedlock's case, since two unrelated murders in a week would seem unlikely in a small town such as

Helston. His death would therefore remain an unfortunate misadventure and the case satisfactorily solved.'

'I think,' Sir James said, 'that His Grace would prefer a solution that condemned the mayor and Mr Lushington.'

'I'm sure he would,' I said. 'I will of course pursue that avenue, too, and if it turns out to be the case I will be very happy to oblige him.'

Anne gave me something of a glare, but I knew Sir James of old, and I didn't think he would waste much time disliking me, any more than promoting my interests with the Foreign Secretary whatever he might say. He would surely understand that my investigation must be fair and thorough if it were to please anyone in Helston at all.

'May I call for you this afternoon, Anne? Will you walk out with me?'

She screwed up her mouth and shook her head with what I hoped was regret. 'Indeed, I cannot this afternoon, Laurence, for I have an engagement.'

'An engagement?' I didn't know she had any acquaintance in Helston at all besides the duke. 'Where are you going?'

'If it answers, I will tell you.' She smiled at my expression. 'Don't look so glum. And perhaps, if you like, I'll walk out with you tomorrow to see the Sapient Hog instead.'

After we parted, I followed George down to the Blue Anchor in its Sunday wickedness. The front door was closed but unlocked. I went inside to find a handful of very old men puffing very large pipes in the taproom of the shabby old inn over tankards of illicit Sunday cider. They were in conversation with George, whom they appeared to know very well, treating him with a marked lack of deference for one so noble. He greeted me with a cheerful smile and jerked his head towards a doorway, whence noise from the skittle alley was washing in and out every time the door was opened. I followed George through to find the alley full of men pinned to the narrow passage between the wall and the smooth boarded skittle slide. As we came in, the pins clattered over, and a man hastened down the slide in his hose to set them upright again.

'Which one this time, Cyrus?'

'Back pin.'

A general hiss of breath was followed by a shout of laughter. 'I'll have thruppence on that. Cyrus do never fail.'

George pushed his way through the throng. 'And a shilling says he won't do it.'

From the way the others protested, that looked a bad bet. The men were farm labourers and workmen, carriers and apprentices, large well-muscled men who must know their business, since a thruppenny stake was a full quarter of their daily wage.

The curate had been right that Cyrus would be here and equally right that he would be betting. His golden curls fell in his face as he bent to his stated intention to topple the backwards-most skittle without disturbing the rest. The onlookers hushed with anticipation, while I kept myself out of the crowd and looked about. Though I had half-thought it a joke, there really was a chalk-board pinned to the wall displaying the odds on each set of candidates for the election, with the wagers of the townspeople chalked in beneath them in small, primitive handwriting.

The odds had changed sharply since old Wedlock's death and John Scorn's collapse. Before that, the odds had favoured the duke, probably on the grounds of precedent. Now, they had swung decisively to Glynn. I scanned my eye down the board. The names were only initials, but I saw GO, presumably George Osborne, who had loyally supported his father's men to the tune of five pounds. This was a huge sum for the townspeople: even Piggy was probably lucky if he earned five pounds a week. Another notable bet, further down the board, had placed a guinea in favour of the mayor. The initials beside it were CB. The curate had been right about that, too: Cyrus had placed the bet before the calamities that had befallen the duke's electors, at the previous longer odds, and stood to make a very large sum if Scorn did not vote.

Cyrus loosed his ball, a general howl of disgust erupted, and a moment later George came back to me triumphantly clutching his winnings. I smiled and tapped his initials on the chalkboard. 'I fear you may do worse in this venture.'

'Who knows? And besides, it hardly signifies.' George was cheerful, apparently as pleased with his shilling wager as he might have been with a hundred guineas. I thought it boded rather well for a future duke to be so admirably prudent.

It was impossible to beard Cyrus now but having satisfied myself that the curate's portrait of his character was a true one, at least to all outward appearance, I left them all to their pleasures. When I came out into the street, Piggy was approaching from the direction of the Coinage Hall. He had been to his old widow and her ears, and he looked very unhappy about it. He paused to tell me what had happened, while the scant Sunday pedestrians passed by on their way to collect their Sunday roast from the baker's oven or to visit their relations.

'I have just had the most perplexing interview with the old woman,' he said, looking particularly mournful and doggy. 'When I came in, she positively threw up her hands in horror. "Mercy," she said. "I called for Dr Johns."

'I explained that the doctor was not in town, nor had been these two months. "I am very sorry to disappoint you," I said. "I should have been delighted to let Dr Johns have the honour of emptying your ears." But when I bade her call the maid with the warm water and the jug she looked terribly uneasy. "I believe I have changed my mind," she said. "Perhaps I shall wait until Dr Johns returns."

'I hate ears, Laurence, but I hated her reluctance even more. Old people can take against new doctors in a tiresome way. "Nonsense," I said. "You wished to have the business done and I am here to do it. Shall I ring for the maid?"'

Piggy now looked pink and shamefaced. 'There followed a short but extremely unseemly tussle over the handbell on the table by her chair. I only let go when I saw that she would not. "Forgive me," I said, "I assure you I have attended many an ear before, and am most practised at the matter, if that is what troubles you."

'"No, no," she said and, good Lord, she clutched that confounded bell to her chest and rang it as if her life depended on it. "'Tis not that, Doctor. I'm afeared—" But then her maid came in and so she did not tell me what she was afraid of, only said that I was leaving and put me out of doors.'

He looked at me sadly.

'Don't mind it,' I said. 'When a man deals with the public, I suppose he must endure its stupidity as well as its thanks.'

He shook his head. 'There was something so meaning in her look, Laurence, and I don't know what it signified.'

12

AFTERNOON

UNFORTUNATELY FOR PIGGY, we were about to find out. A group of brazen Sunday skittlers had come out into the street and were now sitting drinking in full view on the bench outside the Anchor's door. Even while Piggy was telling his tale about the widow I had become conscious that their eyes were on us, and as he finished his doleful story they sloped to their feet like a pack of hungry wolves, crossed the pavement, and surrounded us. I glanced about in hope of seeing Philpott's burly figure, but perhaps he was still detained with the curate or had gone off on some whim of his own.

'What's this then, Doctor?' one of the men was saying as the circle closed around us threateningly. 'Some tale o' poisonin' agin John Scorn, we hear? Very lucky for the mayor, I must say. And you up and down from The Willows yesterday, all day long.'

Piggy's pink face had turned pinker but he did not grasp the man's obscure meaning all at once. 'The Willows? Yes indeed. Mr Lushington is certainly unwell. I visited him twice yesterday. But I don't quite see—'

'At The Willows one moment; at John Scorn's the next. And you alone with Scorn when he took bad.'

'Nonsense.' Piggy began to catch the man's drift and looked alarmed. 'It was a mercy I was with him, or he might have died. And I want his recovery as soon as possible, I assure you.'

'But see,' another man pushed his shoulder against Piggy's and thrust a finger in his face, 'we hardly know 'ee, bein' an outlander 'ere. Some are sayin' you only come to Helston at all to poison John Scorn, on Glynn's say-so.'

Small neighbourhoods like Helston can get hold of a prejudice against a stranger and worry it as eagerly as a terrier with a rat. I wondered how far this rumour had spread and if it also accounted for the widow's strange fear.

'There's good money on the 'lection, too, as I dare say you do know,' the man went on. 'And any meddlin' a shockin' scandal. If Scorn don't vote before the poll closes tomorrow night, folks will be provoked agin 'ee, Doctor.'

'Believe me,' said Piggy still more anxiously, 'you cannot be more eager for Mr Scorn's recovery than I am. He is my patient, and moreover the duke is just as determined as you are that he shall vote.'

But the men were in drink and weren't listening, and

another fellow, who until now had been watching with silent and rising bad temper, launched himself suddenly into Piggy's waistcoat and began pounding him vigorously in the ribs. A shout went up familiar from my childhood. *Fair play! Fair play! Make a ring!* But under the unexpected onslaught Piggy's feet slipped and I knew without a shadow of a doubt that if he fell down his career in Helston would be over.

I was shamefully slow, frozen by surprise. Luckily the attacker was only swinging wildly, far too drunk to connect his fist squarely with Piggy's jaw. Piggy first tried to catch at his flailing hands but then, despairing of containing the attack, he flung out an unpractised fist in his turn and missed. The momentum took him with horrible inevitability towards a large pile of dung some horse had thoughtfully deposited in the middle of the quiet Sunday street.

I was still of absolutely no use, but just before Piggy's nose could be rubbed in humiliation as well as horseshit, a hand grasped his collar, hauling him upright again in the nick of time. The saviour who had suddenly materialised in our midst like St Michael himself now set about the drunken men with his cane, eliciting yelps of agony. The background noise of excitement in the street, which until now I had barely registered, took on another note. Less baying for Piggy's outlander blood than cheering on our local rescuer. It was the old bog root, Jeb Nettle, aged ninety-six. 'Bugger off,' he was remonstrating to the drunks. 'Goss home with 'ee.'

'Fuck 'ee, bedman.'

But, moodily, they sloped back to their bench outside the Anchor to nurse their stripes while the sexton straightened Piggy's neckcloth. 'I 'ave been hearing some strange tales about 'ee, Doctor. It is all a piece beyond my ken, but ye have a pleasant voice in the choir and I believe you are a good man. Don't fear, I shall always speak up if I 'ear bad words agin 'ee.'

'As shall I,' the curate added. He had come up with Philpott, unseen during the fracas, and was now holding out Piggy's doctor's bag to him, which he had rescued from under the feet of the scuffling combatants. 'I have also just heard these foolish rumours, but you have been nothing but good to all your patients, Dr Jago, and folks with any sense will know it.'

Philpott was also wrinkling his brow at Piggy with kind concern. 'It will all come clear, dear sir, never fret. Truth will out in the end, I assure 'ee.'

Piggy looked rather overcome at these unexpected votes of confidence, but as the sexton and William Wedlock moved on with more expressions of goodwill, George Osborne was now also upon us, probably having heard the brawl from inside the inn.

'I *might* have helped,' he said magnanimously, 'but the old relic was doing so splendidly there seemed no need. I advise you to go carefully, however, Dr Jago. An unpleasant rumour has certainly taken root – I have heard all about it in the Anchor – and I'm afraid it will suit a good many people in town to let it blossom.'

The boy looked Piggy up and down with a combination of amusement and indifference that frightened as much as galled me. I knew exactly how it felt to be falsely accused of a crime that could disgrace you at best and hang you at worst. 'I thought we were to see the interesting spectacle of you doctoring your own black eye,' George went on. 'But you have your partisans, too, I see. I suppose the sexton has a bet on old Scorn and does not wish to see his doctor incapacitated. Or perhaps he is of the Glynn party and thinks you a positive hero for poisoning the old devil.'

Having delivered himself of this commentary on human nature, regrettably cynical in one so young, he sauntered off.

Piggy would not consent to rest quietly at home, and I dared not leave him to wander the town alone, so Philpott and I went with him back to John Scorn's house to assess the new course of stimulation he had prescribed earlier that morning. Loveday was in the stale passageway when we came in, gamely clanging pans outside the old man's chamber door. But Scorn was still utterly insensible to the noise, and if Eleanor had been pinching him it had had no effect either – though

I dare say she might have derived some satisfaction from it, which was something. Piggy applied a new hot mixture of mustard to the old man's shaven scalp. The fumes were so strong they made my own eyes sting, but though a tear stole from under Scorn's eyelid he remained as unmoved as a graven image.

'Where is your mistress?' Piggy asked Loveday, the question necessitating a very welcome interruption to the incessant clanging. I thought if I was Eleanor I would have gone out for a very long walk and been tempted not to return.

'Out with Cyrus,' she said, and this was confirmed by the arrival of the ill-starred couple a few minutes later, hand in hand. Eleanor was certainly not ashamed of her preference; in fact, she introduced Cyrus to us with a slight defiance. My first thought was renewed surprise at his good looks. My second was that he had rather a silly expression.

'Your grandfather has not stirred at all?' Piggy asked Eleanor, as she straightened the bedclothes. The misty rain had cleared and she drew one curtain against the late-afternoon sunlight now falling onto the bed. The other side of the room remained illuminated: Scorn's desk, scattered with papers, and the fireplace with its hideous ornaments.

Eleanor only shook her head and said rather unkindly, 'As dumb as a joint o' mutton, all day.' Meanwhile, Cyrus looked from one to the other of us with the same kind of placid interest young Sidney Osborne had shown when sucking Piggy's finger in his crib. Cyrus might be a handsome man, a fine chorister and a shrewd gambler, but for force of character he did not seem Eleanor's equal at all. Moreover, there was something in his expression I found I did not much like. I remembered his large bet on the chalkboard in the Blue Anchor. He had wagered against his sweetheart's own grandfather, and under that innocent, unfocused blue gaze, he might actually be lost in arithmetic, calculating his coming profits in the event the old man did not recover in time to vote.

He left with us, seeming to have no relish at all for the sick room.

'Arternoon, Loveday,' he said to the maid as we passed her in the hall, and she glanced at him and smiled. Helston was a small place and everyone was acquainted one to the other if not actually related – a fact confirmed when Loveday laid a timid hand on Piggy's sleeve.

'Have you seen my little sister today, Dr Jago? How is she farin'?'

Piggy sighed. 'Less well than I would like, but all is not lost, Loveday. I will do my best for little Jane, I promise you that. I know how your parents dote on the child.'

THE POOR FARMER WITH the infected finger would be waiting for him, Piggy said, and he hastened back to the surgery. But I nudged Philpott. Cyrus was in sight, walking down Meneage Street ahead of us towards the crossroads. The bell had started tolling for Evensong, and he should be making his way thither to earn his coin for singing, but instead of crossing the road, passing the surgery and continuing on up Church Street, he turned left back down towards the Angel and the Anchor.

'Never mind him,' Philpott grumbled, not hurrying after the retreating figure but instead pausing to take out his tobacco and stuff his pipe. 'Laurence, the duke is behind it all, I assure 'ee.'

'You want it to be a political story. You said so yourself.'

'I have it all quite clear in my mind, if you will but listen. His Grace had heard of Thomas Wedlock's intended defection and gave the Angel Inn's tinderbox to John Scorn, instructing him to somehow contrive Wedlock's death. But then the damned fool dropped the tinderbox at the scene and thereby betrayed it was murder, not mere accident. When the duke saw it, damn me if he didn't think it best to silence Scorn, too. The old man could well have cracked under the sheriff's questioning and betrayed him. God damn me, Scorn was terrified enough when we questioned him ourselves.'

'But how in heaven do you propose His Grace could have poisoned the old man even if he wanted to?'

Philpott had indeed been thinking it all out. 'With the brandy he gave him on Friday night, o' course. By the time of the funeral on Saturday, Scorn was already very bad. And your cousin says some poisons only take their effect after many hours.'

'But John Scorn had drunk the duke's brandy before we even found the tinderbox. Besides, if you publish such a libel against the duke we will be obliged to flee these shores, too. We will soon run out of countries.'

Philpott was not to be deflected. 'But what did George Osborne mean, by saying it would suit some folks to see Dr Jago suspected? If I am right, it would certainly suit His Grace, whose mind the boy must know very well, I assure 'ee.'

Despite myself, I was rather impressed by Philpott's reasoning – he had obviously been ruminating on it long and carefully – but, as I had objected, the times did not add up. 'And of course, it would suit Cyrus, too,' I said. 'Remember, the curate told us we were muddying the waters by bringing his grandfather's death into it at all. He believes Wedlock died naturally, or at least by a self-inflicted mishap, and that we have only one victim of malice – Scorn – and therefore only one would-be murderer on the loose – Cyrus Best – whom we are in danger of losing sight of, if you stand here quibbling.'

We turned the corner just in time to see Cyrus go into a shop next door to the Angel. It being Sunday, the shop would certainly be closed, so he must have knocked and been admitted. It was a grocer's shop, and a very affluent one, stocked with a good class of cleaned vegetables in the window and dried hams hanging from hooks in the ceiling shrouded in muslin against the flies. I couldn't see anyone within and, emboldened, I tried the handle but it was locked.

We loitered on down towards the bowling green, whose members seemed more inclined to observe the Sabbath proprieties, for it was empty and deserted. We sat by the side of the quiet green until, five minutes later, Cyrus re-emerged from the shop, now in company with a very thin, very poorly-looking man leaning on his arm. They crossed the road and took the short cut to church by way of Five Wells Lane, a narrow alley that ran between the bottom of Coinagehall and the upper reaches of Church Street.

'That must be poor, dying Julian, the grocer with the tumour, whom the curate and your cousin talked of yesterday,' Philpott said. I admired his memory. I had forgotten all about it.

'What can Cyrus's business be with him?' I wondered aloud. 'Nothing good, I suppose.'

'Or nothing bad.' Philpott shook his head at me. We were at cross-purposes that was certain, both chasing different hares.

WHEN WE GOT BACK to the surgery, Piggy was in the dispensing room in company with his white-faced farmer patient. Johannes Bashers had cut himself on the blade of his plough a fortnight since, Piggy explained, and had carelessly exposed the wound to the air so that, over the course of another week, infection had taken hold. The case was at the same time both bad and good: a pity that it was the useful forefinger, the loss of which was always to be regretted; more satisfactory in that it was his left hand and therefore less necessary to Bashers' daily occupations than if it had been his right. Bashers seemed rather less comforted by this reflection than Piggy might have hoped and also appeared to have taken a good deal of brandy. Anxious beads of sweat stood on his brow, and when Piggy grasped his hand to examine it under the lamp he was decidedly unwilling to be meddled with and apparently eager to change his mind. Philpott murmured that he was needed elsewhere and slid out of the room. I watched with mingled fascination and a rising dread that Piggy was going to rope me in to the business, which, of course, he duly did.

'I have been telling Bashers that a good surgeon can take off a leg in ten seconds,' Piggy said with rather unconvincing good cheer, gesturing me to take hold of the disobliging hand and hold it steady under the light, whatever the farmer's new misgivings on the subject. 'We shall be done here before he can say *Cherokees forever.*'

'Damn that,' said Bashers, with a sad attempt at bravado as Piggy grasped the bad finger and manipulated it gently. 'Damned if I don't dab 'ee down with my good fist, Dr Jago, once I am out of your bleddy clutches.'

'Forgive me, I did not take you for a Mohawk,' Piggy

said calmly, removing the finger at the knuckle before the words were even out of his mouth, having twisted the knife deftly to separate the finger at the joint, without touching the bone at all. Bashers screamed and jerked, but it was already over, and besides upsetting the lamp, no other harm was done.

Piggy pressed a wad of lint to the wound, which was now bleeding rather profusely, and then bound the lint in neatly with a bandage. 'The drainage of the wound is better accomplished without closed stitches I find. Best practice would be to debride the wound daily, but I fancy you will not desire to be peeled with a knife, Johannes, and have better things to do than tramp into town from your farm for the pleasure.' He knotted the bandage and picked up the now redundant finger, which Bashers eyed with some bewildered grief. 'If it takes infection again, Johannes, we will put the maggots back to work, as we tried before.'

'Can't abide 'em,' Bashers said. 'Too much fidgetin' under the bandage.' He gingerly put on his coat again, wincing as his lopped hand passed through the sleeve. 'But you reckon it will heal?'

Piggy was a shade less comforting now than he had been before the procedure. 'As far as that goes, I'm afraid only time will tell. But we have done our best. If we had not acted today, you might have been in your grave by Friday.'

'It stings like the bleddy blazes.'

'I'll make up some opium pills if you'll wait in the parlour.'

Piggy rang the bell for Tirza to show the man through. As Bashers gloomily followed her out into the passage, Bitterweed darted in, jumped onto the table and began to lick with some pleasure at the spattered blood. 'Get away, you cannibal,' Piggy remonstrated fondly, but she ignored him, so I shooed her off the table, upon which she squeezed herself disobligingly under the dresser, with only an unfriendly outstretched claw still visible.

Piggy reached down the ingredients and began to make up the pills. 'It is prudent to keep the bowels open as well as relieve the pain,' he was saying half to himself. 'A little soap in the mix will be a laxative. And some lemon, perhaps, to disguise the taste.'

I sat down on the stool at the counter and watched his large paws roll the pills, releasing a pleasant lemon aroma. He then fetched down a paper wrapper and bound the pills into a tight cylinder, nimbly folding in the last corner to make all secure. After that and just as the Market House clock struck the quarter-hour, Tirza battered in, clogs thumping, to announce a messenger had just come from the Angel, requiring our presence in the duke's chambers forthwith.

UP IN THE DUKE'S ROOMS, His Grace was engaged with his fingernails in a corner, too beside himself with some new displeasure to speak to us. What we had done I couldn't guess until Sir James began to speak and it became apparent that they had a third hare of their very own running, in the shape of Glynn and Lushington, and in flushing it out they had started a new and dreadful fourth. Sir James was looking gravely at Piggy. 'Like many others in town, Dr Jago, His Grace has noticed your intimacy at The Willows and deplores it greatly.'

Piggy looked unhappy. 'Intimacy, sir?'

'You have been there repeatedly this week, both before and after the mishaps which have so unfortunately befallen His Grace's two electors.'

This was certainly undeniable, but there was something in the duke's fury and Sir James's particular blandness that I did not like at all. 'He is courting Mr Glynn's niece, that's all,' I said. 'And he has also been called in to treat Mr Lushington, whom you know is poorly.'

'Indeed.' There was some unpleasantly sceptical meaning in Sir James's tone.

'It is hardly *intimacy* to treat a patient for gout,' I said, a shade more warmly. 'It is a doctor's duty, and he cannot choose where he is called.'

Piggy was listening to us, frowning, his pink face as innocent and awkward as the curate's. 'Forgive me, Sir James,' he said rather meekly, 'I don't quite grasp your meaning. Am I to understand you object to my visits at The Willows? You think I have done something wrong?'

The duke sniffed loudly from his corner, but Sir James was still smooth. 'We only observe events, Dr Jago. You arrived in Helston not long before Parliament was dissolved and are constantly at The Willows where there are men very eager to see the duke's candidates fail. We did not think much of the matter until today when disagreeable rumours came to our ears.'

Piggy turned pinker than ever. 'Rumours?'

I felt obliged to step in again. 'If you mean that unpleasant business in the street this afternoon, it was merely a drunk or two, who chose to vent their frustrations on my cousin. Strangers are always viewed with suspicion in a place like this, as you should know.'

Sir James waved his hand. 'And yet, it is not unreasonable in the town to question his recent movements. It has also come to our attention that not only was Dr Jago alone with John Scorn when he fell ill, but he had also been with Wedlock only an hour before *he* died.'

'This is preposterous,' I said. My legs were suddenly weak, so God knows how Piggy must have felt. 'You cannot think my cousin has had anything to do with any of this. He is a rising physician, at the start of a promising career. His father is a respectable merchant and his grandfather was an alderman of Penzance.' I could see Sir James was unimpressed with this pedigree. 'Besides, the two cases are entirely different and you know it. One a death by fire, the other a case of poison.'

'Entirely different?' The duke finally raised his head from his fingernails and examined me with much disgust. 'Entirely different, you say? Indeed, sir, they are not. Scorn fell into a terrible frenzy shortly before he succumbed, I gather. What, then, is more likely than Wedlock was in a similar state of intoxicated excitement when he burned the papers? Why else would he do such a crazy thing, especially since he meant to vote against me and could therefore hardly wish the poll book destroyed?'

This was more or less the same question Philpott had asked the sexton yesterday, and to which Jeb Nettle had had no useful answer. Wedlock had indeed acted in a way no one could explain and when I remembered John Scorn's strange, distracted passion the duke's words seemed disturbingly plausible.

Piggy spoke up. 'But I still don't see—'

Yes, the duke had birthed and matured his new hare and was mighty attached to it now. He fixed Piggy with a hostile gaze. 'It is perfectly plain. If Wedlock was running mad like Scorn, then he had likely been poisoned, too. You, Dr Jago, are naturally in possession of many drugs which you yourself admit may be toxic if taken in excess. You were alone with both men before they fell ill. As such, you are the one link between these events and presently provide the only likely explanation of how all this mischief has been done.'

'But poor Dr Jago has been tireless in his attendance on your old man,' the duchess objected from the window. How she might know anything of the matter wasn't clear, but I was still grateful to her for coming to

Piggy's defence. It was only now that I had time to look for Anne and realised that she was not in her usual place. She had had an *engagement* she'd said, this morning after church, and must be still absent.

But the duke was not to be deprived of a pincushion to skewer with his anger, the pincushion in this instance being not Sir James but Piggy. 'A zeal one might interpret in more than one way,' he said. 'More than one way, I say. It is hardly nonsense to question whether he has played some mischievous role in the affair. A fire, a death and a poisoning all since he arrived in Helston. I am quite decided, Sir James. We must certainly take another look at Thomas Wedlock.'

'At Wedlock?' Piggy was immediately astonished out of his horrified apprehensions. 'What possible good can that do?'

'If a dissection shows there is evidence of poisoning then the sheriff will be obliged to halt the poll whether he likes it or not and you, sir, will hang.'

Piggy looked fit to faint and sat down abruptly. I was furious.

'And if it doesn't show it? What then?'

The duke only spread his hands with a look that told me such an eventuality was, to his mind, beyond the bounds of all possibility. I glanced at Piggy and then fixed my eyes on the duke. 'I'll tell you *what then*, Your Grace. If the dissection shows that Wedlock died of natural causes, or merely in a fire of his own making, then my cousin must be exonerated. The whole theory of a political conspiracy will fall, and instead we will see that we are dealing only with one attempted murder against John Scorn for which my cousin has no motive and for which another man does, according to the very respectable testimony of the curate.' I hesitated, looking again at Piggy's pained face. 'Yes, Piggy, my dear man, remarkable though it seems, His Grace is right. We must exhume the old man's body and prove it was not murder for once and all.'

Instead of sharing my sudden hope, Piggy only closed his eyes and pinched his nose wearily between his fingers. 'I have too many living patients to waste time with a dead one.'

'But you wanted to open Wedlock's corpse the night he died,' I urged him. 'You asked for his family's permission.'

He opened his eyes and looked at me. 'But that was two days ago, Laurence. Time and heat and burial will have wrought changes to the corpse by now that will make the whole business much more difficult. And besides, when I wanted to open him on Friday, I thought it merely a medical curiosity. I didn't expect to find answers.'

If I hadn't been so distracted I might have reflected that Mrs Wedlock had therefore been quite right to call it *slicing him up for your own diversion*. 'But you will surely be able to tell something?' I persisted.

'I will be able to see if there is any blackening to the lungs from smoke – and if so how much and therefore how fatal. I will perhaps be able to tell if, alternatively, his heart ruptured from *angina pectoris* under some extreme excitement.'

'And what of poison? Will you be able to tell if he was struck down in the same way as John Scorn, as the duke believes?'

Piggy shrugged. 'I can open the stomach and look. Odours have sometimes been detected, I believe, and damage to the stomach lining from a caustic poison would also be apparent.'

And so the coroner was duly called. Roskruge proved cautiously amenable to the suggestion in these perplexing circumstances and only concerned with its execution. It was unfortunate that the newly suspected doctor was himself the only man in town capable of carrying out the dissection, so he would send word to Camborne overnight for a second opinion, and if that failed he himself had a smattering of medical knowledge gleaned over the years and would ensure that all was fair. Sir James might also like to attend to represent His Grace.

The exhumation should be accomplished under shadow of darkness, Roskruge went on, so that the old man's family would not get wind of the fact their wishes had been overruled, and the town would not run mad with new rumours about resurrection men on the loose in St Michael's graveyard. For my own part, I thought that far from keeping the dissection quiet, we would do better to trumpet it about the town and let

everyone know due justice was being done and thereafter that Piggy had been fairly exonerated and all the
swirling rumours baseless. But I was also overruled and
instead instructed to find the sexton, who would have to
see to the disinterment of the body. I would find him at
Evensong, the coroner said, and bade me convey the
news of this new, disagreeable task to him when the
service ended.

13

EVENING

CHURCH TWICE IN A day was more than I usually bargained for, but when I came into the churchyard a fugue was wafting down from the choir gallery, its beauty making the hairs stand up on my arms as I slipped inside to listen, loitering in the evening gloom of the quiet nave. The men could certainly sing, and old Nettle as well as any, whatever his years, the state of his teeth or his lack of political information. They produced a formidable sound and I surrendered myself to it, closing my eyes until the last notes dissipated into the still, musty air.

Only the very devout were here, a small and sober congregation which included the thin old grocer Cyrus had brought with him. The curate had thought him too weak to attend church, I remembered, and yesterday had given him Communion at his shop. But if ever a man might be forgiven for excessive piety it was one so near to death. Cyrus took charge of him when he descended from the choir gallery and led him off. I wished he had not looked at the old man so kindly, since it rather disturbed my suspicions. After they were gone I intercepted the sexton when he descended the steps in his turn, and led him into a corner of the graveyard where we might not be overheard. Thomas Wedlock's grave was close by, and still raw, but the brief afternoon sunshine had already capped a crust over it.

'I am come with a message from the coroner,' I said. 'I'm afraid he thinks it imperative that Dr Jago takes another look at Mr Wedlock's corpse.'

Old Nettle gazed at me impassively, leaning on his cane, his mouth ajar. His yellow teeth were faintly visible, and his tongue moved as he swallowed.

I was slightly abashed by this preternatural silence but there was nothing to do save press on. 'Mr Roskruge requests that you exhume the coffin as soon as may be. Tonight, by dark, he thinks will be best, if you can get your men together. The longer we wait the less the doctor will be able to judge from the state of the corpse.'

The old bog oak's face slowly twisted as he pursed his lips over his teeth and ruminated quietly on this development. 'Exhume the coffin?' he said at length.

'Yes, sir.'

'Up and down like a man with the skits from the privy, is it?'

'I suppose you might say that.'

I watched Nettle's features writhe again as he considered the question. He didn't say anything for a long moment, but when he did it turned out that the writhing had accompanied violent mental arithmetic. 'Six ton. Six ton of earth and more, what we have just digged up. And filled in. And now to dig up again.' He paused, ruminatively. 'And then to fill in again.'

'I'm afraid so.'

'Six ton, moved four times is—'

I gaped at him. I had done much Latin and Greek with Reverend Willoughby in my youth, but my arithmetic had scarcely gone past the village dame school and I had not much needed it since, save in calculations of pounds, shillings and pence.

'Twenty-four.' He glared at my ignorance. But his mind now moved on from the *how much* to the *when*. 'Tonight, 'ee say, by dark?'

'That is the coroner's hope.'

The sexton tapped his cane thoughtfully. 'So as folks won't be none the wiser, I suppose?'

'Exactly,' I said. 'If we could dig him up before daylight and have him laid out in the vestry for examination before anyone in town is stirring, Mr Roskruge would be most obliged. It is a stroke of luck that it is election day. The whole town will be busy with the Sapient Hog and the hustings. With a fair wind, scarcely anyone will notice what we are up to at all, especially if we rebury him again after dark tomorrow.'

The sexton had hardly been listening, still ruminating on numbers. 'Six ton to dig up out o' the ground again and toss in a heap. Even loose as 'tis now, 'twill take half the night for three men by turns.' He looked about him. 'I don't see my men 'ere, and don't even know where I'll find 'em.'

'I'll fetch them for you if you tell me where they live.'

He now examined me more carefully, and under his fossilised features I thought there was kindness. 'Ye are all of a lather, young man, I can see that. Has this something more to do with yon doctor o' yourn? Is he in more trouble?'

'He might be,' I said, 'if we don't exhume Thomas Wedlock by morning.'

The root bent stiffly on its cane like a thorn tree bowed against a stiff wind, and the yellow teeth appeared again in the mouth opening. 'Don't trouble yourself; I'll send a lad to find the gravediggers,' he said at last. 'But tell Roskruge I want flagons of cider brought on the hour, every hour, and double pay for my men.' He looked at me sternly. 'Double pay for both the diggin' out *and* the fillin' in, mind. And flagons on the hour.'

Back at the surgery another message had come in, this time from The Willows, requesting Piggy's presence at once.

'From Lushington?' Piggy asked.

'From Miss Glynn, I think. Something about her dog, God save us.'

'You cannot go,' I said. 'With all this swirling suspicion you must keep away from them, Piggy.'

But he had already leapt up, electrified, and begun looking for his hat. 'Sarah would not call me to her dog if it was not serious, Laurence.'

I thought on the contrary it was exactly what she might do and said so. He frowned at me, all docile stubbornness in the lamplight. 'But you'd not have poor Claudia die on account of all this other ridiculous business?'

'Decidedly not. But forgive me, I am even less eager to see you hanged.'

It was no use and there could be no stopping him, being a grown man. He banged out with his doctor's case and, remembering the poor little pug, I went to the door and called good luck after him after all. As he raised a hand and hastened away up Church Street, I saw Glynn coming around the market hall from the direction of the Guildhall steps, deep in conversation with Mr Nicholson, the owner of the Sapient Hog.

PHILPOTT AND I SPENT a quiet couple of hours together in the parlour, me lying on my back on the sofa running my mind over all the events of the past days – and, even amid my fright for Piggy, still having time to wonder where Anne could have gone this afternoon, having no friends that I knew of in Helston at all. Meanwhile, Philpott smoked his pipe and read the

London papers. I had been angry with him for weeks, but though we were still at loggerheads in our suspicions about the Helston case, my ill will towards him was fading. He had not left Mr Gibbs behind on purpose, I knew that. And it was true he had had six children to marshal aboard our hurried ship out of Philadelphia.

Piggy returned shortly before eleven, swaying on his feet from weariness and yet somehow strangely radiant. 'Poor little Claudia,' he said, sitting down with a weary thump. 'She had produced five puppies without much difficulty before I got there, but had been straining and pushing to deliver the sixth for more than an hour. Sarah had feared to insult my physician's dignity by asking me for help, but of course I was eager to see what I could do.'

I smiled at this, though I was still vexed with him for risking his reputation for Sarah Glynn's sake.

'The pug was in the scullery,' he went on. 'The five puppies were already squirming about like slugs, but poor Claudia was in a bad way, her eyes bulging and her sides sucking in and out like little bellows. Fortunately, there was only one pup left unborn, and its head was pushing at the cervix, which was another blessing, since it was at least approaching the world the right way about. But I could feel the narrowness of Claudia's pelvis and I realised she had done well to deliver the five live puppies at all.

'I felt about for the pup's head inside the narrow passage with my fingers. For a horrible moment I thought I had pushed it back into the womb, and all Claudia's pains for naught, but then, heaven be praised, I found an ear – something to grip hold of – and began to pull. The passage was really too tight, but the other five puppies had made it through somehow and what alternative was there? I pulled again, harder, and all at once the puppy was out and Claudia suddenly quite herself again, licking and suckling her six infants as if nothing at all had happened.' Piggy shook his head. 'Birth is a constant miracle. Tragedy so close to joy in every confinement.'

'And was Miss Glynn pleased?' I asked him, at which he turned a sudden and very entertaining shade of scarlet.

'She wept and kissed the puppies. And then she kissed me.' He looked extremely coy. 'I am sure it was an accident, but we were close together and she turned her head so the corner of her mouth met the corner of mine. Her hair against my cheek was as soft as a cloud.'

'Lord help us,' Philpott said. 'I'll remind you of this when you have six children along with your six puppies.' He looked at me. 'But see here, Laurence, this is providential. You must have one of the pups. I'm sure it will cheer you up. About,' he looked shifty, 'that other matter, you know.'

'Have one of the pups?' I was all at once icy, not to say all at once furious, all my brief goodwill towards him dispelled. 'As if one might merely replace one animal with another? As if living creatures were interchangeable? Will you swap one of your children for another man's, sir?'

I thought from the look on his face he was going to joke that he certainly would. But to his credit he saw my expression and realised it was not a moment for jesting. Nevertheless, it had the effect of dampening the mood and after Piggy had gone wearily to bed, Philpott flung himself down on the horsehair sofa and turned his back on me.

I WENT TO MY OWN chamber but I couldn't sleep. The Market House clock was mournfully striking half past eleven and the streets were very quiet. Most of the townsfolk were abed, either from native good sense or from a desire to hoard their pennies and gusto for the wild excitements of the next day's election. Only the gravediggers would be at work by lantern light up at the church. I leaned out of my window to see if I could glimpse those lights or hear the sound of shovelling, but of course I was too far away, and the men would be working quietly as I had instructed.

I left the window open, went back to bed, and stared at the ceiling, listening to the night noises from the darkened gardens. Cats were fighting. A dog barked. Owls were hooting in the trees right outside my window. I thought I could hear the constant grizzling cries of a baby somewhere further off and the rattle of a late cart far away.

I turned on my left shoulder, away from the window.

It was exactly in these sleepless circumstances that I had begun my slippery acquaintance with Godfrey's Cordial – Godfrey's Cordial, with its most benign and contemptible amount of opium suitable only for teething infants. I thought of going down to the parlour but then I remembered Philpott was asleep on the couch. I turned over again, back towards the window and closed my eyes. The Guildhall clock struck the half-hour and I remembered that flask of laudanum on the quiet shelves of the dispensary – a flask so large that no one would ever detect a missing drop or two.

It would be a terrible defeat, and one among so many previous ones. I sat up and swung my feet out of bed before dressing quietly and opening my chamber door, boots in hand. Piggy was snoring as I crept down the stairs to the hallway – or perhaps it was Tirza Ivey. Philpott was prattling cheerfully in his sleep from the parlour. I laced up my boots and then, steadfastly turning my back on the dispensary, creaked the front door open. Bitterweed slipped out of the parlour into the hall as I did so and followed me into the night.

I WAS THROUGH THE lichgate and in the churchyard before I heard the scrape of shovels and saw the dim orange glow of the lanterns. There was one man in the hole, to his knees, and two others watching, leaning on their shovels. Nettle was also there, though I didn't notice him for a moment since he was sitting on his great-great-uncle's gravestone and smoking a pipe in blatant imitation of the young chorister he had caned for doing exactly the same the previous day.

They thought I was the bearer of cider at first, come gratifyingly early, but swallowed their disappointment and went back to their shovelling while I perched beside old Nettle on the gravestone.

'How long have they been at work?'

He shifted a little to make room for me. 'A good hour. The earth is so dry and loose I begin to think we will manage, and the coffin out of sight in the vestry by three o'clock.'

Old folks sleep very little and the ancient man was remarkably sprightly, considering it was now almost midnight. It also seemed he was minded for a chat.

'In fifty year as the town's bedman, I have never known such a thing afore. I have dug up old bones when digging new graves and moved old graves to make room for new graves. But always skelingtons. I have never dug up a coffin entire or opened the lid to see what the worms have been up to while the dead 'un still had flesh on his bones.'

I shivered. It was preposterously eerie in the midnight graveyard with the yews sighing above our heads. 'The worms won't have broken in yet, surely?'

'P'raps not.' The sexton shook his head but then brightened. 'But the flies will have found him out afore he were berried, I am sure. And the maggots will likely have hatched by now. 'Ess, 'ess, 'twill be quite a curious ending to my calling.' He sounded surprisingly charmed at the idea of the maggots, given that he would likely be lying in this earth himself within five years.

'There surely must have been many another strange death in your time, fit for a doctor's examination? Although, I suppose it's rare to get as far as actually burying a man before the decision to dissect him is taken.'

'The town would never have stood for it in times past,' Nettle said. 'But in these godless days, seems a man's body is no more than a lump o' meat.'

Every old man thinks the world has gone to the devil, so I said nothing.

'We have had murders and self-murder and child-destruction in the womb,' he said, after a moment's pause. ''Ess, 'ess, Helston has seen its share of trouble all right.'

'Did you bury that man that fell down the well, all those years back?'

The sexton took out his tobacco pouch. 'No, he went back to Illogen to be berried alongside his folks. Terrible afflicted they were, the body being so dreadful mashed.'

'Did you see it?'

'I did.' He stuffed more tobacco in his pipe and sucked furiously. The smoke drifted past me, sweet and rich. He sighed and took the pipe back out of his mouth to examine its glowing heart in the darkness. ''Ess, 'ess, I did.'

There was a short silence in which I gathered he was not going to tell me more. It must have been dreadful indeed to upset a man whose whole business was dead bodies.

'And what was the truth of it?' I asked after a moment. 'My mother says Tirza Ivey made up some shocking tale. But then there's also the official story that he only mistook his step in the dark.'

Another puff, another cloud of tobacco smoke drifted by me. 'No one knows the whole truth of it, sir. But, as your doctor friend has found out, that don't stop rumour. Your mother is probably right to doubt Tirza, though the woman keeps a sharp eye out and ain't always wrong. The man had been drinkin' without a doubt and argyfyin' with other men in the Angel. But the likely truth is he fell by mishap, poor devil, as the coroner ruled.'

'Arguing with other men?'

'Ay facks, those were different days. From all accounts half the town was argyfyin' that night. There was some nasty talk about John Scorn, howsumever, since he was the one to raise the alarm. Been out in the courtyard, too, see? And the man that died had been courtin' his daughter, much to Scorn's disgust.'

I shifted to look at him. 'The same daughter who went on to marry against his wishes?'

Nettle nodded. 'John Scorn was a blockhead. That man was a better one than she ended up weddin'. But he is just the same about young Eleanor. Worse, in fact, and it looks plain the same story will be told again, what with the parson and all.'

'I beg your pardon?'

The sexton looked at me by the light of his pipe. 'Have you not met him? I'm sure you have, for you have been at church three times already. A fidgety, timmersome young man, with shockin' untidy hair which I should much like to take my scissors to. He's always had a fancy for Eleanor. Known her all his life since they were childern. But, as I 'spect you know, the Wedlocks and the Scorns were always at each other's throats and Scorn won't have him any more than that young rogue Cyrus, while old Wedlock, the curate's grandfer, felt quite the same about Eleanor.'

William Wedlock wanted Eleanor? No wonder he hated Cyrus Best. But he was also a clergyman – and therefore surely he was the last man to break the ninth commandment and bear false witness against his neighbour? Besides, I remembered the curate's earnest excitement when he told us the story; his overwhelming desire to see justice done had seemed entirely genuine.

I had seen Cyrus in the choir and at the skittles; a strange presence at Eleanor's house and a kind one with the old grocer. Now here was another reason to doubt my suspicions. But though both the curate and myself might have our own reasons for wanting Cyrus to be guilty, that still didn't mean Cyrus wasn't.

The world had changed for the worse, Nettle thought, as all old men think. Glynn disagreed, seeing Helston on the march to an enlightened new place in the wider world, and even Sir James had observed that poison was too archaic a political method for these rational days. The feuding of Scorns and Wedlocks might be ancient history now, but the town was riven again into tribes. How much had the world changed really? The political meeting on Friday night had been a powder keg, and two old men were dead and dying amid it all. In the dark churchyard, under the yews by flickering lantern light, I could almost think myself in Sarah Glynn's gruesome medieval novel. I should not have been the least surprised if Nettle had hopped off the gravestone, pulled a lever, and revealed a flight of stairs disappearing down into the earth, lit only by flaming torches.

Monday
30 May 1796
Election Day

Lay downe, lay downe the corps, she sayd,
That I may look upon him

14

MORNING

THE NOISE OF THE crowd woke me. Though it was scarcely eight o'clock, the town was already on the move ready for the excitements of the day ahead: the Sapient Hog at noon and then the hustings, where Glynn's thirty-two new electors would cast their votes and show both the town and Parliament how far Helston had changed.

We had agreed to meet Sir James and the coroner at church at half past nine, but Piggy had risen early and gone out to his patients first. I glanced in the appointment book in the dispensary and saw he had scribbled down *Jane Landeryou*, Loveday's little sister with scarlatina, and beneath that, *John Scorn*. I woke Philpott, who was snoring on the sofa unmolested by Bitterweed, who still appeared to be absent after leaving the house with me in the depths of night.

'Piggy is in danger of showing himself the rebel,' I said. 'He has already skipped out to treat his living patients and I'm afraid he'll play truant from the coroner altogether if we don't go and fetch him.'

We slurped down a pot of tea and Philpott stuffed a saffron bun in his pocket in preparation for a swift departure. We were hampered in this intent, however, by the discovery that Bitterweed's absence had been freighted with ominous meaning. She had made herself scarce, having pissed in Philpott's hat while he slept: a fact he did not discover until a fraction too late. He was obliged to scrub his head under the yard pump and afterwards, looking very pink, set out with me in the direction of John Scorn's house where we hoped to find Piggy at his ministrations.

It was market day, as well as election day, and the town was crammed with racket and congestion. Wagons thundered up and down the street, a peril to any unwary pedestrian. The shop girls had ribbons in their caps and wore their best clothes, coming in and out of their shadowed doorways on whatever pretext they could think of, calling out arch remarks to shy young farm lads in from the country. There were knotted groups of farmers standing about the Guildhall steps and livestock auctions in progress in the market yard. A score of red cows browsed hay from a wooden rack, while very early lambs ready for the butcher pulled at the grass growing up between the paving slabs, happily innocent of their approaching fate.

The morning sun was already warm, yesterday's clouds dispelled, and a lad was throwing buckets of water about, to settle the dust raised by the animals' hooves.

Under the auctioneer's babble, other private sales were also in progress. A burly man was opening the lid of a basket to show the contents to another. 'Take a look at these little beauties and tell me you won't have one.' Kittens, puppies, ferrets? I would never know, for Philpott had now touched my arm and pointed out the red flags draped over the Guildhall entrance for the new corporation, while a couple of other men were stringing blue bunting across the doorway of the Angel for the duke. Ribbons and cockades in the same colours were everywhere. We were scarcely past the crossroads when we met Sarah Glynn and Eleanor Scorn coming down Meneage Street together. Eleanor looked tired, but glad to be out in the fresh air, and her perpetual scowl had faded to a mild look of ill humour.

'We were just coming to your grandfather,' I said. 'How is he? Is there any sign of wakefulness this morning?'

'He has moved his foot,' she said with admirable brevity and absolutely no show of joy at this development – if development it was, or only an involuntary nervous spasm. I had once thought his death would leave her stranded, but I knew better than that now. Sarah had said she would be better off without him. If he died she could certainly have Cyrus. If he lived, she might end up with no one.

'I have dragged her out for a breath of air,' Sarah put in, 'and a look at my puppies before she must go back to her nasty old dungeon. Pythagoras told her to come with me to admire them. He is quite the proud father.'

I still wished he had not gone back to The Willows against my advice, but Sarah was laughing innocently, and if he had not gone she would not have kissed him. I could hardly begrudge him that small joy amid all this trouble.

'Who is with your grandfather now?'

'Loveday and the doctor.'

But Piggy was already leaving John Scorn's house as we came up. The man's body was restless, he said, but his mind still quite insensate. What that might signify in this puzzling case was unclear, but movement of any kind was to be welcomed and he would return within the hour to examine him again.

'But you are going to Wedlock now?' I said, as we turned with him back down towards the crossroads through the cheerful crowd. 'Everyone will be waiting for you at church, in the vestry.'

Piggy frowned at me. 'I should really go back to little Jane Landeryou. I believe the crisis will come this afternoon and her fate be decided one way or the other.'

'Then there is nothing you can do until then,' I said, stopping him with a hand on his sleeve. 'Piggy, the coroner required you to open the corpse at half past nine, and by doing so you will show all suspicions groundless and remain at liberty, able to help all your patients for years to come.'

He still looked doubtful. 'If you will not do it for yourself, do it for me,' I added. 'I have taken it upon myself to support the duke's ridiculous whim against the wishes of Sir James, and if you don't attend to the business after all the trouble the sexton has taken I will look like a fool. Let's get it over with.'

WHEN WE GOT TO the church Wedlock's opened grave had hurdles laid across it, scattered with soil, so that at a casual glance the works of the night were not very obvious. The coffin was in the vestry, and a large old table at which the curate doubtless wrote his sermons had been cleared. William Wedlock was sitting in a corner, white-faced, keeping vigil with his grandfather's body. He broke off from his prayers and stood up to greet us, wearing a look of resolution to meet the coming horror that I thought was rather admirable, while the coroner bustled up full of the news that another doctor had not been forthcoming and that he and Sir James were therefore required to be vigilant onlookers. Sir James was sitting in a corner looking very far from pleased with this unasked-for duty. Meanwhile, Piggy had hastened over to the curate.

'I am sorry to have kept you waiting.' He put his large paw on the curate's arm and looked remorseful that his morning's procrastination had, after all, caused another man a few minutes' unnecessary suffering. 'Be sure that I will treat your grandfather with all the tenderness he deserves. But,' he now looked particularly St Bernard-like and kind, 'I hardly think *you* will like to observe the procedure, William. See, Mr Roskruge and Sir James are both here to bear witness, and Mr Jago and Mr Philpott will no doubt ably assist me. I advise you to leave us to the task – and I promise you that by tonight when he is reburied we will have made our very best enquiries.'

'Thank you,' William Wedlock said. His white face had turned grey, probably at the thought of the dreadful operation in prospect. 'I know you will do right, Dr Jago. You always do. And I will indeed leave you, being of no use and likely only a hindrance if I stay.'

Once he was gone, Piggy set down the wooden chest he had exchanged for his usual doctor's bag at the surgery on our way to church. He opened it to reveal a selection of tools that looked more suitable to a carpenter than a surgeon. The coroner had seated himself by Sir James for these preliminaries but Philpott at once got out his notebook and licked his pencil.

'Now then, my dear sir, will you tell me what it is you have in that there handsome box, and its purpose, so that I may set it all down for the *Cannon*? The readers will vastly enjoy it, I assure 'ee, being persons of a remarkably inquisitive bent o' mind.'

The first item Piggy obediently produced was a

sharpening stone, set on a wooden handle. The next was a scalpel, which he honed to a razor-sharpness on the stone. I knew the scalpel's disquieting efficacy from the poor farmer's case the previous evening. But Philpott, having missed that instructive use of the instrument, was quite charmed by its appearance now, and would have made some experimental cuts on the vestry curtains if Piggy hadn't frowned and put the blade safely back in its place.

Piggy next sharpened a small saw. 'Once I have opened the body with the blade, I carefully tease the skin, fat and muscle from the bones, and peel it back, to open the body like a book.' He glanced up at Philpott who was still writing busily. 'If you feel about your own chest, you will observe that under that thin layer of skin, fat and muscle lies the ribcage, beneath which all the vital organs are protected. I will use this saw to remove the ribs thus gaining access to the heart and lungs. If we believe Wedlock died either from a stroke of *angina pectoris* or from the inhalation of smoke, this will be confirmed or denied by an examination of those organs. A stroke to the heart can be indicated by many things: ossification of the arteries, softening of the heart muscle, or the rupture of one or both of the heart's chambers. If suffocation by smoke is the cause, we will see soot in the bronchi and alveoli – the myriad small air sacs of which the lung is composed.'

Philpott was nodding and scribbling frantically, and

I wondered how his spelling of the *bronchi* and *alveoli* would come out.

All this time Jeb Nettle had been gently working at the nails in the coffin lid, attempting to ease them out without damaging the wood. At length the lid came off, and a rank odour met our nostrils. Philpott picked up Piggy's saw and tried it against his finger, looking suddenly thoughtful. 'Yes, yes, 'tis merely the knacker's art, that's all. And have I not seen more lambs and pigs butchered than Dr Jago could throw his books at? It will be of no great surprise to *me* to see Thomas Wedlock opened, I assure 'ee.'

'Very well then,' said Piggy. 'Let us begin.'

The sexton departed, Roskruge and Sir James shifted uneasily in their seats, and I helped Piggy lay a linen sheet over the vestry table before following him to the coffin. Piggy tutted. 'And this is why I did not like the prospect,' he said. 'See how, with every passing hour, his body decays.'

I myself had once seen a body left to hang for three days, but not at such close quarters as this. I swallowed a rising sourness in my throat and went to the corpse's feet as Piggy directed me. I noticed that Philpott was now standing further off by the coroner and Sir James, murmuring something about giving us room to manoeuvre the dead body out of its coffin. On the count of three we lifted it. The *rigor* had passed off and Wedlock's middle sagged. Piggy snapped at me sharply to be quick and the corpse thumped down on the table with less deference than the curate might have liked. But at least the thing was done and Thomas Wedlock himself would neither know nor care.

The corpse was dressed in a woollen shroud, tied below the feet like a parcel. On its head was a cap, on its hands woollen gloves, and its jaw was tied up with a linen band. One of the pennies that had still been on the eyelids had fallen on the floor in the course of our ungainly man-handling and rolled over to where Philpott was standing. 'Bring me that penny, will you?' I said. When he didn't answer I turned to look. His eyes were fixed on the body as he bent at my command as stiffly as an automaton. He got so far as picking up the penny but then his mecha-nism seemed to run down and he remained bent where he was, entirely motionless. I had to go to him and take the penny forcefully from his lifeless fingers.

Meanwhile, Piggy was undoing the shroud which was buttoned like a shirt, and I next helped him ease it off the dead shoulders and pull it down about the waist. Piggy lifted the body and I slipped the shroud off entirely. 'We will put it back on afterwards,' he said. 'No one will ever see what we have done. Philpott, will you hand me the scalpel?'

Philpott's steps came to my ears slow and halting. Then, as I put the penny back on the dead eye I saw a movement under the lid and, to the probable satisfaction of the sexton if he had still been there, a solitary maggot crawled out from between the old eyelashes.

'The scalpel, if you'll be so good,' Piggy was saying to Philpott again, holding out his hand without looking at him. Philpott made no movement nor reply. When I turned to him he was utterly still, one hand holding his notebook to his forehead, and his eyes, staring at the squirming maggot, as fixed as John Scorn's drugged ones on his sickbed.

I touched his arm. 'Philpott?'

He stared only into futurity like a dead man.

'Philpott!' I shook him again and then slowly, gracefully, he tipped forwards. This time there was no friendly hand to catch at his collar. Piggy wasn't looking and, as yesterday, I was a fraction too slow. Philpott landed flat on the vestry floor face down, only the notebook saving his nose from a mashing I should never otherwise have heard the end of.

PHILPOTT HAD BEEN right about one thing, however. The dissection really was like butchering an animal, even if his confidence that he would therefore like it had been misplaced. When Piggy sawed through the ribs it was exactly like my brother splitting mutton chops, and though I didn't think I would ever eat that article again (even if this meant starvation, mutton chops being the staple fare in every tavern in Christendom) I managed to keep my feet, while Philpott recovered his wits in dignified privacy lying on a pew in the church.

Sir James looked equally determined to stave off faintness and did so by asking endless questions as the heart and lungs were carefully removed and placed on the table beside the corpse for closer examination by and by. 'His Grace is most interested in the stomach,' he reminded Piggy. 'I'd be obliged if you'd proceed to that directly. Only then will the heart and lungs be of any interest.'

Piggy glanced up at him. 'You won't like it, sir, I assure you.'

'I dislike the whole foul business,' Sir James answered curtly. He was pale but quite as admirably resolute as the curate had looked when we came in. 'Let us get it over with, sir, and be done with it.'

All this time, the distant sounds of revelry had been floating up to us from the town through the open window of the vestry, while we ourselves, about our abstruse mysteries, seemed entirely removed from the concerns of that ordinary world. In point of fact, I was too busy not fainting myself to notice when sounds nearer at hand came wafting into the vestry. The patter of footsteps in the churchyard and then a dull, rhythmic pounding like someone felling a tree at some considerable distance.

The stomach was a fair-sized purse-shaped object and, after Piggy had tied off the entrance and exit pipes from the gullet and guts respectively, he cut through those tubes and removed it, laying it down beside the heart and lungs. A new and indescribable odour crept out from the guts, now opened like the gates of hell.

I held my nose and breathed through my mouth, but only succeeded in swallowing the stench and, despite all my former resolutions, I retched. Sir James, God bless him, did not.

Piggy fetched another cloth on which he laid the plump purse of the stomach. 'I would not have the contents contaminate all else,' he said by way of explanation, an explanation that I did not like the sound of at all. My mind boggled at the idea of *the contents*. Piggy hesitated his scalpel over it for another moment and then cut swiftly. We all cried out. The rancid remains of what looked like a Cornish pasty spewed out at the cut, along with an odour of unimaginable awfulness: a stench I fervently hope never to smell again, though I fear it will haunt my worst dreams till I am as dead as Thomas Wedlock.

'I'm afraid there is no possibility of detecting the scent we smelled on John Scorn's breath,' Piggy remarked mildly, poking about among the decomposing stomach contents. 'But I will spoon it all out and examine the lining if you wish.'

A strange sound was coming from the door to the nave and I fell away from the table with more alacrity than I have ever shown at any other period of my life. But it was only Philpott, scratching like a dog, and announcing through the hinges that the Sapient Hog was making mischief in Wedlock's grave and should we do something about it?

'You are dreaming,' I said, my eyes drawn unwillingly

but inexorably back to Piggy's foul work. 'Lie down again, for God's sake.'

He obeyed meekly, his footsteps pattering unsteadily away. But a moment later he was back at the door, scratching again.

'I am not dreaming, Laurence, I assure 'ee,' he croaked, in a hoarse, spiritual voice that did not much convince me. 'Come and look. Come and see, my boy.'

Piggy nodded at me, and Roskruge came nearer to assist him in my place. I slipped thankfully out through the door into the body of the church where Philpott was waiting, swaying slightly on his feet. I breathed in the musty church air with as much pleasure as if it had been a bracing Atlantic breeze, and looked at the quiet pews with some longing. Just such a narrow shelf had been my bunk aboard ship these past six weeks where I had been rocked peacefully to sleep.

'You should be lying down,' I said. 'Piggy says you need to rest else you may faint again.'

'Never mind that.' He made a sepulchral sign, beckoning me to follow him towards the door. 'Come and look.'

However unlikely his story had sounded, I was obliged to agree that the miscreant rifling through the heap of earth excavated from Wedlock's grave overnight was indeed the Sapient Hog. On his porcine face was a look of joy it was hard to begrudge him. His sleek, glossy coat was smeared brown with earth, his snout was thrusting in the mud, making that same strange, muffled thumping

I had heard inside the vestry, and his long eyelashes were fluttering in a positive ecstasy. Poor thing. I suppose in the gilded courts of London and Europe – and in his own sty, however palatial – such simple pleasures of worms and roots and weeds were too often denied him.

We watched as he snuffled and snorted amid the piled-up earth, seeking out the choicest titbits, the very picture of a happy pig. Down in the town the clock was striking half past eleven and the noise of a large crowd gathering floated up to us clearly through the morning air.

'God damn me, he has slipped his leash,' Philpott said, with much satisfaction. 'And him supposed to be performing in half an hour, by God! The most remarkable thing I ever saw in my life.' His face was recovering, I thought, and he looked much less dazed.

'He certainly shows remarkable *sapience* to seek out the best midden in Helston.' I sighed at the prospect of a whole new set of problems. 'What are we to do?'

'We could leave him be.' Philpott eyed me experimentally to see how I would take such a subversive notion. 'I dare say they will find him eventually, but meanwhile he will have had his fun, the dear creature.'

'But there will certainly be search parties already in pursuit of him, and Roskruge will be vexed if our business is therefore discovered. And besides, what if he starts digging up the other graves?'

At this Philpott looked serious, probably remembering

as I had suddenly done, the children newly buried here. 'God forbid.' He shook his head. 'And so must end all our little joys, Laurence, at the altar of duty to others not to mention common decency. Still …' He smiled. 'I dare say it would be a dreadful shame to miss his show again. Shall we catch him?'

It was typical of Philpott to talk of this task as something easily accomplished. But, God bless him, he was right, for it only took a length of rope the workmen had left lying about after lifting up the coffin, and the saffron bun in Philpott's pocket to bring the poor pig's little spree of freedom to a close.

He was affectionately attached to the mud, however, and surprisingly strong in his resistance to being parted from it. It took both of us pulling the rope to divide snout from earth, and when he came, he came with a rush, and then sat down rather suddenly on his haunches. We looked into his small eyes and I wondered what he was thinking. He was smiling, or he appeared to be, and after a moment he rolled onto his side with a look of beatific tranquillity.

We got him reluctantly to his feet again and began to pull him towards the lichgate. Once back in Church Street, his peaceful smile vanished. Evidently invigorated by the change of scene, he raised his snout as if suddenly electrified by a new smell, woofed three times, and then set off at a gallop down the hill towards the town. We could not hold him and we let go of the rope slipped around his collar. It waved like a banner for a moment before he sloughed it off. His plump hams twinkled away from us down towards the crossroads where the crowd was waiting.

'They will catch him,' Philpott said with confidence.

'I think he smelled something he liked,' I said.

'His master, perhaps?'

'It would be pleasant to think so.'

We hurried down the road after the errant hog. I had abandoned my post with Piggy and, though I loved him dearly, just now I would not consent to return to that awful spectacle unless someone came and positively dragged me back on the end of a rope myself.

15

NOON

HALFWAY DOWN THE HILL, outside the confectioner's shop, I recognised our family market stall, set out with wheels of cheese, clotted cream pots, and primrose-coloured pats of butter wrapped in muslin. But Mother was not there. A woman I didn't recognise was standing in for her, she said, Mother being needed elsewhere this morning at short notice.

'Not at the farm?' Philpott asked, with a slight look of alarm. 'There has been no trouble there, I hope? No infants drowned or fallen off sheep?' He glanced at me. 'When I left the farm, Laurence, Margaret was quite bent on riding 'em.'

The woman assured us that, so far as she knew, my mother's business was not with any sick or injured person, but she knew no more than that, she said. She had had a good morning so far – had cleared ten shillings – but her custom was thinning now as the crowd gathered more and more thickly outside the Angel for the Sapient Hog's performance. The pig had been caught, as Philpott had predicted, and was now being groomed and prepared by Mr Nicholson in the market yard, periodically jumping excitedly off all four trotters at once, apparently still delighted with his brief escape from tiresome duty. When we came round the corner into Coinagehall Street we saw that the crowd had arranged itself in a dense semicircle around an affair of hurdles and boxes that had been flung up as a stage, and which would later also serve as the hustings.

I looked for Eleanor and Sarah Glynn, wondering if there was any further news of John Scorn that we had missed while up at the church, but I didn't see them. I couldn't see much of the stage either: we were arrived too late for a good view. I was wondering reluctantly if we should go back to Piggy, when I heard a voice shout our names and, looking up, I saw Sarah Glynn in the window of an attorney's first-floor office, beckoning us up with a pleasant smile. At once Philpott began to push through the crowd towards the attorney's door between shopfronts. I glanced at the Angel, where I could see the duke's party also at their windows. I would have preferred Anne's company, but the crowd was now as thick as it had been on Friday night at the political meeting and it would take sharper elbows than mine to make my way across the street to the inn. Instead, I followed

Philpott to the attorney's door and mounted the echoing stairwell to the first floor, telling myself I could at least question Sarah a little more about the relations between Eleanor and Cyrus and the curate.

There was a huddle of bodies in the attorney's sash window, looking down on the entertainment in the street. Apart from the lawyerly gentleman I supposed was our host, I knew the rest of the party. Lushington, sitting in a padded velvet chair which had been carried to the window, Glynn the mayor, Sarah his niece, and Philpott newly arrived and perspiring gently from the exertion of the stairs.

Sarah was coming over, her face bright with welcome, and she tucked her arm in mine. 'I was looking for Pythagoras, but I suppose he is b-busy as usual,' she said confidingly as she led me to the window. 'Do you know where he is?'

'Engaged with a patient,' I answered as I looked down on the seething crowd below in the street. Opposite, in the window of the Angel, Charles Burges was leaning dangerously far out, his mouth agape. Anne had a hand on his collar, and George Osborne was there, too. He saw me, smiled, and raised a hand in greeting.

'Extraordinary thing,' the attorney was exulting. He seemed very inclined to take credit for the whole entertainment. 'What a splendid view we shall have of the Sapient Hog!'

We could indeed see Mr Nicholson in his striped coat

and tall hat very well as he leapt gracefully on to the make-shift stage, leading a rather less agile Sapient Hog by the leash that was once again attached to his broad leather collar. The pig did not heed Nicholson's pulling at once, instead turning in a circle that contrived to tangle the leash, gazing in apparent wonder at the crowd as if he had never seen such a thing before in his whole short life. Nicholson tugged at his collar again with a frown and the Hog abandoned his marvelling examination of the audience and clambered awkwardly up the steps to the platform behind him without an ounce of the grace he had shown when flying down the street only half an hour earlier.

Sarah Glynn was leaning forward out of our open window, as eagerly as the child across the street. 'He is never wrong, or so they claim. When we saw him at the Assembly Room, I asked him if my b-book was to be as famous as Miss Radcliffe's and he said indeed it was.'

'A politic answer,' Glynn said with good-natured cynicism. 'But I fancy we shall see quite enough here to settle our minds as to the pig's abilities – and his true political opinions.'

Lushington kept his own counsel, his blotched hands folded together in his lap and his face only quietly amused.

As the crowd flowed and ebbed as it had done on Friday night, but now in far better humour and without the brawling, I saw washed up at the front of the throng Loveday, Eleanor's maid, with Cyrus Best, Eleanor's lover. Their faces were close together and animated with the fun of the occasion. They kept turning their heads to whisper in each other's ears, their hair touching, their cheeks scarcely a lip's breadth apart, and I was pretty certain that they weren't discussing the Sapient Hog but something of a much more personal interest. Good God, they were in league somehow, unknown to Eleanor, and when I remembered Philpott's question as to how Cyrus could possibly have administered poison to John Scorn, a new answer presented itself. The conveniently broken china in the dunny heap. I imagined Loveday's sweet voice this time. *Poor master. Do have a nice cup o' tea.*

I glanced at Sarah, wondering if she had also seen them, and then at Philpott, wondering if I should point them out to him. The duke believed Piggy the man with the best opportunity to do wrong, but this, thank God, showed otherwise. But Nicholson was now setting out alphabet and number cards in a semicircle before the Sapient Hog, whose wonder at the crowd had deserted him and who looked suddenly tired to death. After a moment watching his master's preparations without much interest, he slowly sank to his belly, legs splayed out on either side like a starfish. Mr Nicholson, not noticing this lapse of porcine dignity, turned towards the audience, with a well-practised and rather balletic flourish.

'Ladies and gentlemen,' he cried out in a booming voice, 'I am honoured to present the Sapient Hog, celebrated in London, Paris and all the capitals of Europe.

He has been displaying his extraordinary genius these many years, and I am sure that by now you have all heard of his superlative gifts. You may even doubt that the tales can be true. You may have formerly chosen to scoff at such things. But today, all your doubts will be exploded, and you shall depart from this place with a lifetime's tales with which to delight those of your friends and families so unlucky to miss this stupendous exhibition.'

He turned to his prodigy, who was now snoring gently. He poked the Sapient Hog with his pointed toe and the pig woke blearily and struggled to his feet again, seeming dimly to remember the required choreography of his familiar performance. But it was an effort, and he shook his ears rather like a drunk trying to clear his head, which made a ripple of amusement run through the crowd. There was a rustle of Sunday-best dresses as women turned to each other to laugh and whisper. Mr Nicholson's look of quizzical displeasure suggested this was not a usual part of the performance. He tugged at Toby's collar again, and the Hog gamely lumbered forwards towards the cards laid out before him.

'Let us begin with a simple demonstration of Toby's alphabetical genius. Call out your names, ladies and gentlemen, and he will spell them without a single mistake.'

'Thomas Smith,' someone shouted immediately from the crowd.

'Oh, far too easy,' Sarah said at my elbow. 'The p-pig must have spelled that name a thousand times.'

This did not, in fact, appear to be so, however, if the Hog's perplexity was any guide. In fact, he seemed utterly confounded by the whole affair. He looked at his master and waggled his ears again. Mr Nicholson said something sternly under his breath and the pig wobbled along the semicircle of letters to pick out a T with more careful deliberation than was likely to impress the audience in the way Mr Nicholson had hoped.

But after that one letter the Sapient Hog was stumped. He swayed up and down the alphabet as if, like the audience, he had never seen the cards before. If, as I had formerly wondered, the Sapient Hog was, like the monarchy, an institution inhabited by a succession of creatures of differing abilities, this one was certainly a dud.

There was a general rustling in the crowd now, and a hum of rising voices as neighbours asked each other if this promised entertainment was to be a disappointing failure. I looked across at the duke, the patron of the feast. He was frowning horribly. Then, evidently tiring of the pig's poor spelling, a voice called out from the crowd, 'Where shall I put my wager, Toby? Will John Scorn wake in time to make his vote or no?'

Mr Nicholson looked displeased again, this surely being a question he had not schooled his already unsatisfactory hog to answer. But perhaps the pig's dull wits recognised the shout as a question. And to a question there were only ever two possible answers, easy enough for even his inferior sapience. He picked up two cards delicately by the corner and laid them at Mr Nicholson's feet.

N O

At this first hint that the pig not only understood English after all, but actually had his trotter on the pulse of the town's affairs, there was finally a minor sensation in the crowd: an outburst of clapping from the Mohawks and booing and hissing from the Cherokees there assembled. The pig raised his snout again at the noise, seeming stimulated by this brief success, and emitted three short woofs as he had done earlier in the street.

And as before, woofing was the prelude to wild activity very much at odds with the strange lethargy that had lately overtaken him. Then it had been his rapid flight down the hill to the town; now it was his wits that, having seemed so dull, burst into a sudden dazzling display of fireworks. Unfortunately, as he began haring up and down the alphabet at lightning speed, it transpired to be a firework display where all the rockets had been knocked somehow out of true and exploded at all angles like errant squibs.

H E R
G R A C E
A T
T H E
B L U E

He spelled with sudden confidence, but then paused a moment reflectively and shook his ears for a third time.

AND
SIR
JA ...
JAM ...

He was having trouble with the spelling of this name but it was no matter since the town took his meaning well enough. Her Grace and Sir James! These being personages never to be seen at so humble an establishment as the Blue Anchor – the crowd leaned forward with a new interest.

'Here we go,' Glynn said with some satisfaction. 'Keep your eye on the duke and enjoy his discomfiture, Lushington. We shall have our ten guineas' worth and more, I hope.'

The pig's trotters were now positively flying, as he rushed from card to card, Nicholson calling out the words he spelled, which grew more and more truncated the faster he flew, like an old lady's oft-told tale, full of ellipses and all run together pell-mell and hugger-mugger.

LOCK
THE
DOOR

HER
GRAC...
AN...
SIR

SCR...
IN
TH...
CUPB...

Over in the Angel window the duke's frown was
deepening, while the duchess looked extremely surprised
and had fixed the pig and its master with a reproachful
gaze. She had paid it a small sum to be kind to her
husband, but it now appeared that Glynn had paid ten
guineas for it to be cruel to herself. For its part, the crowd
found it all mighty amusing. A rising tide of whoops and
laughter from half the throng was being shushed by the
other half, leaning forward to catch every last syllable.
Meanwhile, Mr Nicholson had a look of slight panic on
his face, which suggested the Hog was out of control and
might now do anything with the words so laboriously
taught him.

Sarah Glynn was turning to me with a furrowed
brow. 'I understand most of it, Mr Jago, but what can he
mean by the duchess and Sir James? And what of SCR?
SCRummaging? Or SCRabbling? And in a cupboard!
Whatever for?'

Meanwhile, Glynn was laughing quietly in Lushington's ear. 'I told Nicholson that ridicule is always a better answer to power than argument. The town won't forget Her Grace and Sir James in a hurry, even if the pig does turn out to be a disappointing specimen.'

A disappointing specimen indeed, for now, after all this brief yet frantic motion, the pig was slowing again. Whatever mania had gripped him was wearing off as quickly as it had come.

C U P ...
D O O R
S C R ...
J A ...

The pig's dash between letters turned to a trot, then a walk, and finally, to a stumble. His ears drooped.

H E R
G R ...
S I R
J A ...
S C R ...
L O C K
C U P B ...

The Sapient Hog paused, looked around at his audience for another moment with a kind of wild conjecture, and then fell down with a tremendous thump. There was a brief, dreadful silence when we all thought the poor thing had expired before our eyes, but then the Sapient Hog gave one last feeble *woof* and began snoring again loudly.

IF MY ELBOWS HAD not been sharp enough to part the crowd, Philpott's were. We arrived just as the pig was being carried by a handful of cheerful men into the peace of the alley beside the dying grocer's shop. Mr Nicholson was stroking the pig's head and sobbing endearments. Philpott lumbered to his knees beside them while I tried to keep the interested onlookers at bay.

'Poor Toby,' Mr Nicholson was saying brokenly. 'To think I thought him disobedient, when he was really ill.'

'He was not ill an hour ago, when he was running about the graveyard.' Philpott lifted Toby's eyelid as Piggy had done John Scorn's. 'Laurence, come here and tell me what you see. And tell me what you smell.'

I knelt down to peer into the piggy eye. It was fixed and dilated. Moreover, there was the same strange smell about him that had lingered on Scorn's breath but fresher and much stronger now. 'Good God. The pig has been poisoned, too,' I said. 'Why the devil? And what *is* that smell?'

''Tis nutmeg,' a quavering voice said behind us, and I turned to see the dying old grocer, Julian, at my elbow, probably roused out of his shop by all the sudden commotion. 'I sells it, sir. I knows it very well.'

I stood up. 'Will you show me?'

He nodded and leaving Philpott still in tender attendance on the pig, I followed the grocer into his shop, which was pervaded by the warm aroma of coffee beans and tea leaves.

'You are very well placed.' I looked about me in admiration at the shop's affluent cleanliness and style. 'The Angel Inn next door and lawyer's chambers across the street.'

'Yes, yes, we have a good class of customer, sir,' Julian answered without much enthusiasm. 'But they do always want fancy goods that cost much more to buy, so I sometimes reckon I'm no better off for their business. However, it's for that reason I have the nutmeg at all.'

I had already caught the scent of spices, not an exact match for what we'd smelled on John Scorn's breath, but scents that made me think of punch as the nutmeg had done. I was following my nose to the dim far corner of the shop where spices in jars and spices loose in boxes were displayed. But the grocer's voice called me back. 'I keep the nutmeg here behind the counter, being too valuable to leave out for folks to thieve.'

'Valuable?'

'Yes, sir. A very rare commodity is nutmeg. Four or five guineas a pound – depending on the market, I should say.'

As he spoke Julian reached down a jar from the shelves behind his head and handed it to me. I unscrewed the lid and saw a handful of whole nutmegs in the jar, along with a small drawstring bag which I fished out and opened. It contained some of the nutmeg grated, and as I sniffed I realised that, though perhaps a little faded from its long sojourn in the cloth bag, this was, at last, the exact match for the scent I remembered on Scorn's breath and had just now smelled again on the pig's.

'Do the Scorns ever buy your spices?'

'Betimes. At Faddy Day, I suppose. Saffron, too, o' course, for their buns, but saffron may be had at any shop in Helston, being so very necessary for the baking. Can't say I remember Loveday buying nutmeg, howsumever, not for a long time.'

'Does anyone else sell it in town?'

'John Richards, up Meneage Street, may 'ave it, but as you observed, sir, this shop has a very good class of customer as can afford it. I doubt many other grocers in town could stretch to stock it.'

'Can you mind who has bought nutmeg from you recently?'

The grocer wrinkled his forehead in a frown. 'No one at all, that I can call to mind, save Dr Jago for his dispensary. Three nuts he had of me last week.'

This was extremely tiresome. Whether nutmeg had anything to do with the poisoning or not, our conversation here was bound to get out the minute I left the shop.

'I don't suppose Cyrus Best has had any from you?' I asked as I screwed the lid back on the jar. 'I saw him at your shop last night.'

'He is my nevvy,' Julian said. 'And he wouldn't know nutmeg if a ton of it fell on his head and pressed him squat.'

I TOLD PHILPOTT WHAT the grocer had said and, since he was no use but a positive hindrance at the dissection, I bid him go about the town's other grocers, to see if nutmeg were to be had elsewhere, while I reluctantly went back to Piggy.

After the noisy crowd it was eerily quiet up at the church. Sir James was gone and Roskruge had sat down in his corner again, while Piggy was sewing up the old man's chest with all the various organs inside, so that come Judgement Day Thomas Wedlock would not be missing any essential body parts. Piggy looked up at me as I came in with a tired smile.

'You have finished?' I came over to watch the needle go in and out through the purpled dead flesh. The awful smells had dissipated into a general but bearable miasma. 'What did you find?'

'A good deal.' Piggy paused in his work to pat my arm. 'You were right, Laurence, it was the proper thing to do after all. We now know the cause of his death for certain, and I find it is a comfort to my mind. I hope his family will feel the same in time and forgive us for our meddling. And of course it answers the duke's questions, too.'

'Well?' I perched on the edge of the table to watch.

'No damage to the heart at all. A remarkably healthy organ for such an aged man. But as for his lungs ...' Piggy shook his head. 'Every man's lungs darken gradually with age, and especially in one so old. A lifetime of open fires and smoking pipes causes a remarkable change from the pink lung of the child to the grey one of the man. But Wedlock's were black with soot. There was soot, too, in his airways and throat – even some in his stomach. He had breathed in a copious amount, Laurence, and swallowed it, too. Far more than any human frame could support. The fire was doused so quickly afterwards that he did not burn, thank God, but he certainly died from suffocation by the fumes. Mr Roskruge has updated his report, and the sheriff will know by teatime. Wedlock will be buried again by midnight, and everything will be resolved.'

He had finished his sewing and was beckoning me to bring him the shroud. 'As for his stomach, there was no corrosion to the lining and, of course, no possibility of identifying the scent we smelled on John Scorn amid all that stink of decay.'

I was opening my mouth to tell him I had at least solved the mystery of that smell – though whether the nutmeg had flavoured a misused tonic or a devilled kidney was still unclear – when the door to the vestry opened and the sheriff himself came in. Piggy nodded to him cordially and the coroner stood up.

'We have determined the cause of death, sir,' Roskruge said with unfeigned relief. 'Misadventure by the inhalation of smoke just as we first thought, and no sign at all of poison or any other mischief.'

But Hitchens was boggling his large eye at us in a strange way, and I realised he was in a state of some nervous excitement. 'Not at all, sir,' he jangled at the coroner gruffly, his chest worse than ever. 'Not in the slightest.' His eye blinked rapidly and he put out a hand to grasp Piggy's sleeve. 'Dr Jago, I am obliged to arrest you on suspicion of Thomas Wedlock's murder.'

'What?' I started forward to shake his hand from Piggy's arm. 'What are you talking about?'

'New evidence,' the sheriff wheezed at me, resisting my hand, while Piggy looked at him, amazed. 'As you know, sirs, the door to the Guildhall cupboard was locked and the clerks were obliged to break down the door. Yet, though we searched high and low, we found no key within the room. We have not spoken of it widely, fearing to apprise the murderer of our suspicions. But now it is all made plain, even if I don't understand it for the life of me.'

'Understand what?' I said.

'Why the doctor should have locked Thomas Wedlock in the cupboard and left him to die.'

I looked from Hitchens to Roskruge, and then to

Piggy. They all looked equally shocked.

'But even supposing the cupboard was locked from the outside, what makes you think my cousin did it?' I was angry, perplexed, perhaps too violent. The coroner put a restraining hand on my arm and the sheriff's frightful eye turned on me in a way that made me quail.

'I do not *think* it, sir, I know it. His housekeeper, Tirza Ivey, has just found the key to the Guildhall cupboard in the doctor's bag.'

16

'In his bag?' I echoed. 'For God's sake, Pythagoras, tell Hitchens how it got there.'

Piggy was rubbing his head, looking rumpled and perplexed. 'I can't … I don't …'

'Dr Jago, you must come with me,' the sheriff said. To do him justice, he did not look as if he liked this turn of events any more than I did. 'Roskruge will finish matters here and the sexton will make all right.'

I went straight to the duke, but he was not at home, Sir James said, as he cut me off at the door. In fact, the duke was very much at home, for Sir James was coming out with the coal scuttle brimming with broken china, while the duke's angry voice carried as clearly through the panelled door as if I had been inside. The words *cuckold* and *nonsense*, and George's appreciative hoots of laughter, drifted out to us.

Sir James seemed to have survived the unpleasant experience of the dissection better than I had. He remained his usual calm, collected self, if only slightly harassed, while his patron was running mad in the adjoining room – *bastard son* and *how dare you say so* were now wafting through the door, the duke apparently having taken the duchess's *SCRummaging* and *SCRabbling* with Sir James in some unknown cupboard more seriously than was absolutely reasonable from the mouth of a performing pig. But, of course, Glynn had known it was a raw nerve and no doubt George was busy poking it.

'But I must speak to him,' I said. 'My cousin has been arrested on suspicion of Wedlock's murder, which is nonsense for you know very well that he had just found it was not poison.'

Sir James raised an eyebrow. 'So he said. And very convenient for him.' But his determined calm was slightly disturbed as he flinched at the sound of a sharp report inside the duke's rooms, followed by the tinkling of broken glass.

'You will not help my cousin?'

'I will let justice take its course, Jago. If Hitchens has evidence good enough to arrest him, I am sure he is quite within his rights.'

When Sir James and the duke heard the concrete nature of that evidence, in the stubborn form of a key among Piggy's possessions, there would be no mercy for him at all. Behind the door the duchess was now giving

the duke a very shrill and circumstantial account of all
her clandestine dealings with Glynn's thirty-two electors
and telling him that if he would not be a man and bribe
them, she would. *And as for Sir James*, she added, rising
to a climax . . .

Sir James promptly steered me down the steps and out
into the courtyard of the inn. He handed the coal scuttle
to a passing servant, who took it philosophically, and we
loitered at the brink of that infernal knee-high well.

'There are others with far better reasons to harm John
Scorn than Glynn,' I said. 'I will prove it to you all, and
you will be obliged to apologise to my cousin before the
end.'

'Use your brains, Jago,' Sir James replied. 'Don't make
a fool of yourself again when you have the chance of a
new career in Whitehall, not to mention—'

I was turning away, loath to have Anne's name dragged
into all this, when a breathless voice called from the
upstairs window that the duke was took very bad. Sir
James and I looked at each other for a moment and he
made no objection to my following him back upstairs.
I don't know what I expected. My mind was so full of
death and poison I half-thought he would be lying pros-
trate on the rug like John Scorn or the Sapient Hog. But
when we came in, His Grace was only lolling in a chair,
arms wrapped about his ribs, his face very red. He was
dying, he informed us dolefully as we came in, suffering
from a sudden terrible pain in his chest.

'It is only the heartburn, Your Grace,' Sir James reassured him. 'You know the doctor always says so. Probably the result of all this general excitement.' That was one way to describe the wreckage of the duke's wrath scattered across the carpet, not to mention the coming wreckage of my cousin's whole life.

'But this here.' The duke put his fingers to his breast-bone and looked at us soulfully. 'This here, I say. Such a fluttering and a sinking in my heart. Fluttering and sinking and fire from stem to stern.'

'That is why they call it a heartburn, Your Grace,' Sir James answered stolidly. 'The doctor has told you so a dozen times.'

'And so I also told him,' the duchess observed from the sofa. 'But he must always be singular.' There was high colour in her face and she was engaged in angry embroidery, biting through her thread as she cast her husband a withering glance. 'He thinks himself far too grand for a little trapped wind.'

The duke rested his head against the chair back, closing his eyes and looking aggrieved. 'I think I have every right to be struck down, after all that I have suffered.' He opened his eyes again to look at us. 'Every right to be struck down, I say. Hey, hey, Sir James, wouldn't you say so? Wouldn't you say I am quite as ill used as Wedlock or old man Scorn?'

'At least *you* ain't been poisoned yet,' George said cheerfully as he got up from his chair. The entertainment

274

of the row between his parents being ended he was probably going in search of other amusements.

The duke was instantly angry and struggled upright. 'Poisoned? No, no, George, it is worse than that. I have been stabbed in the back by all these damned ungrateful townsmen.'

But George was gone with a serene wave of his hand, and the duke was obliged to turn his ire back on the rest of us. 'All my money, all my care, all my damned journeys from the north to the west country at such cost of time and expense. Stabbed in the back, I say, God damn them.'

At this juncture the door opened and Anne slipped in, probably having noticed the cessation of the duke's wrath through the thin walls and surmising herself safe from flying objects, at least for the present. In this she might have been premature, for the duke was now recovering his spirits and sprang up from his chair, beginning to pace again, broken glass crackling under his shoes. His fingers twitched as if he wanted to throw something else but, looking about, I saw that every movable object had already been smashed, and if he wanted to vent his feelings on something inanimate it would now need to be a chair or a table. Frankly, in his present mood, I wouldn't have put that past him.

'And now, at the very close, to be thwarted,' he was saying. 'Ten to one Parliament would have supported Scorn again if he had voted, for they cannot change their minds without a very good reason. Ten to one, I say, they would have supported me. Without my elector's vote it cannot be right to allow the election to stand, whatever that damned sheriff may think. It cannot be right, I say, in any degree.'

From the direction of the crossroads the Market House clock was striking a quarter to three. The duke flapped at Sir James. 'For God's sake, fetch the paper, will you? Fetch the paper, I say.'

Sir James obediently went to the desk and a moment later I found he was thrusting a sheet of paper into my hand. It was the ballot slip, supposed to be signed by John Scorn if he ever woke.

'Take it to him, Jago, for God's sake, take it to him I say, and tell his granddaughter to have him sign at the very first hint of consciousness.' He looked at me significantly. '*At the very first hint*, I say. If he so much as twitches, tell her to guide his hand.'

I thought I had misheard him. 'Your Grace?'

'Don't look so innocent, Jago. You know exactly what I mean.'

I remembered Anne telling George that forgery was a hanging offence. The duke saw the look on my face and grew impatient. 'I am not asking *you* to do it, Jago, though in your own peculiar position you might well reflect upon where your loyalties lie. But if his granddaughter is found out in such deception folks will only say she is a strange young woman as outlandish as her grandfather.' He scowled horribly at me. 'In any event, and however you do it, you must make sure it is signed by the time Hitchens calls to collect it after the polls close tonight.'

Had I been a more ruthless man I suppose I might have made much capital of this. I might have demanded payment, or position – or even a seat in the House of Commons, if the duke still had such a thing to bestow. On the other hand, I rather thought this was indeed what he was offering – or at least some of it. An appointment back in Whitehall. The clearing of my name at home and abroad. I took the paper, mechanically folded it up, and put it in my pocket.

O F C O U R S E I W O U L D do no such thing as His Grace hinted, and all the episode had taught me was that there was no help forthcoming from the duke or Sir James as I had stupidly hoped. With this damned Guildhall key against him, it was more than ever imperative that I prove John Scorn's poisoning the work of someone other than Piggy. I had shuddered at the notion that Eleanor or Loveday could be involved, but quite frankly I would now welcome the news he had been poisoned by the family cat. Not that I had seen any animals in the Scorn household – another aspect of its grim, unhappy chill, and that miasma of ill will that the old man radiated even from his sickbed.

'Where is Eleanor?' I asked when Loveday opened Scorn's door.

'Out walking again with Miss Glynn.'

'Can I see your master? I'm afraid the doctor can't come to him just at present.'

Loveday led me into the old man's chamber without demur. It was dark and stuffy and the maid went to the window, opened the curtains, and threw up the sash to admit some afternoon light and air. The clock was striking three and there was still a tremendous racket from the merry-making crowds outside.

'How is he?' I crossed to the bed and touched John Scorn's shoulder. His eyes moved under the lids and I leaned over him, tapping his shoulder again. 'Mr Scorn? Mr Scorn, sir. Are you with us?' But alas, he was still far from consciousness. I pulled out the voting slip from my pocket and propped it against the wooden tobacco jar on the mantelpiece. With this, I had done my best for the duke, and felt myself discharged, though I now wished heartily that Scorn would indeed vote and Piggy be thereby credited with saving instead of killing him.

There were two chairs either side of the bed and Loveday had sat down in the furthest one with a basket of darning. She bent her head over her work, not looking at me as I paced the room, before plumping myself down in the other chair. 'I saw you with Cyrus Best at the pig show,' I said. 'I did not know you were so intimately acquainted with him.'

She kept her head down, but I could see a flush rising up

her cheeks and her hand twitched at her darning. 'Yessir,' she muttered cautiously. 'Our families was always friendly.'

'I have heard strange tales about him, Loveday.'

She did not answer, for she had at that moment stabbed her finger with her needle. She put it to her mouth with a little cry of pain. Her eyes met mine as she sucked the beads of blood from the wound and I saw her breath was short and her look anxious. My heart skipped a beat. 'Loveday, if there has been any mischief here, you must tell me, you know.'

'Mischief?' Her voice was faint. 'Oh, sir …'

Yes, there really was some secret, I could see it plainly now in her face. She glanced at the old man on the bed involuntarily as he gave a snort and pushed at his covers restlessly with his old hands.

'Tell me about it, Loveday,' I said. 'There is no reason for you to be implicated in whatever Cyrus has done, if you only speak frankly and tell me the truth.'

She didn't answer for a minute. 'The whole town's run croony,' she said after a pause, her voice scarcely above a whisper. 'I do want to go 'ome.' She looked at me earnestly. 'Do you not think I might go 'ome for an hour or two, sir, and see my poor little sister, Jane? Will you tell Miss Eleanor I shall be back in time for tea? And that I have been dosing the master with the nutmeg physic, just as Dr Jago told us.'

'Nutmeg?' I was puzzled. 'You have been giving your master nutmeg?'

'Yessir. Dr Jago was very pressin' upon it. Master will be due his next dose at six o'clock, so if you'll tell Miss Eleanor I'll be much obliged.'

But instead I made some excuse and left her, walking back down Meneage Street to the surgery in a daze. Nutmeg mentioned twice! First by the grocer, and now Loveday. But even if the spice had been used to disguise whatever poison had been administered to both pig and man, surely it must be mere coincidence that my cousin had also prescribed it to his old patient.

The market was over and the town slipping inexorably into debauch ahead of the poll. The whole place was simmering as I reached the crossroads. News of Piggy's arrest had seeped out and the Sapient Hog's collapse was another matter for gleeful alarm, I could hear all around me from the chattering voices of the pressing mob. A group of insolent wits had been as quick to take the Hog's hints about the duchess as the duke had, and they had given an old song new words.

If for the Duke of Leeds you will poll
You may tickle the Duchess's TOL DE ROL LOL.
When the Duchess of Leeds the THING takes in hand,
What man can refuse at her QUARTERS to stand?

Tirza was serious and perhaps defiant as she opened the surgery door to me, probably expecting blame for betraying my cousin to the sheriff. But I hadn't time for anger now; what I wanted were facts. And so it seemed did Anne, for she was there in the horrible parlour and rose from the horsehair sofa to greet me.

I threw my coat onto a chair. 'Anne! Good God! What are you doing here?'

She smiled at me as Tirza went out and shut the door. We were alone for the first time in years. 'A lady may visit a doctor's surgery without impropriety, I think.'

I crossed the three strides between us and took her in my arms. Her lips were warm. Her body was slight and cool and trembling. I threw my spectacles on the chair with my coat, all the while kissing her as if my life depended on it. Anne hesitated a moment, then her hands tangled in my hair. But Tirza's voice, singing some lugubrious dirge, was approaching from the direction of the kitchen and we broke apart, brought to our senses and in my case rather out of breath. For a moment Anne gazed at me, her eyes huge. But then, as the singing receded again, she drew me to the sofa and curled into my shoulder as if she had always belonged there.

'I came because I heard about your cousin,' she said. 'I'm so sorry, Laurence.'

Despite everything else it was a miracle to touch her, and even more to sit like this in a loving, unhurried embrace. Not in all these years had I stroked her silky hair or buried my nose in its softness. I was as smitten as Piggy, but our history was much longer and more complicated than his sweet courtship up at The Willows.

'It must all be a mistake, Anne,' I said. 'Although …' With a sigh I told her about the pig and the nutmeg and the grocer and Loveday's description of the tonic Piggy had prescribed. 'But where were you yesterday, Anne? What was your mysterious *engagement*?'

She still wouldn't tell me. She only said, 'It was your cousin's maidservant who found the key?' And withdrawing herself gracefully from my arms, she stood up from the sofa, smoothed her hair at the glass, and went to call Tirza.

Piggy had left his bag open in the hall that morning, Tirza told us, and I remembered this was true, for I had watched Piggy drop it on the floor by the door when we called in to collect his dissection chest on the way up to the church. He had opened it to rummage about inside for some forgotten item.

'I did tell him a dozen times not to leave it lyin' about, I did indeed, but he did not listen and that blasted cat had done it again, I could tell, when I come through to take in a parcel about one o'clock. I know it was one, for the clock was chimin' and the carrier said, "Not long till the polls close now, Mistress Ivey, and the pig says old John Scorn won't vote. Best tell your master to be quick and rouse him."' She looked at us confidingly. 'He had a bet on the vote, I think, and wanted to know if he was to lose his money.'

'But you were speaking of the bag?' Anne said.

'Pissed in 'un, han't she? Shockin' stink there was, and

the doctor's things all spoiled. I took it into the scullery to empty out afore I washed it under the pump. And there was a key tucked in a little pocket inside. Bless me, I did not know it, so I laid it on the parlour table, meanin' to ask the doctor what it was when he come back. But then the curate come in. Said he'd been at John Scorn's house and did the doctor know the old man was twitchin' like an 'orse with flies? I said I was sure he would know and warn't he there? He said no, he warn't there. But then he saw the key on the table and asked me what it was. I told him I'd found it in the doctor's bag and han't the first idea where it belonged to. He did look a bit queer at that and went off to fetch a clerk from the Guildhall. Bless me, the clerk turned quite gashly white, and they tore off with the key without so much as a by-your-leave.'

She was enjoying it all rather too much for my taste but I couldn't blame her for being made the way she was, and the sexton had said she was no fool. 'What kind of key was it, Tirza?'

'A lerrupin' old thing.' She shook her head. 'Like to a castle or some such.'

The only building in Helston that could possibly answer that description was the ancient Guildhall. It therefore wouldn't have been hard for the curate to put two and two together, recognise what the key must be, and call for the clerk. How astonished and horrified William Wedlock must have been to think Piggy guilty of his own grandfather's death, especially when they had worked together, caring for the town's dying children, and Piggy was at that very moment cutting up the old man himself. Surely the curate couldn't believe it any more than I could.

'Piggy will have some explanation,' I said to Anne after Tirza had gone. 'I'm sure he will. Either that or he has been misused most dreadfully. After all, John Scorn's poisoner must have heard the rumours against Piggy just as we have. Perhaps he somehow slipped the key into Piggy's bag to incriminate him further.'

'It's possible,' Anne said, her brows contracting. 'But who, and how? Who has had access to your cousin's bag?' She hesitated. 'And then, you know, Laurence, there is also this business of the nutmeg that your cousin had prescribed.'

'A tonic, I am sure of it,' I said. 'Piggy's books are full of cinnamon tonics, he told me so. Why not nutmeg, too?'

But when we went into the dispensary and consulted the dispensing book, there was no mention of nutmeg prescribed to anyone, still less Scorn. 'But, look, the last entry was two days ago,' I said. 'Piggy has been running around the town, and probably has fallen behind with his accounts.'

We looked about us at the shelves and their array of jars. I saw my old friend the laudanum, and bark for fevers, but there were also some shockingly old-fashioned ingredients in dusty pots, including viper wine *for deafness*, one bottle announced on a label grown brown with age. I scouted along the shelves until I found the jar labelled *nutmeg*. It was empty. I opened the lid to be sure, and a very stale version of the spice's scent met my nose. Far too stale to have struck either Piggy or I when we sniffed at John Scorn's breath, or Philpott when he sniffed the Sapient Hog's. But the grocer had said that Piggy had had three fresh nuts of him recently. Tirza had laid the washed contents of Piggy's bag neatly on the bench to dry. There was a bottle of *sal volatile*, another of laudanum and a pouch containing bark among his things, but no nutmegs.

The medical volumes he had been consulting lay in a pile on the bench beside the dispensing book and Anne began to look through them for nutmeg remedies. Distilled, ground or expressed into an oil, it was indeed a common ingredient of physic, she showed me, and differed not much in its effects from cinnamon, the *Royal Dispensatory* remarked. Combined with powdered crab claws and sugar it apparently made a soothing pastil for a sore throat.

I carried on searching the shelves while she read out the recipes to me, which was when I found another book tucked in at the end of the shelf of jars. I took it down, set it on the bench beside Anne and opened it. The covers were stiff as if it were very new and scarcely read. The author was one William Cullen, and the title *A Treatise of the Materia Medica*. There was only one entry for nutmeg in the index, also clothed in the respectability of a Latin name. When we turned to the indicated page, the appearance, character and application of *Nux Moschata* were observed upon briefly before Cullen turned to what he considered its most interesting characteristic.

> Some writers have mentioned its hypnotic power. BONTIUS speaks of it as a matter of frequent occurrence in the East Indies which has often fallen under his own observation. I have myself had an accidental occasion of observing its soporific and stupefying power. A person by mistake took two drams or a little more of powdered nutmeg; he felt it warm in his stomach, without any uneasiness; but in about an hour after he had taken it, he was seized with a drowsiness, which gradually increased to a complete stupor and insensibility; and not long after, he was found fallen from his chair, lying on the floor of his chamber.

I closed the book with a thump and stared at Anne.

'How much is a dram of nutmeg?' she asked in a rather shaken voice. 'How much is two? Would three nuts amount to such a measure, do you think?'

'Nonsense.'

I went back to the dispensary book, but we had been right the first time. On paper at least Piggy had not prescribed nutmeg to anyone, though three nutmegs were certainly missing.

'If he wished to conceal his prescription of the drug, he would not write it down,' Anne said sombrely.

'It is only a coincidence. It must be, whatever we have now learned.'

Whatever we have now learned. What, really, had Piggy learned? And what had he already known? Had he already read this book of Cullen's on nutmeg long before John Scorn's collapse?

Moreover, why was the book not in the pile of volumes he had brought to the parlour table but instead hidden away in this corner? The only charitable surmise was that it had lain there forgotten for a long time. I went back to the shelf, which was very dusty, and took up a jar to find a neat ring of clean polished wood beneath it where the dust had not settled. If the book had stood there for any length of time it too would have left its mark, but there was none. I began to feel very uneasy. The Guildhall key. The hypnotic power of nutmeg. The missing nutmegs from the dispensary shelves.

'And then there is Sarah Glynn,' Anne said from behind me.

'Sarah Glynn?' But I remembered only too well my own words from yesterday. *He is courting Mr Glynn's niece, that's all.* And Sir James's bland reply. *Indeed.* I now remembered Piggy telling me of Glynn and Sarah over our buttered saffron buns the night I arrived. *Though I dislike the man, I must appease him … The town is divided, but tendrils run through it like fungus, connecting us one to the other …*

Perhaps Piggy's love affair was no simpler than my own, after all. He had been to The Willows twice on Saturday, the day Scorn fell ill. Once in the morning and once again in the afternoon, ostensibly to treat Lushington's gout. John Scorn had certainly been unwell when Philpott and I left him on Saturday afternoon, but it was alone with Piggy that he had actually collapsed. And since then, Lushington had had no further need of my cousin at all.

And Thomas Wedlock? Quite apart from Piggy's self-confessed visit to see the old man only an hour before he ran mad in the Guildhall, my cousin had also already been at the Market House when Philpott and I arrived at the cupboard door on Friday night. Though I had asked Sarah where all her party had been before the political meeting I had not asked Piggy the same question. Why should I have done? There had been no reason even to think of it. But someone had locked the cupboard door on Wedlock and left him to die, and Piggy had the key to that door.

Anne was looking at me, her forehead furrowed again with concern. 'It is painful, Laurence, but I think you must tell Sir James all this, whether Dr Jago is your cousin or not.'

She twined her fingers through mine but I pulled away. 'I cannot.'

'You must.' She was calm, quiet, composed again after the first brief shock of discovery. She did not know or love Piggy – why should she? She was thinking only of me. 'If you are ever to be a respectable man again and find your rightful place in the world, you cannot pick and choose. You must act honestly at last.'

'*They* pick and choose,' I said stubbornly. 'The duke would not see his own family disgraced. He would contrive it somehow.'

But, in fact, the duke had divorced his wife in full view of the world's eyes to save his own reputation. She had gone off with Byron; he had braved the ridicule and eventually found himself a new wife. But would he have recovered his reputation so well if he were not a nobleman of the first water – as a duke only next in prestige to royalty? Would a common man like myself be applauded for putting the law of the land above blood relations or shamed as Piggy's kinsman, nonetheless? A duke could get away with more than I could, I had reflected, when he handed me the ballot and desired me to see it forged. He would never go to the gallows himself if he could blame someone else, I had thought, and conniving at an act of fraud in company with a duke would never end well for a common man.

But what did the opinion of the world matter beside my own conscience? What course of action would allow me to look in the mirror with any degree of confidence or pride? If I shielded Piggy I was an accomplice, who must live for ever more with the possibility of being found out. If I betrayed him I knew in my heart I would be for ever despised by other men even if they pretended to applaud my disinterested justice. And more to the point, I would despise myself.

I had thought Anne would not expect Quakerish honesty of me, but when I looked at her again it seemed I was wrong. 'Leave me,' I said. 'I can't think straight when you are looking at me like that.' And, continuing an old train of thought sparked by reading *Paradise Lost* aboard ship last year, I might also have said, while she was whispering in my ear tempting words to save myself whatever the cost to others.

She pursed her lips. 'Laurence—'

'Go back to the Angel, Anne. I love you, but I must work this out in my own mind alone. Don't say anything to Sir James just yet.'

'I will be flesh of your flesh, Laurence, and mind of your mind if we marry.'

'I know,' I said, and now something in my tone made her angry. What had she heard in my voice? A scintilla of doubt? She had rejected me a dozen times before, but her words had been tantamount to a proposal and, like George Canning, I had drawn back. She went out, shutting the door firmly behind her.

17

I SNATCHED UP MY COAT and ventured out again into the streets. I went first to the Guildhall. Later tonight the poll book would be brought here from the hustings and the return authorised by the sheriff for dispatch to London. But just now the building was eerily empty. I walked through its quiet corridors, past the cupboard where Wedlock had died. The door was back on its hinges and mended but it was still unlocked and I opened it to see all its contents neatly back in place. Even the smell of smoke and wet paper had dissipated. I closed the door again and walked on in search of human life. I found some eventually, at the very far end of the corridor, behind another massy old oak door. The clerks' voices within were very muffled, and when the door was opened at my knock, there were only two young lads holding the fort and looking sulky at missing all the fun. Neither was the man that had found Thomas Wedlock, and neither could tell me if Dr Jago had been seen in the premises on Friday night before the political meeting.

But one thing was clear. On that day, as this, most of the clerks would have been out in the crowd enjoying the spectacle; and that day as this, any man might therefore have wandered in unseen as I had just now done.

I went back out to the street and walked down past the lusty *tol de rol lols* to the grocer's shop, where Piggy had bought his nutmegs. I wanted to quiz the man again, but the door was locked and there was no answer to my knock. I paused in his doorway, watching the general festivities flow by me. The mayor and a collection of aldermen had gathered about the steps to the hustings, deep in conversation, while the sheriff was on the platform already holding the poll book, preparing to take the votes of the electors and mark each one down in the empty column I had seen beside the names. The radicals thought a secret ballot would let men vote as they really wished, though such an arrangement would be scant comfort in this case, Glynn's electors being presented with a very poor sort of choice at all. In any event, Thomas Wedlock had been brave indeed to announce he was changing sides in the teeth of the Cherokees' ire.

I glanced down Coinagehall Street towards the Blue Anchor and caught a glimpse of a porkish figure skipping along on sprightly trotters. The man holding its leash and being dragged along faster than was probably quite pleasant was Philpott. The Sapient Hog had recovered from his indisposition far more quickly than John

Scorn, and Philpott had abandoned me to frolic with him. Did he even know Piggy had been arrested? Hog and man disappeared into the alley of Five Wells Lane and I felt suddenly quite alone.

When I turned my eyes back to the hustings, I saw with some surprise that the duke was now there and also the duchess, whom I would have expected to keep well away, since a thunderous rendition of the *tol de rol lol* had been taken up again, the singers very insistent on the *thing* she was taking in hand. I thought she must be able to hear them, but she was determined to brazen it out with a brilliant smile.

She had taken up a stance by the steps to the platform and, as the first of the electors drew near to mount and make his vote, I could see her lips moving. The fellow was a clergyman and I imagined her whisper to consist of something like, *Remember that living in Yorkshire we have the gift of. Switch your vote to the duke and be a man!* But Glynn was waiting at the other side of the steps, greeting the reverend with his own meaningful nod, and the allurements of Yorkshire must seem very far away. At any rate, the reverend put his hand on the Bible, muttered something inaudible and then scuttled back down the steps. '*Lushington and Elliot!*' Hitchens announced and the duchess laughed, a clear, derisive and musical peal that made everyone startle.

The crowd was seething like a boiling pot, spitting the voters forwards by turns, and rearranging the onlookers as revellers pushed through the throng and sent it surging. After one such rearrangement I saw Cyrus washed up at the front in his Sunday-best suit – looking magnificent, there was no denying it – but now alone. I launched myself from the shelter of the grocer's doorway and pushed through the mob to where he was standing.

'I saw you with Loveday this morning,' I said in a tone sufficiently accusatory to make him open his mouth as if to deny it, but then look glum.

'We were childhood friends,' he answered sullenly. 'And the poor maid needs cheerin' up, what with nursin' that old devil all hours.' He hesitated; the whites of his eyes as doleful as a spaniel's as he looked at me. 'But you'll not tell 'er now? She will give Loveday such a shockin' earful o' spleen.'

'Her? She? You mean Eleanor, I suppose? Eleanor, who would not wish to see you dallying with her maid?' I'm afraid I sounded more than a little like a virgin aunt in a mob cap. But it served a kind of purpose for Cyrus wilted, just as he might have done before some such fierce old lady.

'Miss Scorn would not like it, no, sir. Not with the whole history of the affair.'

'History? What do you mean by that? That you were once Loveday's sweetheart, too, I suppose?'

'Oh no.' He squirmed uncomfortably. 'No, no, not zactly that. We was childern, sir. A childish kiss or two is surely neither here nor there. Or so I tell Miss Scorn.' He looked even more gloomy. 'So I tell her often and often.'

My dislike of him was probably irrational, I knew, based on some instinctive distrust of his extraordinary good looks, along with his vacuous expression and the curate's dreadful accusations – which I now knew might be only born of jealousy if old Nettle's story was true. But for Piggy's sake I needed him to be guilty and if Cyrus was dallying with Loveday as well as stringing Eleanor along, he was certainly a liar if nothing else. 'You find Eleanor a troublesome sweetheart? You prefer her maid?'

He didn't answer me directly. 'Miss Scorn is dreadful aggravated by this affair with her grandfer.'

'Is she?' I said. 'And what about you? Are you *aggravated*, Cyrus?'

'Me?' If anything he looked now like a beaten dog. 'I do keep my mouth shut, sir, that's what I do. She is a very violent, *headstrong* woman, see. I do find it unwise to rile her.'

It began to dawn on me, then, that Eleanor's determination to marry Cyrus might be as unwelcome to the man himself as to her grandfather. If so, the edifice I had constructed concerning his desire for John Scorn's money began to crumble a little, and at this moment he certainly did not look at all like a murderer.

He did not wait for me to ask further questions but slunk away through the crowd. I was about to follow him when another hand touched my sleeve. It was Sarah Glynn and her cheeks were tearstained. 'How is

Pythagoras? Have you seen him? Oh, Mr Jago, it is all turning out far too much like a novel with him locked up in dungeon deep.'

Was she being flippant, amid Piggy's very real danger? But perhaps she was so habituated to be witty and arch that the true horror of his circumstances had not yet wrought a change to her manner. There were the tears on her cheeks to show true feeling after all, and I squeezed her hand. 'I have not seen him yet, Miss Glynn. I have been too busy trying to clear his name. Tell me. Has he ever said anything to you of nutmeg?'

'Nutmeg?'

'Forgive me, I know it sounds absurd—'

'The p-poison has turned out to be nutmeg?' She frowned, then smiled. 'Well, after all, I am hardly surprised.'

I stared at her. 'I beg your pardon? You know something of it?'

'Oh, yes. Its toxic qualities are known to half the town, I should think, and I have even put it in my b-book.'

With a sinking heart I remembered her say that Piggy had provided unusual deaths for her novel. 'And was it Piggy that told you of this?'

'No, no.' She looked surprised. 'It is Mr Lushington's favourite dinner-party anecdote, that's all, for he is addicted to grating nutmeg on all his food.'

I remembered Piggy say he had chided Lushington for his silver nutmeg grater and overindulgence in spices.

'Anecdote?' I echoed. 'What exactly does he say?'

Sarah had now forgotten her tears. 'He tells how the natives of the East Indies are forever intoxicating themselves with the stuff. The nuts growing on trees there, you know, thick as b-blackberries. Shockingly potent it is, and they die of it ever so often.'

'Then why do they eat them?'

'For the interesting effects, I b-believe. Visions, and so on.'

Lushington knew nutmeg's poisonous character, had some of it in his possession, and had called Piggy to him twice the day John Scorn was poisoned. Quite apart from the grocer's supply, it was looking blacker and blacker for my cousin by the moment.

'And what do you mean when you say half the town knows about it? Who exactly has Lushington told?'

She looked at me blankly. 'Oh, every guest we have had at uncle's table since Mr Lushington arrived, I should think. As I told you, he is very fond of the story.'

Before I had time to digest this information and decide whether it further damned Piggy by association with Lushington or opened up the field of suspects to every man that had dined at The Willows this past fortnight, yet another hand touched my sleeve. This time it was the poor old grocer and, as I turned to him, Sarah swirled away into the vortex of the crowd and was swallowed up at once.

'Mr Jago.' Julian looked dreadful and I wondered what

could possibly have brought him out into this bruising mob of bodies. Apparently it was me. 'I counted out those nutmegs after you left. Somethin' didn't look quite right to me when we opened the jar. Damn me, there were more missin' than three. Seems like some villen must have put his hand in when I weren't lookin' and snatched a few.'

'But you keep the jar behind the counter, do you not?'

'I do.' He shook his head. 'And I wouldn't trust any man but the doctor to help himself.'

I didn't quite understand him. 'The doctor?'

'He counted out his nutmegs and told me what he'd taken, but in a general way I be very careful. Howsumever, I think someone must have got to the jar somehow when I weren't looking and did filch some.'

'Can you remember a time it might have happened? When you were called away from the counter, for instance?'

He shook his head. 'I don't know. But it is a damned mort o' money to have lost, sir. That much is certain.'

Though it was bad that Piggy had been suffered to count out his own nutmegs, the story filled me with a faint hope, nonetheless. Lushington's anecdote would surely have travelled far beyond those who had sat at his table, to their families and friends and servants. 'Your nephew Cyrus has been often in your shop, I think?'

'He do help me to church now and then. Painted the shop for me last week.'

'And when he was painting was he ever left alone?'

'I dare say. Being family.'

Five minutes ago I had thought Cyrus a sorry figure, but I still wanted him to be guilty nonetheless, and now at last here was proof he could have heard of the poison and availed himself of it, too. I didn't know where he was now, but I would go back to John Scorn's house and quiz Eleanor and Loveday as to Cyrus's movements on Saturday. Though my belief in his motive had been shaken by his apparent reluctance to marry Eleanor, the means by which he could have carried out the attack on her grandfather were now clear. That at least was something.

I found Loveday alone, still darning by the old man's bedside, having failed to make her desired escape. But she looked far more cheerful than before and when I asked her, she said her uncle had called in with the news that Jane was no worse, thank God, even if not positively improving. I remembered persuading Piggy to go to the coroner and the corpse that morning and leave the child till later. Subsequent events, in the unexpected form of Piggy's imprisonment, had prevented him from visiting the poor thing at all. I was glad for my own sake that she still lived.

Though it was only six o'clock, the sun had tipped down behind the houses on Meneage Street, the shadows were lengthening outside, and the north-facing room was dusky. John Scorn groaned as I came in and muttered thickly, his eyelids fluttering though they did not open. I went to the bed and shook him as I had done before. So much would be solved if he could but wake between now and the conclusion of the poll down at the hustings.

Scorn kicked irritably at my touch, but though he was achingly close to waking, gliding the delicate margin between consciousness and stupor, he could not yet swim to the surface. He had not the strength to break the film and push through. Once the poll closed in Coinagehall Street the sheriff would make his way here directly. There was probably only a half-hour remaining until whoever had poisoned John Scorn could cheerfully toast the success of their stratagem and damn my cousin doubly, having failed to cure the old man as well as being a suspect in Wedlock's death.

'Cyrus told me you were sweethearts once,' I said. 'Loveday, did you poison your master at Cyrus's bidding?'

'Poison master?' She looked at me astonished.

'Or did Cyrus do it himself? Was he ever alone with him? Or did he give you any food or drink to pass on to him on Saturday?'

She had actually begun to laugh with the same tolerant amusement with which the grocer had doubted Cyrus would recognise nutmeg if a ton of it fell on his head. 'If anyone would have the nerve to poison master in this 'ouse, it would be Miss Eleanor, not Cyrus—' she caught herself up with a sly look. 'Mr Best, I should say.'

That was certainly true from everything I knew of

Eleanor – *a violent, headstrong woman*, as Cyrus himself had said. And wasn't he in her clutches, it transpired, not she in his? And now Eleanor herself was coming in with a lamp, gimlet-eyed and unreadable as ever. She set it down beside Loveday to aid her darning, and then came to look at her grandfather.

At the sound of her footsteps he drifted once more to the surface of his stupor, his eyes moving under the lids, his hand twitching. She took hold of it and with a tenderness I had never seen before, put it to her cheek. 'Poor bleddy fool. Blazin' old sourpuss,' she said almost fondly and then looked up at me. 'He is wakin', I am sure of it, Mr Jago. All that infernal bangin' and thumpin' seem to have been o' some use after all. I never believed it,' she added in a very quiet voice, her eyes suddenly damp. 'I thought he was to die no matter what the doctor did.'

''Tis time for the caudle, ma'am.' Loveday began to stir, but Eleanor nodded, dashed the tears from her eyes and banged out again before the maid could even put down her darning. Perhaps she was ashamed of showing such human weakness. From somewhere down at the crossroads came a distant cheer. The voting of the thirty-two at the hustings had probably concluded. If so, it wouldn't be long before Hitchens arrived. I felt like a child playing at blind man's bluff, reaching out into the darkness with stretching hands grasping at nothing.

'I have never seen Miss Scorn so softened,' I said. 'Can she really love her grandfather after all?'

'Oh yes, sir, they are tight as two peas in a pod – and will be argyfyin' again within the week, I don't doubt. All this pop and touse with Cyrus – Mr Best, I mean – and with the curate.' Loveday slipped the darning basket under the bed and got to her feet. 'Everyone's been so teasy for so many months,' she added, with a flash of sudden bad temper. 'Cyrus so glum – Mr Best, I mean – and Miss Eleanor so peevish. And Reverend Wedlock far too vexed with her for all her play actin'.'

'Play acting?'

'I tell her she shams lovin' Cyrus with o'er much relish for the curate's peace o' mind but she do never listen.'

I stared at her. '*Shams* loving him? What do you mean?'

Loveday opened her eyes very wide, probably realising her indiscretion as she came around the bed towards the door. She was suddenly bent on escape again. 'Oh, sir. I must not say.'

'I think you must.' I reached out and grasped hold of her hand to stop her. 'Are you telling me Eleanor feigns her love for Cyrus? But why on earth would she do that?'

In truth, it was a foolish question, since it would annoy her grandfather and annoying her grandfather seemed to be Eleanor's one vocation in life. But Loveday's alarm had now turned to round-eyed eagerness to impart the secret. Even so, she cast a look at the bed and her voice dropped to a whisper for all the old man was lying as still as a corpse. 'So as to make Reverend Wedlock seem the better man in her grandfer's eyes, see?'

'Your mistress *wants* to marry the curate?'

Loveday nodded. 'Ever since they were childern, sir. But the Wedlocks and the Scorns ...'

I began foggily to understand what she was telling me. I had already guessed that Cyrus did not want to marry Eleanor. Now, it appeared she did not want to marry him either. If the edifice of my suspicions had been crumbling under the first discovery, it collapsed around me with the second. Cyrus would surely be positively glad if John Scorn woke and prevented the marriage he himself did not want. There was still his bet, of course, but even that made a kind of sense – perhaps a cry of defiance against the unwanted entanglement he had found himself caught up in.

Yet what was I to think of Eleanor herself? In truth, Loveday's story made little difference to her. It only meant that if her grandfather died, she would be free to marry Reverend William Wedlock instead of Cyrus Best. And yet, she seemed full of tenderness to the old man now. I wished I could talk to Anne or Philpott, but I had offended the one and the other was amusing himself with the Sapient Hog.

Eleanor was coming back in with a steaming bowl that smelled pleasantly of nutmeg custard. John Scorn shifted and moaned, but she paid it little heed for I accosted her before she was even halfway inside the door. 'Miss Scorn, I have just been hearing all about your tricks with Cyrus Best and Reverend Wedlock.'

That stopped her dead. She fixed me with her hard eyes, still glossed with unshed tears, her face inscrutable. 'Mort o' bleddy gossip in this town.'

'I made Loveday tell me. It seems you have been aggravating a good many men, Miss Scorn.'

'No more than any on 'em deserve. There's naught against William Wedlock save his name. If Grandfer dies, his old feuds don't mean nothin'. If he lives, he may finally see they never should have.'

'But what made you think of doing such a thing?'

She set down the caudle to cool by the bedside and sat in Loveday's empty chair while the maid hovered about. 'I remembered my poor aunt's tale and thought to frighten Grandfer with the chance of losing me, too. For all we argue, he loves me dearly, Mr Jago. Says I am the only true Scorn left. I took up with Cyrus to vex him and Cyrus dared not refuse me.' Eleanor smiled. 'Poor devil, he is quite besotted with Loveday and she turments him about it dreadful. She talks about our weddin' and the flowers, and the children we shall have, but when Grandfer sees sense and it is all over, she will tell him the truth.'

'Dearovim,' Loveday said softly, 'he'll be that relieved, and it will be my weddin' and my flowers and my childern in the end, sir.'

I was struggling to take in this whole new complexion on the affair. 'Does Reverend Wedlock know of this plan?'

'Not at all, and he is as jealous as a cat,' Loveday said eagerly, before Eleanor could answer.

I frowned. 'The curate came to me and Philpott with a terrible story about Cyrus, Miss Scorn.'

'Did he?' She smiled. 'Poor William.'

'Poor Cyrus if I had believed the story.'

My pious glare did not work so well on Eleanor as it had on her reluctant lover. 'Cyrus Best is the kind o' man that will sail through life, Mr Jago, smiling his bleddy way out of trouble and wasting all his money.'

There was a moment's pause in which Eleanor turned her eyes tenderly on her grandfather. I went to the window, thinking hard. In all truth I was no nearer a solution to this mystery of Wedlock's death and John Scorn's poisoning than I had ever been. Or rather, the answers I had wanted to be true were false. Philpott's theory about the duke was unproveable hot air; Cyrus Best and Eleanor seemed exonerated by this story, for Cyrus had no reason to kill Scorn and Eleanor evidently loved her grandfather after all, despite all previous appearances to the contrary.

Only one solution remained and during the course of the afternoon had grown more plausible. Lushington at The Willows, and Piggy himself, alone had the means, the knowledge and the motive to do harm to John Scorn. I was still sure Piggy must be innocent, but the net of circumstantial evidence was narrowing, closing around him. *If Scorn don't vote before the poll closes tomorrow night, folks will be provoked agin 'ee, Doctor.* And now I could see a movement coming up the street like a wave. A knot of official-looking men and among them the sheriff.

The ballot paper which only waited for the old man's signature was still on the mantelpiece propped against the tobacco jar. I took it up, noticing with one abstracted part of my mind that the design upon the jar was rather familiar.

'What are you doing?' Eleanor asked me. There was a knock at the street door.

'Go out into the hall, both of you,' I said. 'But do not let those men in until I tell you.'

I went back to the bed. 'Mr Scorn! They are here. You must wake now or they will have won.'

He was so achingly close to wakefulness. Another hour and he might be strong enough to set his hand to the paper himself, in defiance of whoever had meant to silence his old, inconvenient voice. It was so arbitrary, so unfair to my poor cousin. *If he so much as twitches, tell her to guide his hand.* I would never have done that. Why should Eleanor be made a part of this whole horrible affair? In the end it concerned only me, Piggy and the duke. His Grace had made veiled promises to me if I did his bidding and forged the paper. I should have asked him outright if he would see Piggy cleared in return for my committing a felony on his behalf. But it was too late for that now.

All I knew for certain was that if John Scorn did not

vote, the duke would pursue the case through the sheriff, the courts and Parliament, claiming malfeasance and demanding the election be void. If, on the other hand, Scorn somehow voted, the duke would lose interest in the whole affair at once. Piggy would be hailed as a hero for saving the old man, and whatever ridiculous mistake had seen the key placed in Piggy's bag would be eventually explained. And in the worst case – if Piggy had indeed killed Thomas Wedlock and poisoned John Scorn? Well, I could smooth over one half of that with a stroke of the pen.

There was another knock at the door as I carried the ballot paper to the desk, littered with papers and among them surely a specimen of the old man's signature. The duke had already written the names of his two candidates in a firm hand: Sir James Burges and the absent Charles Abbot of the *felicific calculus*. There was a space left for the voter's mark, and another space for the signature of a witness. I dipped Scorn's quill in the ink pot and rummaged among the papers until I found a letter signed *John Scorn Esq.* I copied it beneath the two candidates' names and then signed my own name as witness.

Even as I blotted the ink dry, there was a third, peremptory knock and I called out to the women to let the sheriff in. There was an influx of noise from the street along with the stamping of official feet in the hallway. The front door closed again and the street's noise was muffled. I went out into the hall and handed Hitchens the paper.

'He is sleeping again now,' I said. 'But you will be pleased to see he recovered sufficiently to make his vote. He came to his senses half an hour ago and though, as we expected, he was far too weak to come to the hustings, he was still very eager to make his mark.'

The women stared at me from behind the sheriff's back as he opened the paper, jangling a veritable symphony of astonishment and boggling his strange eye at the signature. 'Well, Mr Jago.' He looked up at me and scratched his head. 'This makes matters a sight worse and a sight better, I suppose. I shall now have the headache of managing the double return and sending it off to Parliament to be adjudicated after all. But on the other hand whatever happened to old Wedlock, at least John Scorn was not stopped from voting. His Grace and Parliament will be very pleased to hear it.'

With the slam of the front door behind him, the full realisation of what I had done hit me and then, beyond all the bounds of possible belief, a hoarse voice was calling from John Scorn's chamber.

'*Eleanor?*' And then more loudly, more angrily, '*Eleanor!* Where the devil are 'ee? And where the devil am I?'

Eleanor stared at me a moment, clearly struck quite as amazed as I was, but then went to him swiftly. 'At 'ome, in yer bed.' I could hear her voice from where I stood in the hall. 'You have been poorly, you daft old bugger. But you will be well now. The doctor has seen to 'ee.'

I went to the doorway and looked into the room.

Eleanor was sitting on the bed. She put out a hand to stroke her grandfather's cheek but he only batted her away weakly, trying to sit up. 'What day is it?'

'Monday.'

'Election day?' He began to struggle weakly against his blankets. 'I must go make my vote, maid.'

'Hush,' she said. 'The hustings are over.'

'Hustings over?' He clutched at her arm with remarkable passion. 'But I shan't live to see another election, girl. 'Twas my last shot. And the duke—'

'Silly old fool,' Eleanor said fondly. 'You don't think we'd let 'ee down? The sheriff has just collected yer vote.'

The old man stared at her. 'What do you say now? What bleddy bilge are you talkin'?'

'Someone poisoned you,' she said. 'You come 'ome from Wedlock's burial on Saturday and fell down with a thump like a sack o' spuds. And then it turned out that old Wedlock had been murdered to stop him votin', too. The duke had arranged a written ballot for you to sign if you woke. We have just given it to the sheriff.'

Under this barrage of extraordinary news – which anyone but Eleanor might have delivered more cautiously – John Scorn began to cough as he had done in church on Saturday, a fit that worsened by the moment, his shoulders convulsing. Good God, had she killed him after all? One shock too many amid all the rest? 'Get out,' he gasped. 'Get out, God damn me. I shall see ye all hanged.'

Eleanor looked at him a moment, with a deal less anxiety than I was feeling, likely judging it merely one of his usual fits of anger. She came out of his room, took my arm, and led me to the door. 'Don't fret,' she said quietly. 'His very first thought on waking was to vote, and you have only done what he would have done himself if he had not been knocked on the head by Glynn and Lushington.'

'You really believe them the culprits?'

'Who else can it be?'

And if that was the general view of the town, and Scorn had not voted, Piggy as their instrument would certainly have been done for. I had done the right thing, whatever the cost might prove to be. Anne's counsel had been sincere by her own indomitable lights, but my life had been so murky for so long that to do as I had done was really, when you thought about it, the only action I could have taken and remained true to my own unruly self.

18

EVENING

Bᴜᴛ ɪ ᴘᴜsʜᴇᴅ ʙᴀᴄᴋ through the crowds to the surgery, hardly knowing what I had done and, as my excitement subsided, fearful of the consequences. By what stroke of an unfriendly deity had John Scorn woken only a moment too late? I had shaken his shoulder and told him it was his last chance – had those words finally brought him to wakefulness? If I had waited a moment more he could have given Hitchens his vote himself and spared me so much danger. But it was over and done now, for better or worse.

The atmosphere in the town had changed again, for with the onset of evening the cumulative effect of all the drink had reached a pitch and the Rodney was full to overflowing with drunken working men, while drunken working women shrieked together on the pavement outside. The men with red-painted faces were on the prowl, once more seeking trouble, and everywhere scarlet ribbons seemed in the ascendant. On arriving in Helston I had thought their case was a better one. Three days later, I had done my best to prevent their illegal victory. Scarlet Town or Blue, Helston itself was sick and could only ever be cured by a purging draught of thorough parliamentary reform.

I met George Osborne at the crossroads, looking as bright and unruffled as ever. 'The sheriff is with father, who would be glad if you'd step up to his rooms, Mr Jago. He wants to thank you for what you have done tonight.'

'I have done nothing,' I said. 'You should thank my cousin for nursing John Scorn back to health in time to vote.'

From the look on George's face, I wasn't sure the boy believed in this miraculous recovery a jot. 'Well, Papa is jubilant, in any case,' he said. 'You might enjoy basking in his enthusiastic praise for a change.' He was smiling at me, his boyish smile. 'And what did you make of the Sapient Hog this noon? A most amusing interlude, I thought, though it rather scuppered my stepmother's hopes of stealing the mayor's voters.'

'I am very sorry she was so insulted. How does she bear it?'

'Exceeding ill,' George said with another sunny smile. 'But not for the reason you might suppose. In the course of her quarrel with my father, it turned out that he had been doing as she directed him all week, and all her own efforts and expense had been entirely superfluous. She was not pleased.'

When I got to the surgery I sat down in the parlour wondering what to do next. By voting on John Scorn's behalf I had hoped to neutralise one part of the affair as it bore on Piggy. But there was still the matter of the key. Should I now go to Glynn and confront him with all my suspicions? If I frightened him enough he might agree to arrange Piggy's release and see him exonerated in return for my silence. It would not be pleasant. Glynn was so smooth and so pleased with himself, and Lushington was so powerful a man, that to take them on would be another horrible moment of *déjà vu*, for had I not once tried to confront my masters in Whitehall and failed dismally to my own cost? And besides, it was all conjecture. I still had no actual proof they had done anything wrong. All the evidence I had concerned poor Piggy. As with the duke, the mayor and his candidate had contrived to keep themselves safely above the shabby doings of us insects who toiled on their behalf.

I was saved by the entrance of Philpott, looking remarkably dishevelled. He had mud on his cheek and was nursing a wounded hand which was quite as bloody as Johannes Bashers' finger and dripping freely on to the doctor's grubby old turkey rug. I jumped to my feet. 'Good God, Philpott, what has happened to you?'

He was, in fact, very cheerful, chuckling almost too

much for a coherent word. 'I am quite in a muddle, Laurence, I do confess.'

'What's happened? Where have you been all day? And who has attacked you?' I snatched up a napkin from the table and wrapped his hand in it, with a very poor imitation of Piggy's skill at bandaging.

He looked at me fondly. 'My dear boy, forgive me for abandoning you so long. But I have been finding out very many interesting things. Very many interesting things indeed.'

'Then stop babbling and tell me,' I said. I sat him down in a chair and poured him a brandy hoping it would calm him to take a sip, but he knocked it back in one, and held it out for a refill.

'You mind we found the pig at the grave this morning? And you mind how he acted so very peculiar afterwards at his show and then fell down insensible, stinking o' nutmeg like John Scorn? Well, my boy, I don't know what happened to you – for one minute you was there and the next you was gone – but I visited the grocers as you bid me and found our poor Mr Julian certainly is the only purveyor of the article in town. After that, I stayed with the Hog all afternoon until he recovered his senses. In the course o' which I had a very interesting chat with a chap who told me nutmeg was well known as a poison, God damn me! What do you think of that?'

I doubtless showed less astonishment than he was hoping for. 'Where had the fellow heard that story?'

'Oh, it is all over town,' he said. 'In any event, when the pig finally woke, by God, he was in fine fettle as if naught untoward had happened at all. And he seemed extremely desirous of returning to the graveyard. So I took his leash and off we set at quite a gallop.'

'I saw you disappearing up Five Wells Lane together.'

He nodded. 'When we got back to the church the workmen were gathering to refill the grave, but the pig was not deterred, not a mite, God bless him. I let him loose and he went straight to the spoil heap again, snuffling like a truffle hog among the mud. He tossed it about and made such a mess the men were vexed but there was no pulling him off. Then I saw what he was about. Bless me, there was a nutmeg hidden in the soil and he had sniffed it out and snaffled it up as easy as kiss my hand. I dare say you noticed how excited he was, Laurence, this morning, which was, I suppose, the first time he ate one. He must have much enjoyed the sensation.

'But then I realised I should try to save a nut if there was one left, as proof they were there at all, so I set to.' He looked at his hand and smiled with reminiscent glee. 'We had a rare old tussle, Laurence, you should have been there, I assure 'ee. It was when we both spied a nut at the same moment that I came by this injury. Poor Toby, I am sure he did not mean to hurt me.'

'And did you save the nut?'

He reached in his pocket with his good hand and produced the muddy nutmeg with some triumph. 'Someone threw a parcel of 'em in the grave, Laurence, after Wedlock's funeral, I am persuaded of it. And I am also persuaded that whoever did so is our poisoner seeking to hide the evidence.'

He must be right. 'But who was there?' I asked, my heart sinking. Neither the duke nor Glynn, nor Lushington; only Piggy.

Tirza came in then, with our dinner that was spoiled beyond all conscience, she said as she slapped it down. 'Two days in a row it is you've spoiled my cookin' now. And if you throw your coat about, Mr Jago, you will lose all your possessions,' she added severely. 'Here is John Scorn's tinderbox large as life, I found tumbled in a corner.'

She put the wooden box on the table. It must have fallen out of my coat when I pulled it off before kissing Anne.

'*John Scorn's* tinderbox?' Philpott asked, his eyebrows shooting up as though they were on strings. 'What makes you call it that?'

'It's his sign, ain't it?' She picked up the box again and showed it to him. 'Satan. His old nickname in the town.'

'Nonsense, that is not Satan but the dragon from the Angel sign,' Philpott objected.

''Ess, sir, but the dragon on the Angel sign *is* Satan, what St Michael was fightin' in dragon form.'

'Good God,' I said. 'He has a matching tobacco jar on his mantelpiece. I saw it not an hour ago.'

Tirza nodded. 'The old mayor gave him the set when he was made a freeman and elector of the town, oh, many years ago now. I don't suppose many will remember it howsumever.' She placed the tinderbox down again and tapped it fondly. 'He was a fine man in those days, for all I wouldn't have him.'

We stared at each other after she'd gone out.

'What a fool I am,' I said. 'So much has happened since, I'd quite forgotten that look on Scorn's face when he took Communion on Saturday. His terrible guilt.'

Philpott looked exceedingly smug. 'And so, you will observe, my dear young man, that my theory is the right one after all. John Scorn killed Thomas Wedlock and took the Guildhall key back to his house, I suppose, where someone afterwards slipped it in your poor cousin's bag while he was tending to the old man.'

Would Eleanor have done such a thing to protect her grandfather? Perhaps she might, loving him as she now seemed to. 'But, Philpott, I still don't believe it could have been the duke that poisoned him. He hasn't been anywhere near John Scorn's house.'

'You are forgetting the brandy on Friday night.'

I had not forgotten it, but quite apart from my previous objections, I had known the duke was exonerated as soon as I read Cullen's book. The illness resulting from nutmeg which the book described had come on about an hour after the dose. Friday night was far too early, whatever Philpott might wish. 'The duke wasn't at the funeral.

Nor was Sir James. They could not have been the ones to throw the nutmegs in the grave either.'

No, alone of all my suspects, Piggy had been there.

Tirza was back at the door, looking extremely curious. For a moment I thought she had been eavesdropping, but in fact she was here with yet another message. John Scorn was awake and demanding an immediate meeting with the sheriff, the duke, the Willows party, and myself at the Angel Inn.

'Philpott,' I said, 'there's something I should tell you.'

But he was getting to his feet, seeming bent on coming to the Angel with me, and laughing again, in a way that made me wonder if his faint earlier in the day had left him silly, or if he had also been at the nutmeg. 'And so have I, Laurence, something to tell *you*, but it will keep, I think. Actions speak louder than words, as they say.'

I asked him what the devil he meant, but he only shook his head and steered me out of the door, across the road and into the Angel yard. What did it matter? I thought, as I hurried after him towards the reckoning. If John Scorn was bent on exposing my fraud, Philpott would understand it all, soon enough.

A SEDAN CHAIR WAS emerging out of the Angel courtyard as we came up and it trotted away down the street while we hesitated for a moment under the archway. The yard was dusky, being beyond the reach of the setting sun or the streetlamps being rather precariously lit by a poor lamp man up his ladder amid all the drunken crowds.

It seemed Scorn had been brought hither in the sedan, being too weak to walk, and to my surprise I saw now that the curate was with him. Under the roar of the crowd in the street we could only catch snippets of their conversation. The aged man's irascible grumbling, the younger voice replying, kindly bidding old Scorn take his arm. I couldn't imagine why the curate had also been called to the meeting, but here he was.

'Keep me away from that damned well,' John Scorn was saying to him querulously, his voice rising above the street's clamour for a moment with remarkable vigour for one so lately near death. 'God damn it, my eyes are queer and I have a shockin' fear of falling.'

The curate gave a murmured answer, too low to catch, and then they stopped dead. I thought that, despite his warning, the old man's foot had actually touched the low coping of the well.

'Hogwash,' he said. 'The steps are in yon corner, you young fool.'

Then there was a flurry of activity behind us, occasioned by the arrival of the whole Willows party. Lamplight spilled into the yard as servants hastened out of the inn to help the two invalids, Lushington and Scorn, up to the duke's apartments. I looked for Philpott before following them, but he was engaged in some confidential and excessively cheerful consultation with one of the servants and so I went upstairs without him.

The duke's rooms looked very bare after the depredations of his destructive wrath earlier in the day, but at least the broken glass had been swept up out of the carpet. His Grace and Sir James were sitting at the same table where the duchess had made her lists on Saturday. John Scorn was guided to one chair, Lushington to another, in the course of which Philpott slipped into the room and sat down beside me with a wink.

His incomprehensible high spirits grated painfully on my nerves. I stared at Scorn who was trembling dreadfully, just as he had done on Saturday, before his collapse. I could not pity him now. Amid all my other doubts, Philpott and Tirza between them had at least convinced me that it was John Scorn who had set the fire and locked Wedlock in to die, however obscure his motives and whatever the matter of the key in Piggy's bag might otherwise suggest. Good God, I realised now, I had risked everything for Piggy and in doing so had acted in the interests of a man who was certainly a murderer.

Anne was concealed in the window curtains again, watching us quietly with a look of clear-eyed judgement, like some goddess far above the human fray. She would soon discover I had acted in direct defiance of all her advice. But I would always fail her, however warm my feelings and however blameless my intentions. She was too good or at least too inhumanly pitiless for me, and it was perhaps as well that we had quarrelled.

For his part, Lushington looked very much invigorated by the exertion of the short journey from The Willows to the Angel, and evidently bent on directing the meeting, for when the duke took out his snuffbox he snapped, 'Put that damned thing away,' and, for a miracle, stunned at such unprecedented impertinence, the duke obeyed him.

Meanwhile, the sheriff was coming in and, good God, Piggy was following behind him. It was no wonder that my cousin looked tired and anxious, but the tidiness of his dress told me he had been kept quietly under guard in some decent rooms, rather than in the town gaol to the total destruction of his reputation. I didn't exactly know why Hitchens had brought him. Perhaps as a witness to whatever business had called the rest of us here; perhaps as the accused alongside myself. One poisoner. One forger. A fine pair of cousins.

Hitchens sat down at the head of the table and without any further ado took John Scorn's ballot slip from his pocket and laid it down, smoothing it out with anxious fingers, his bad lungs rattling. 'Thank you for coming, gentlemen. We are faced with a devilish awkward circumstance, I'm afraid. A written vote is an uncommon thing and thank God for it, I say, since Mr Scorn has just informed me that this paper, which I received supposedly from his hand, has in fact been forged.

Given the heated nature of things in town I thought it best to consult quietly with the parties most likely to have been involved.'

We all knew who he meant. Glynn's eyes shot at once to the duke with a look of utter and delighted triumph. Not only was the duke's one vote now surely about to be annulled, but Glynn could also crucify him in public opinion with this revelation of forgery, just as Anne had warned George. Glynn was yet to discover my involvement, and no doubt His Grace would disclaim all knowledge of the crime, but folks would likely still think the duke behind it all somehow.

'Remarkably,' the sheriff was jangling inexorably on to my ruin, 'it seems that this forgery was performed by Mr Jago and for no good reason the elector can imagine. Mr Jago has acted in a disgraceful way, not to mention committed a felony that, as I dare say you all know, attracts the gravest penalty.'

There was no point in denying it, when my signature was on the paper as witness. Glynn's eyes had now turned from the duke to me; but I didn't return his gaze, not wishing to see either his contempt of me as the duke's lackey or his sanctimonious disapproval of a deed which, I was certain, he would have had no compunction in doing himself if the shoe had been on the other foot.

I wasn't sure if Piggy was taking in anything much, for he sat slumped, a most dejected dog, entirely lost in his own misery. I couldn't look anyone else in the eye, especially not Philpott, whose body had stiffened beside me. He was probably thinking that he had expended too much of his affection and time on a man irredeemably stupid if not absolutely venal.

Meanwhile, John Scorn's fingers were dancing on the arm of his chair again, as they had done under our questioning on Saturday, but this time he did not seem to be seeing ghosts. His hoarse voice was stubborn. 'Yes, yes, Jago must certainly hang, God damn him. Stealing my vote – 'tis a damned disgrace. I will have it back and have his felony exposed to all the world.'

Hitchens examined the irascible old face, looking troubled. 'Those are harsh words, Mr Scorn. You'd see Jago hang, even though he voted exactly as you would have wished to do yourself, had you been conscious? It seems a trifle queer.'

'Exactly as I wished?' Scorn laughed roughly. 'What do any of you know about my wishes? *I* meant to vote for Glynn.'

19

THE HORRIBLE OLD MAN stared around at us with what seemed like grim triumph. Our faces looked variously surprised, shocked and, in the duke's case, suddenly dismayed. At least there was no longer any reason to wonder why Scorn was so angry with me.

'I can vote for whom I damn well please; that's my right, I suppose.'

In fact, there was a protesting whine to his voice that made me think even he was a little afraid of his own insubordination against the duke. But he had embarked on a mutinous course and was not going to be deflected now.

'I have sold it to His Grace this fifteen year, but Glynn is offering a better price. So I want that damned paper burned and change my vote.'

'A better price?' I echoed faintly.

'Two 'undred guineas. That's what Glynn and Lushington offered me. The damned duke don't never go above ten pounds.'

'You'll hang Laurence for two hundred guineas?' Philpott, God bless him, was suddenly furious. 'Damn me, sir, you are not *Satan* at all. You are but Judas, selling another man for thirty pieces of silver.'

John Scorn threw up an angry hand. 'That's all-well-a-fine, but do you think I'd pass up such a sum to save *his* neck? A man I don't know and don't care a damn for? A man who has stolen my vote and given it entirely against my wishes?'

Though I was looking at Scorn I was very conscious now of Anne's large eyes fixed upon me from her place in the window. I had called her too good for me, but I found I still desired her forgiveness if not her understanding. 'I only meant to let you speak, Scorn, since someone else so clearly meant to silence you.'

The duke was also looking at me and beneath his anger at the prospect of losing his one remaining vote I thought, God forbid, he was rather pleased with me. 'I took the paper to Scorn's house and left it there,' I said to him, trying to explain. 'I wanted nothing to do with any of you. But then later—'

The sheriff wasn't listening to my excuses. He was still boggling at Scorn's declaration, which had caused a very general stir of murmured conversation around the table. 'And when did you come to this agreement with Glynn and Lushington, Mr Scorn?'

'Over a week ago, sir.' John Scorn was taking great pleasure in his revelations, so disagreeable to his former patron. 'Glynn pointed out that to split the duke's vote would see Lushington safely returned, and I had nothing to say against it. Wedlock would look like a fool and be humiliated along with the duke, which made it all the better, God damn them both.'

Hitchens jangled in quiet alarm, probably heartily wishing he had served his term as sheriff quite another day, quite another month, quite another year. He turned to the East India man, whose face, alone among the rest of us, was impassive. 'Mr Lushington, can all this be true?'

'Why not?' Lushington seemed genuinely surprised at the question and still quite serene. 'I dare say treating may be frowned on, but it's done from Land's End to John O'Groats, as you well know.'

'And as Scorn has told you, the duke does just the same,' Glynn put in. 'He is only more tight-fisted about it, that's all.'

Lushington was now looking thoughtful, however, and his serenity slipped a little. 'Yes, it's quite the done thing, I gather, but if there is going to be a scandal, I would be extremely unwise to be involved. I believe I will therefore retract my offer.'

'A gentleman's word is his bond,' John Scorn barked angrily.

'So I have often heard. But as we are neither of us gentlemen, Mr Scorn, but merchants quite used to the vicissitudes of trade, we are a little more inured to disappointment – and to disappointing others, I think.'

For his part, the duke was looking remarkably virtuous, given the fact he had instructed me to forge Scorn's signature only that afternoon.

'Lushington should never have undertaken so shameless a bribe and Glynn should not have encouraged it,' he observed primly. I wondered if it was a case of flagrant hypocrisy or merely self-deception of the highest degree. 'Indeed,' he went on, 'I would have expected Mr Glynn to have informed me of my voters' intentions to betray me, the thieves having also already pocketed my own treat.'

'I confess it, I was wrong,' Glynn said. 'I allowed my amusement at your dismay to cloud my better judgement. But now we are all acquainted with the details of the affair, what do you make of it, Your Grace?'

At this the duke looked extremely judicious. 'I think we had better keep quiet and let the matter stand. Let the matter stand, I say. I do not see any good reason to withdraw the present vote since, like Mr Lushington, I have no relish for scandal attached to my name.'

'Nor I,' Glynn agreed. He exchanged a glance with Lushington, who nodded, and then turned to Scorn. 'That being so, I'm afraid, sir, if you disavow your vote and send a foolish young man to the gallows, you will have no support from us and certainly no money.'

'God damn you all,' John Scorn said morosely. He was deflated now, and all he could do was grunt like an angry old hog. 'I always knew you were devils worse than

Wedlocks. But you'll not silence me. I'll tell of Glynn's bribery and Jago's crime and you cannot stop me.'

Things would have been looking very bad for me now, except that I had a trump card to play. John Scorn might threaten and bluster – might trash my good name before Piggy, Philpott and Anne, and ruin my hopes of a return to Whitehall – but I could still silence him with one incendiary item, and what he had just told us made the true circumstances of Wedlock's death clear to me at last.

'Jeb Nettle, the sexton, saw Wedlock consulting with the thirty-two electors last week,' I said. 'And when he asked Wedlock what he was doing, Wedlock said he had also decided to change his vote to Glynn. In his case, however, he did it on principle, not for a bribe. Am I right, Mr Lushington?'

'I certainly did not offer Mr Wedlock any money,' Lushington said. 'Only one vote was needed, so why pay for two?'

'But if Wedlock changed his vote, there was no longer any need to pay John Scorn either. An even better out-come for you, I imagine.'

'Your point, sir?' Hitchens asked. I looked about at the others and briefly at Anne, half-hidden in the curtains, her eyes fixed on me.

'I think John Scorn heard that Wedlock meant to vote for Lushington,' I said, 'and that therefore the bribe they had offered *him* was now needless. Perhaps Lushington told him he had changed his mind and would no longer pay. Perhaps John Scorn only guessed as much. At any rate, we all know he and Wedlock have been feuding for more than fifty years, and I dare say Scorn much begrudged the loss of such a large sum only on account of his old enemy.

'We have all of us wondered why Wedlock meant to burn the poll book, when he intended to vote, and I now believe he never did. It was Scorn who lured Wedlock to the Guildhall, not the other way about.'

'Admirable reasoning.' Philpott slapped his hand delightedly on the table. 'Even a dog rolls in shit for a reason, after all, my boy.'

This observation was doubtless obscure to the rest of the company, but I didn't pause to explain.

'I went to the Guildhall this morning,' I said. 'It was quite as deserted as it must have been on Friday night. I listened for voices and eventually heard two clerks talking through a closed door. But their voices were so muffled I could not have identified them even if they had been my own brothers.'

I looked at Scorn. 'It was *your* voice the clerks heard through the closed cupboard door, taunting Wedlock that you meant to burn the poll book and stop the election. But later, when they only found old Wedlock inside, they naturally assumed it was his voice they had heard.'

'You have been busy about the town, I see,' Scorn said, his fingers drumming nervously on his chair arm.

'What happened then, I don't know,' I went on.

'Perhaps you struggled together but, if so, it must have been feebly since Piggy found no marks of injury on old Wedlock. Perhaps the smoke overcame him before it did you, and he only fell unconscious. But you came out into the deserted corridor while the clerk was gone in search of help, and for some reason you locked the door on Wedlock.'

'Baseless conjecture.' Glynn was impatient. 'Mr Jago, I don't wish to hang you, but you had better have some proof for all this.'

I took out the tinderbox and laid it on the table before Scorn. 'You dropped your tinderbox there, sir. I know it is yours now, since I saw a tobacco jar on your mantelpiece that exactly matches it in both colour and design. It was a pair, presented to you in happier days, Tirza Ivey tells me. She will testify it belongs to you.'

John Scorn only stared at me levelly. 'Bugger you, Mr Jago. Bugger Tirza Ivey. And bugger that fucking tenderbox, too, I say.'

'Go carefully, sir,' I said. 'I know I have done a foolish thing in forging your vote and you are entitled to expose my wrongdoing. But you have done an evil thing, which I will trumpet out as far as I can, not merely for my own sake but for my cousin's. That key in his bag must have come somehow from your house and been planted on his person to save your neck.'

At this, John Scorn looked puzzled, and I realised this sleight of hand was news to him. He had been unconscious when the key found its way into Piggy's bag, and the thing had been done by another hand – probably Eleanor's, I now thought, though it seemed shabby when Piggy had been caring for her grandfather with such tenderness.

I felt no tenderness towards the horrible old creature myself. 'The sheriff is writing all this down, Scorn. It is the result of my official investigation, on the coroner's behalf, and will be brought in testimony against you at the assizes if you persist in exposing the rest of us, in defiance of both the duke and the mayor. I don't know if you meant to kill Thomas Wedlock any more than you meant to kill that farmer, twenty-five years ago, down the Angel well. But to lock the door, even if in a panic or a daze, was murder, sir, nonetheless.'

Piggy had finally looked up from his inward reverie and was watching me along with everyone else. Hitchens had, in actual fact, been listening open mouthed and not writing anything. He now bent his head and began to scribble disjointed phrases but John Scorn had begun laughing in a way very well calculated to grate on everyone's nerves.

'Pushed the farmer down the well? You may think yourself very wise, Mr Jago, but that weren't me. That was old Wedlock himself, and I can prove it, just as I told the curate.'

20

REVEREND WILLIAM WEDLOCK mewled in distress, rather more like a kitten than a puppy, but it was Hitchens who broke the astonished silence.

'*Told the curate*? Pray, what exactly did you tell Reverend Wedlock, sir, and when?'

John Scorn was now looking at the curate with undisguised loathing. 'On Saturday morn, after our first meeting with you, sir, at The Willows, when that damned clerk Jago showed us the tinderbox and Glynn tried to make it seem the duke was behind the fire.

'The curate walked back down to town with me after the meeting. He told me Mr Jago had come to his grandfer's the previous evening, with the doctor and the coroner, to examine the body. Jago had showed him the tinderbox and, though he had said nothing, he had thought it was mine. He said my face at the sight of it, just then at the meeting, had convinced him he was right.

'He said he would tell on me to you, Sheriff, and have me arrested for his grandfer's murder.' Scorn bared his teeth. 'More fool him, he should a done it at once instead of gloatin' over me, like a damned Wedlock, for I told him directly that if he did breathe so much as a word about it, I would tell you in my turn about his grandfer. Young Reverend Wedlock would never rise above the rank o' curate if I did that, I told him, and his poor mother would be disgraced for ever in the town.'

As yet, Scorn's was an obscure tale, but my eyes had snagged on William Wedlock. I remembered the scene just now, when we arrived in the courtyard, and the episode took on a whole new meaning.

But meanwhile Hitchens was trying to make sense of John Scorn's story. 'You say you can prove old Wedlock killed that farmer all those years ago? If so, you had best explain yourself, sir.'

John Scorn seemed only too pleased to do so. His old face was animated with more than anxiety now. Instead, he glowed with venom. 'Saw the whole thing with my own eyes, didn't I? I was there that night, twenty-five year ago, and was comin' out of the privy when I saw Wedlock and the farmer argyfyin'. Wedlock had turned oogly and had his face pushed in the other man's. Said the man had been screwin' his son's wife and that she was with child. I'd hung back in the shadows to listen, and the next thing I knew, the man was fallen down the well and Wedlock had run off, in through the back stairs to the snug, so as to come out with all the rest when I raised the alarm.'

'That is an interesting story,' Philpott said. 'But where's the proof you claim to have?'

'Nine months later.' John Scorn jabbed his finger at the curate. 'He was born. As any old Helstoner who was there that night will tell 'ee, the dead man had a white streak in his hair like his father before him, and *his* father before that, no doubt. When William Wedlock was born, dang it if he hadn't just the same streak in his babby hair. They took care to hide it after, but I saw what I saw.'

He reached suddenly across the table and swept William Wedlock's hair from where it hung low over his brow. The curate resisted, but we all glimpsed the pure white lock hidden under the thick curtain fringe.

John Scorn sat back and showed his teeth again in what I now realised was an awful kind of smile. 'Grandfer a murderer, and him a bastard! No, no, he wouldn't go far once that was out, I told 'im. No Wedlock must ever prosper, sirs, for they are villains. Always have been, always will be, clergyman or no.'

It wasn't exactly *proof*, as John Scorn had claimed, but it was a malicious story nonetheless that could certainly do the curate great harm.

'So you took your revenge,' I said to William Wedlock slowly. 'You now saw that you could not hand over John Scorn to the sheriff, as you had meant to. If you did, he would tell this horrible story. So, instead, you tried to kill him. By God, sir, you may not look it – may not even be it by blood – but under your churchman's dignity you are certainly a Wedlock by disposition.'

Hitchens jangled heatedly. 'What are you sayin' now, Mr Jago?'

I pitied the sheriff for the trouble all this affair would place in his hands, just as I had once pitied William Wedlock for having to conduct his own grandfather's funeral. The curate had been particularly pink and squirming that day as he smoothed out his funeral stole and said his prayers.

'I think the curate is our mysterious poisoner, sir,' I said. 'Like everyone else he had heard of the nutmeg's properties from Lushington and gave some to John Scorn. He hid the evidence in the grave before it was refilled. Good God, I heard the nutmegs clatter off the coffin from his very hand. I thought they were clods of earth.'

'You have all run croony,' Reverend William Wedlock said, suddenly sounding far more Cornish in the old style. His puppyish squirming had a little of the bulldog in it now. 'How could I have ever heard of such a thing as nutmeg poison? How could I ever have got nutmeg at all?'

Glynn looked grave. 'You heard of it at my table, sir. I remember you were there with the rector on Thursday night and heard Lushington tell the whole room about it.'

'And you were visiting at the grocer on Saturday, less than

an hour after John Scorn had told you this disagreeable tale,' I added. 'You went there on the pretext of giving Julian Holy Communion. The man trusts scarcely anyone alone in his shop, but I dare say he would make an exception for a man of the cloth just as he does for the doctor. You sent him out on some pretext and while he was gone you stole a number of nutmegs from the jar behind his counter.'

William Wedlock's face was stormy and I was sure I was right.

'But how you then poisoned Scorn, I don't know.'

'I do,' John Scorn said. It was remarkable how much he had cheered up at the prospect of ruining one Wedlock, even if he himself was going to be hanged for killing another one. 'I almost choked on that wafer he gave me in church at the berryin', not half an hour before I fell ill. Stands to reason there was a poisoned one meant for me among the others on the dish.'

'It's certainly possible,' I said, remembering the curate's hand that day as it proffered the wafers one by one to the worshippers.

'No, it isn't possible, Laurence.' Anne's voice came from where she was sitting among the curtains. She sounded very cool and very remote. It appeared that she had forgiven me neither for our argument that afternoon nor for my subsequent felony. 'Dr Jago's book said the dose was two drams or more. There is no earthly possibility a wafer could hold so much and not be noticeably different from the others on the plate.'

'Two drams?' Philpott asked. 'How much is that in plain English?'

'Over an ounce,' Piggy answered, though I wasn't sure he was really following the conversation.

'Then Mrs Bellingham is right,' Philpott said. 'Unless the curate's kitchen maid makes his wafers as large as gold guineas.'

'So it must have been the wine,' I said, my mind still lingering at the ceremony in question. 'Scorn was last. The Communion cup was almost empty. When Scorn began to choke, the curate refilled the cup from a bottle on the altar. The nutmeg must have been in that.'

'He could not know that Scorn would choke on the wafer,' Philpott objected.

'Pepper, perhaps,' Anne said, again from her curtains. 'A good sprinkling of pepper or cayenne on the wafer would do it.'

'Howsumever it was,' Scorn said, 'I would have spat it all out, except that coming after his great lecture on hellfire, I was damned if he should think I had choked because I feared myself a sinner.'

'But you did fear it afterwards,' I said. 'You saw Thomas Wedlock's ghost in the corner of the room when the nutmeg began to send you mad.'

'Not Wedlock,' Scorn barked. 'Never a Wedlock. I would not give him the pleasure. That old serpent, Satan, that's who I saw.'

'And you saw *him* because you always knew you was

bound for hell,' William Wedlock said hotly. The storm that had broken across his face under my accusations had now resolved into the same righteous rage he had shown against Cyrus.

'You tried to make me believe Cyrus Best had poisoned the old man,' I said to the curate. 'Good God, and I thought it must be true, because even if you loved Eleanor and hated Cyrus as a consequence, a clergyman would never bear false witness against his neighbour.'

'Cyrus Best *is* a scoundrel,' the curate answered moodily, settling back into his seat and folding his arms.

Philpott's face had been purpling and he now thumped his fist on the table in a fit of tremendous dudgeon. 'God damn me, you are a shocking scrub, Wedlock. You saw I did not believe your preposterous tale against Cyrus. So, fearing discovery, you looked about for yet another scapegoat.' Philpott was suddenly furious. 'Very convenient for you, 'twas the next day folks began to talk about Dr Jago. Somehow or other you got the Guildhall key from Scorn and put it in the doctor's bag.'

It was all growing clear to me now. 'Wedlock took the key from Scorn's house on one of his visits,' I said. How foul it was to think that the curate had poisoned John Scorn and then visited him afterwards in the guise of a kindly clergyman. 'But as for when it was planted on my cousin—'

'When those men attacked me in the street, I suppose.' There were tears in Piggy's eyes. He had suffered dreadfully over the business, far more dreadfully than the rest of us, even Thomas Wedlock, for the old man could have known very little of the smoke that killed him. 'The curate rescued my bag,' Piggy said, 'and returned it to me after the fight was over. And he said such kind things. Said he would always stand up for me against baseless rumour.'

I remembered him say so. The sexton and Philpott had been genuine in their condolences. William Wedlock had been lying through his teeth.

'And, finally,' I said, 'the curate tried his hand against John Scorn one last time, tonight. The old man came here alone in a sedan and was met in the courtyard by William Wedlock, who kindly offered him his arm. I wondered at the time why the curate was here, and who had invited him, but I think now that no one had.

'He had heard of this meeting by chance and had come to exact his final revenge for his grandfather's death, if he could. Philpott and I happened upon them just as the curate was about to push John Scorn down the well after his own poor father. What a crew of villains they all are! But then the rest of the party arrived, thank God, and interrupted him. No one else noticed amid all the fuss, and I did not understand it until now, when everything else is explained.'

I hesitated and turned to the sheriff. 'My cousin has never done *anything* wrong. I hope you see that now, as I do.' I looked at Piggy remorsefully. 'I found out the poison quite independently of Lushington,' I said to him. 'It was in a book in your dispensary, Piggy. By a man named Cullen.'

I should not have called him Piggy before these men. But he actually smiled, the dear old dog. 'The *Materia Medica*? The carrier has brought it, then? I have been expecting it every day this week.'

Tirza had found the Guildhall key in his doctor's bag when she went to the door to take delivery of a parcel. The parcel must have been this book, which with her customary inquisitiveness she had unwrapped and then left on the shelf in the dispensary for him. And I knew for a fact he had not been home since. But there was one more question to be asked and again, in all the excitement, I forgot to address him more formally. 'Piggy, where are the nutmegs you bought from the grocer?'

He reached in his waistcoat pocket and produced a small drawstring cloth bag, kin to the one I had seen earlier that day in the grocer's shop. He pulled it open and shook two nutmegs into his hand.

'I took the bag to Scorn's house this morning and gave one nut to Loveday to grate into a caudle. But why do you ask?' He saw the look on my face. 'Bless me, Laurence—'

'I did not believe it,' I protested, perhaps too much. 'But I *was* terribly afraid.'

I F YOUNG REVEREND WILLIAM WEDLOCK ever meant to confess, it was not going to be to us. Perhaps in the quiet of the church he might one day confide in his Maker, but I wasn't sure about that either. He was a Wedlock through and through, by temperament if not, ironically, by blood. He sat, arms still crossed, and stared out at us through his too-long fringe saying nothing.

A strange new noise was now emanating from the direction of my elbow. It was Philpott, chuckling to himself.

'I am glad you find this business amusing, sir,' Sir James said to him stiffly. 'I am sure such unpleasantness is much in your line.'

Philpott was not in the least offended by the disdain in Sir James's voice. 'So it is, so it is, sir, I assure 'ee. But you know, the ins and outs are so interestin', when you think of 'em.'

'Ins and outs?' Despite himself, Sir James was curious. Philpott nodded around the table at the rest of us.

'Do you not see, sirs, that once John Scorn had killed Thomas Wedlock, Glynn and Lushington were back to square one? The duke's vote could no longer be split, and if Scorn voted for His Grace after all, the new corporation was no further forward. As well as dispatching an old enemy, no doubt to his vast enjoyment, John Scorn had also made himself valuable again. Am I right, Mr Lushington?'

21

LUSHINGTON HESITATED, but as we had already cleared him of Wedlock's murder and Scorn's poisoning there was really no further need for him to dissemble. He shrugged. 'Mr Scorn was certainly still eager to vote for me and by doing so have his reward after all. He came to me on Saturday morning before that first meeting at The Willows with the sheriff and demanded a still larger sum of money in return for his vote. But I confess I was doubtful after all that had happened with Wedlock. I said I thought Scorn should stick by the duke after all, and we'd say no more about it.'

Philpott was nodding. He had already guessed as much.

'But Scorn didn't like that,' Lushington went on. 'He foresaw that now he was the only one voter remaining for the duke, Parliament was bound to decide against His Grace, and along with the duke he himself would suffer a dreadful humiliation in the town.'

Lushington smiled briefly. 'John Scorn is a very proud, stiff-necked man, and for that I quite like him, even though he threatened to expose our whole transaction if I didn't pay him as we had previously agreed before Wedlock's death.

'In the end, I agreed to give the same sum as before, but this time only on the understanding that he would not vote at all. In that way the duke would fail and I would certainly be returned to Parliament. But there could be no suspicion of my involvement in an old man's temporary indisposition.'

He frowned and shifted uncomfortably in his chair. Perhaps his gout was troubling him. It certainly did not seem to be his conscience, for he was as calm as ever.

'I was surprised when Scorn fell ill that same afternoon, however. We had agreed on a much shorter and less peculiar spell of illness and I rather cursed him for drawing so much unwanted attention to himself. But I see now that, quite by chance, the curate was equally bent on incapacitating him, and only acted a little earlier than we had intended to do ourselves.'

I remembered Scorn's strange restlessness this afternoon, despite his apparent *coma*. 'You were awake all day today,' I said. 'Good God, you were shamming.'

Scorn didn't deny it. 'Seems a Wedlock can't even poison a body and do it right.' He looked at the curate with utter contempt. 'He only knocked me out until Sunday evenin'. Woke up with a poundin' headache and hungry as the devil.' He looked brooding. 'Still *am* hungry as the devil, damn it, having pretended to be asleep a whole night and day, and with all the confounded smells of the kitchen waftin' in and out.'

I remembered him groan at the scent of the nutmeg caudle. I also remembered Piggy say Scorn's eyes had recovered from their strange dilation as early as Sunday morning. The Sapient Hog had also recovered quickly from his nutmeg intoxication, but how could I have guessed that John Scorn would sham unconsciousness or that he had had, all along, no intention of voting at all?

'But if you were awake, why didn't you prevent me forging your vote?' I asked him. Scorn scowled, and for the first time he looked chagrined.

'Didn't know about the ballot slip, did I? How should I? No one spoke of it in my presence. I heard you rummagin' about the room, but I did not know what you was about. You went out, and I heard the sheriff leave, and I thought then that it was all over and I could safely wake.'

Hitchens' internal symphony chimed quietly in the following silence while we all contemplated *the ins and outs* of the whole affair, as Philpott had put it.

The sheriff pushed the ballot paper about the table with a disconsolate finger and looked glum. 'I wish to God all this did not fall to my charge,' he said eventually. 'I am but a Cornish gentleman as you know, sirs, and am hardly equipped to pronounce on such a deplorable set of crimes. Of course, the assizes might make a better job of it.'

He rubbed his forehead with his fingers. 'It seems to me that the only man in this room who has acted properly throughout is the one man we have had locked up all afternoon. Mr Glynn and Mr Lushington have offered large bribes in pursuit of their own personal interests. Reverend Wedlock has disgraced every idea of the Church and what a clergyman owes to his flock. And, whatever his motives may have been, Mr Jago has acted in a way quite at odds with his position as a supposed gentleman.'

His eye was particularly stern as it bulged about at us by turns. 'But I confess I have no great desire to see this sorry business get out. I would not have a respectable market town like Helston exposed as such a nest of vipers. After all, Cornwall is the front line in our battle with the French, as all coastal places are. And besides,' he came to the true nub of his gloom, 'my tenure in this position ends on Midsummer's Day and I have very little desire to be caught up in this muddle for months afterwards.'

'But you cannot allow all these crimes to go unpunished,' I said, forgetting my own neck for a moment. But no one answered me. Hitchens only looked mournful.

In the end it was Lushington who saw the matter with the clarity of someone no doubt well used to a thorny negotiation.

'I would cheerfully hang John Scorn,' he said, 'but I fear he will have no compunction at all in taking everyone else down with him – and hanging you, too, Mr Jago, while he is about it.' He smiled at me. 'That being the case, I think a tactful settlement is indeed for the best and, if it is also calculated to spare the sheriff much trouble, who are we to object?'

'Quite right.' The duke had been uncommonly silent throughout all these revelations but it seemed that, if he had allowed Lushington to best him in the matter of his snuff, he was now determined not to let the East India man lord it over us any longer. 'But you can hardly be the one to settle matters, Mr Lushington, being yourself a most egregiously guilty party in the affair.'

His Grace now looked remarkably smug. 'I think Hitchens will find that I alone, like the good doctor, have acted honourably amid this whole sorry chronicle of events. That being the case – and as I am also the man of highest rank among us – I think it is naturally my place to settle matters. Settle matters, I say, if the sheriff will allow me.'

Hitchens looked positively delighted and waved a hand as if to say, *By all means.* The duke leaned his elbows on the table and looked more animated than I had ever seen him. Perhaps this was how he had imagined himself as Prime Minister at the Cabinet table.

'The fact that Scorn killed old Wedlock seems clear – quite clear, I say – but as Mr Lushington observes, the benefits of punishing that crime are outweighed by the costs. In any event, if Wedlock was himself also once a murderer, one might even call Scorn's act a kind of justice, if it suited one to think so.'

It was clear that in the duke's opinion this should certainly suit us, and to the devil with any finer moral judgements.

'Then there is young Reverend Wedlock,' he honked on, 'who has disgraced the cloth, that is true, disgraced the cloth shamefully, I say. But though he undoubtedly meant to *harm* Scorn, we cannot conclude with absolute certainty that he meant to *kill* him. And regardless of whether he did or not, the fact is that Scorn did not die.'

The duke looked at us firmly. 'Did *not* die, I say. I believe, therefore, that a quiet word in the rector's ear, and by thence to the Bishop, will be punishment enough for Reverend Wedlock – for as Scorn himself observed, the curate will never go far with such a cloud over him.'

I must say I was rather taken aback by the duke's sudden attack of natural authority, as was Sir James, who was staring at his patron positively open-mouthed.

'And so, having dispensed with the murder and the curate's attempted revenge, we come finally to the far more important matter of the vote,' the duke went on. 'The matter of the vote, I say. I think we are all agreed that despite Glynn's disgraceful attempts to thwart me, the present written vote must stand unchallenged, which will have the incidental and happy effect of also saving Mr Jago's neck – and not for the first time, I gather.'

John Scorn growled. The duke ignored him and turned to look Glynn directly in the eye.

'But though we may patch up the affair in this way, the sheriff is quite right to say that you and Lushington have behaved most improperly. Most improperly, I say. If any rumour of your bribery were to get out, I dare say it would surprise no one, but it would nonetheless be highly damaging to yourselves and your business.' He looked pitying. 'You are not – forgive me – peers of the realm, and therefore above all such petty trifles, as I am. This being so, it seems to me that we might make what you would call a gentlemen's agreement, if I may stoop to that level.'

They hated him but listened anyway. The duke steepled his fingers and looked wise. 'I fancy I shall let it be known in Westminster that I accept the thirty-two new electors and their vote for Mr Lushington after all. I will tell Parliament that John Scorn is quite senile and I regret putting my honour in the hands of such a poor old creature.

'You will get your victory in Helston, Mr Glynn, and Lushington will get his seat. But after that, I think there will be occasion for a new settlement. I have paid the poor rates and maintained the church like my father before me for many years, and I am well disposed to continue the tradition. In return, you will accept my patronage of the town and next time Parliament is dissolved you will instruct your thirty-two electors to vote for candidates of my choosing. My choosing, I say.'

The duke's *gentlemen's agreement* was no more than courteous blackmail. Do as he bid them or have their misconduct exposed.

But I did not much pity them. Instead, I had my eyes on Sir James, to see how he would take the news that he was now to be abruptly deserted by his patron in favour of Lushington, and that all his happy hopes of a seat in Parliament were summarily dashed.

His self-possession was almost perfect, I was thinking with some admiration, when William Wedlock jumped to his feet, his face ablaze with avenging, feuding passion.

'See there, Scorn! You'll be shamed in Parliament after all, as a stupid old man no one wants any more, just like you feared. It will be in all the newspapers, too, you old bastard, and everyone in Helston will know it. God damn me, that's sweet, whatever else.'

'Oh, no,' the duke objected magnanimously. 'I think we must let old Scorn keep some shred of dignity. I fancy I will not demand the return of the ten guineas I paid him for his vote. I may even make it twenty, if it will make certain of shutting his mouth for good. He did, after all, vote for Sir James whether he meant to or not.'

Sir James had taken his defeat with his usual dignity, and Lushington was quite tranquil – once this week was over he likely would have no dealings with the town or the mayor ever again, for at the next election he could always buy himself another seat somewhere less troublesome. But all this was gall to Glynn. He had taken on the duke and lost.

'I suppose I must agree,' he said with some bitterness. 'There will be half a dozen shameful things you have also done, Your Grace, but they have not come to light as yet. When they do, I swear I will have my revenge.

'But in the meantime, I will accept your offer. Not merely for myself, but for my niece, Sarah, who wants Dr Jago to husband. A family connection to a forger would be highly disagreeable.'

Piggy had been listening to everything, but he still seemed too overwrought and bewildered by the political horse-trading going on all around him to understand much. Nevertheless, at Sarah's name he blushed. He would be happy again, I thought, when all this was over. The pressure at my heart on his account, at least, began to lessen.

'Yes, yes, dear Dr Jago,' Lushington said, turning to him with an affectionate smile. 'He has got off to a bad start in Helston through no fault of his own. And I'm afraid that if no one is ever hanged for Wedlock's death and no one accused of John Scorn's poisoning either, the stories against him will not be banished so quickly as he might wish.

'So, if he will accept, I would have him come to town and set up in Harley Street. I will be his first patient, and through my recommendation he will soon have a stream of wealthy patients banging on his door. That being so, the wedding may be sooner, rather than later, and all will be happy and hopeful.'

'Thank you, sir.' Piggy was half-choked with emotion. I had spent too long with politicians, become too cynical, for I hadn't believed Piggy when he said Lushington was a decent man after all.

'Well, then.' Hitchens rose to his feet with a musical wheeze. 'If we are all agreed, I believe I will close this meeting. I will speak to the rector about the curate tomorrow – or perhaps the next day – there is no great hurry. Mr Scorn will go home and count his twenty guineas and remember that if he makes any disobliging comments abroad, the matter of the tinderbox will always be remembered.

'Meanwhile, I will send off the double return to Parliament in the morning. It will be for His Grace to smooth that matter over in Westminster next week. But I suppose I may congratulate you, Mr Lushington, on your coming victory at the poll.'

Hitchens looked at Piggy, then, and smiled. 'Last but not least, I advise the doctor to run to The Willows and propose to his sweetheart at once. As an old man to a young one, sir, I recommend you do not tarry.'

But Piggy remained his earnest, conscientious, exasperating self. 'In fact, I must go to see a patient,' he said. 'A child, for whom I feared the worst this afternoon, and from whom all this business has detained me most dreadfully.'

'You mean Loveday's sister, little Jane?' Philpott's face

grew a trace more rosy. 'My dear man, unless you cannot deny yourself the immediate applause of your patients, I believe you may leave the little girl until tomorrow. I spoke to her uncle just now – a servant at the Angel. He told me her fever has passed over, and she is sleeping quite peacefully.'

I remembered Philpott's conversation with the servant in the courtyard before we came up to the duke's rooms. It seemed an age ago now, but that fellow must have been the uncle, and their cheerful intercourse now very agreeably explained.

'Thank God,' I said, not merely for the child's sake, or Loveday's, but for Piggy's too. His days had been filled with failure and despair ever since I had arrived in town and I was heartily glad of this little triumph for him among all the gloom. And who was to say it was a *little* triumph after all? God willing, the child would prosper and a woman's whole, long life would flow from this one instance of his skill and care.

Before he left, the sheriff turned back and fixed his strange eye on Philpott. 'By the by,' he said, 'I have allowed Mr Laurence Jago to run about the town on the say-so of the coroner, who I gather knew him from a lad. But it has come to my ears in the last day that he is also your apprentice, Mr Philpott, and therefore this licence has allowed him to gather materials for a story in your paper that he would not so easily have amassed without my help.'

'Very grateful, Mr Hitchens, I'm sure,' Philpott said easily. 'If you desire it, we will make especial mention of your name as the patron of the feast, so to speak.'

The sheriff glared and jangled more violently than ever before. 'On the contrary, Mr Philpott, I mean to observe that if any word of this affair is breathed in your paper, or elsewhere, I will cheerfully see *you* hanged. Having failed to get justice for anyone else, it would give me a great deal of satisfaction.'

22

A FTER THE COMMOTION involved in removing the invalids to their sedan chairs, only the duke, Sir James, Philpott and I remained sitting at the table.

George slipped into the room, probably having been listening at the hinges quite as shamelessly as Tirza Ivey would have done, and he sat down with Anne in the window. At the general sounds of departure the baby Sidney in the next room started crying.

But we were far too low company for the duke's taste. 'I believe I shall retire,' he said. 'London tomorrow, Sir James. And, though I suppose you will be disappointed, it is still victory, you know. Victory, I say! I have routed my enemies after all.'

He went out, shutting the door with a happy smack, and the crying baby cried louder.

'Well, God bless me,' Philpott said, reaching in his pocket for his tobacco. 'It will take me a little while to rearrange all my ideas, I do confess. The kidneys and the brandy both *red herrings*, you might say, and just as strong smelling, quite sufficient to put the hounds off the true trail, I assure 'ee.'

I frowned, not really listening, and Sir James raised his eyebrows at me.

'What is it, Jago? You have something else to say?'

'Yes, sir,' I said. 'I think we have let the duke off the hook, which is another piece of grit in the very gritty oyster we have been obliged to swallow tonight. I have been remembering that at the very start of this affair you warned me to be careful and were displeased when I first suggested that Wedlock's death was murder.'

'What of it?' Sir James looked mild.

'George told me tonight that the duke had been wooing the thirty-two all along, just as the duchess bade him.'

'Then it seems George is as indiscreet as you are, Mr Jago.'

'It occurs to me,' I said, 'that when the sexton first saw Wedlock *huddling* with the thirty-two, Wedlock was probably offering the duke's terms to them. It was only afterwards he decided to join their ranks.'

'Dialogue is everything in politics, Jago. As witness to the negotiation of a treaty, you should know that.'

'I would have liked the sheriff to know it, too, that's all. It galls me almost more than all the rest that the duke managed to keep himself so high and mighty, and his hands apparently so clean. And God damn it, he has the most infuriating smirk I ever saw.'

Sir James didn't answer. The whole business was stitched up so tight that to reproach these men was of no more use than throwing oneself at a cliff.

I looked at Anne with a pang of regretful sorrow. She had seen me at my worst tonight, accused and with a rope round my neck for the second time. She would certainly despise me again, but I thought on the whole it was as well if she did so. She had been more than a mere dream of love all these years. She had also been a kind of sister, a kind of counsellor too, ever since we were both very young. But we were not suited. She was too ruthless; I was too compromised. Even if the duke did recommend me back in Whitehall, as a reward for committing a crime on his behalf, I did not think I would ever visit Anne at Kensington after all. Better to let the thing die, and the recollection of her lips and arms fade only into a happy memory.

There was, at this juncture, a quiet knock at the door and the servant I had seen with Philpott in the court-yard popped his head around it. He was wearing the same expression of suppressed mirth I had noticed then. Something else in addition to the good news about Loveday's little sister was afoot, that much was clear, as he addressed Philpott in a conspiratorial stage-whisper.

'Is it time, now, sir?'

Philpott looked around at us all, and a strange, happy smile creased up his face in its old familiar way. 'By God, my man, I think it is *exactly* the time, I assure 'ee. Will you send in Mrs Jago, now?'

It was indeed my mother who came in next, looking rather out of place in these lofty rooms. I rose to my feet, wondering what in heaven could possibly have brought her here. I almost forgot Philpott's smile and for a moment feared some dreadful calamity at the farm.

But before I could speak, another shape was following her into the room. Long, and lean, and shaggy as an old wolf. It lifted its nose to look about and then saw me, or smelled me, or perhaps only sensed the joy that had flooded through me.

Mr Gibbs had never been a demonstrative animal. A cursory nose at my hand, a capacity to sleep all night in the crook of my knees – an unthinking belief that where I was, he must also be. But now all his old dignity was forgotten. I was on my knees and he was licking my face as if he would never stop.

Philpott was laughing with much self-congratulation. 'You see! You see, my boy! Did I not assure 'ee it would all come right at last? God damn me, the most delightful thing I ever saw in my life!'

I tried to look at Mother through Mr Gibbs' enthusiastic flurry of fur and tongue. She was laughing, too. 'He arrived yesterday, Laurence. We had word from Falmouth and went to fetch him this morning instead of coming to market. They put him on the very next ship out of America for you.'

Sir James, it unexpectedly transpired, was a dog-lover, too. He was clapping his hands and commanding George to fetch us all a brandy, quite as if the boy wasn't a duke's son and himself not a disappointed civil servant at all.

Gradually the turmoil subsided, and I found myself back at the table. Mr Gibbs, having decided that all right things were now restored, settled himself at my feet and, apparently exhausted by such unusual emotion, went promptly to sleep.

They were all studying me. Philpott still red with pleasure, Mother only happy to see me happy, George cool and amused as ever, and Anne pale, intense and inscrutable. Sir James had a new look on his face. I thought I had seen it dawning before my mother came in with Mr Gibbs.

'I believe America has agreed with you, Jago,' he said. 'You are more canny than you were. A fool no longer, I think.'

'America was part of it,' I said, poking Mr Gibbs with my toe to make sure he was really there. 'But the Foreign Office and now this election business have been far greater teachers. Thanks to you all, I have learned to trust no one and believe nothing. It is not an education I would have sought by choice.'

'But one of admirable use in politics,' Sir James said. 'There is a place for you in Downing Street, you know, if you desire it. Now I am to remain at the Foreign Office instead of taking a seat in the House of Commons, its door will be open to you.'

'Laurence has no need of that,' Philpott said. 'He has

a place at the *Cannon* on Fleet Street, which will be a damn sight more comfortable berth than he would ever find with you.'

Sir James was dismissive. 'He may rise high in Whitehall if he puts his mind to it. Even his French mother, who was formerly a difficulty, begging your pardon, madam,' he bowed to my mother, 'even his French parentage, I say, may be useful in these days of war, if we can now rely on his allegiance.'

They were talking about me in the third person again. This time I wasn't flippant, only shook my head. 'I thank you, Sir James. You are a far better friend than I supposed, but I can't work for the Ministry again. This election has shown me how far everything is tainted in Parliament. And until there is a reform of the representation, and a much wider electorate, it will only remain so.'

'You fancy to be a martyr, then?' Sir James said. 'Preaching to the poor in Spa Fields and inciting riots till they hang you after all?'

'No, sir,' I said. 'I have no desire whatsoever to be hanged.'

I looked at my mother and sighed. She was smiling brightly at me, though I knew the smile hid sadness. She was more than fifty, and I had been away so long. Each time I returned home it felt as if I had never been away, but each time we parted she knew it might be the last time we ever met.

'Mr Gibbs will not like Helston, Laurence,' she said.

'He is a London dog, I think, born and bred.' She looked at Anne. 'And so is Mrs Bellingham. She would not suit a banker's wife in Cross Street, Laurence.'

I looked from her to Anne with absolute astonishment. How the devil could Mother know anything about her?

'I went to your farm, Laurence,' Anne said, cool as a cucumber. 'Yesterday, after church. Your mother and I had a long talk about your future.'

Anne had said my mother should be made to see sense, and not persuade me to renounce London. It had never occurred to me that Anne would take the business on herself. God damn me, I had never even said the words *will you marry me* – though, having made love to her this afternoon, it was certainly churlish of me to object now. And she was smiling at me, tremulously. By God, she had not fallen out of love with me after all.

Perhaps in sending her away this afternoon I had made myself a more valuable prize than I had ever been when I was the constant, suppliant suitor on my knees. Or perhaps – for I must do away with such cynicism if I am ever to be happy – perhaps she really had loved me all along. The thought that immediately followed came unbidden, and as strange to me as the algebra or the *felicific calculus*.

Did I still love her?

Yet what difference could that make? A gentleman could no more withdraw from an engagement with a lady than poison a man with nutmeg. Still, unless I exerted myself now, she would certainly have me, and put me back in Whitehall with Sir James whatever I might think about it. My mind raced over everything she disapproved.

'I do not wish to be hanged,' I said. 'But there are other ways to support reform.'

'Bless me,' Philpott said. 'A weekly column in the *Cannon* would be just the thing, my boy.'

I smiled at him. 'No, sir. Thank you, but I think I shall call on Mr Fox when we are back in London. His followers in Parliament might be few, but as leader of the opposition he has been the standard bearer for parliamentary reform these twenty years, and perhaps when the war is over he will even be Prime Minister. And then there is Sheridan, you know, a most impressive speaker.'

An impressive speaker with wandering hands, as Anne had told me.

Sir James quirked his mouth. 'Good Lord, a mad Foxite Whig!'

'No, sir, only a bare-headed democrat. But working for Mr Fox in Parliament would give me hope again, I think.'

I slid my eyes to Anne to see how she had taken this. She had put her head on one side, her gaze wide and thoughtful. I knew every bone in her body and every thought in her mind. She was too much a part of me not to love her. But, still, I hoped she would think the hated Whigs one step too far and set me free.

'Mr Erskine is a Whig,' she said after a moment. 'And Lord Grenville, too, for all he serves in Pitt's Cabinet.'

'I will not be that kind of Whig, Anne. Not a comfortable member of the Ministry with my nose in the trough. I dare say I shall be poor, for even if Mr Fox or Mr Sheridan employs me, the pay will not be much. Moreover, it will be precarious, not a regular stipend from the Government.'

But God damn me, her love, now finally given, was not to be shaken.

'Politics is politics, Laurence, and whether in power or opposition it is the most glorious career a man can ever pursue. It is lucky that my first husband left me some little money of my own. I expect we shall manage.'

Sir James raised his glass to me. 'Well, it seems congratulations are in order, Mr Jago. And, while I thought you had lost all your naivety, I find I'm not sorry that you are still a dreamer after all. Mr Fox is certainly eloquent against the war, and against Pitt, and against the King, and very romantic in favour of the people, which I dare say will please you. However, I'm afraid you may find your new masters disappoint you in the end, quite as much as we have done.'

New masters! I had once chafed against the Foreign Office and even against Philpott in the end. God only knew how the Whigs and Anne would turn out between them. But there being nothing else for it, I downed my brandy and poked Mr Gibbs with my foot again for courage.

'Well, sir,' I said, 'I suppose we shall just have to wait and see.'

HISTORICAL NOTE

This novel is based loosely on the Helston election of 1790, which saw the culmination of a long tussle between two opposing parties in the West Cornwall town. The mayor and aldermen having been selected for personal and family reasons over many years, the town corporation was rocked by internal division and endless litigation. A decision by Parliament in 1773 had resulted in all the freemen elected over the previous twenty years being struck off as improperly appointed. A new corporation was established with a new body of freemen, but Parliament subsequently decreed that the right to vote in parliamentary elections would remain in the six remaining freemen of the old borough until they died. Which they duly did – in fact, by 1790, the duke only had one voter left, not two as in this story.

When the double return of 1790 went to Parliament, the Duke of Leeds was finally defeated and the new corporation's two candidates, Stephen Lushington and

Gilbert Elliot, were returned as MPs for the town. The last old elector briefly became a freeman of the new corporation but died in August 1791 aged eighty. The duke afterwards reasserted his patronage of the town, which was only relinquished by his son George in later years when it became too expensive to continue due to the large financial demands of the freemen in return for their unreliable votes.

I have moved this story to 1796, while the general portrait of Helston presented in these pages is taken from *Bailey's Western and Midland Directory, or Merchant's and Tradesman's Useful Companion, for the year 1783* and the census of 1841, which constitutes the first detailed description of the town. While mixing all these periods together, I have tried to place shops and families in the homes and premises they really occupied in those various days.

The story of the poisoning and the murders are all invention, so I have renamed the old electors and invented the guilty parties. As far as the real characters in this story are concerned, the Duke of Leeds was famously difficult and bad tempered, and Sir James really was known as his pincushion in Whitehall. The duke did divorce George's mother for an affair with Mad Jack Byron in 1779, but George was certainly the duke's legitimate son as the affair post-dated his birth in 1775.

Stephen Lushington, chairman of the East India Company, did stand for Helston on the invitation of

Thomas Glynn the mayor. Lushington was indeed incapacitated by gout, but whether he was acquainted with the effects of nutmeg is unknown. There is no record that either man bribed anyone, but amid the extraordinary corruption of the times only wealthy men could ever afford the considerable expense involved in standing for Parliament.

The last old elector's daughter does appear to have married a man he did not esteem, but in reality there is no record that his granddaughter, Eleanor, ever married at all. In earlier times, when three electors remained, one of them, being outvoted, did set fire to Helston's parish records. Finally, a man did die from falling down a well in Helston, but the real event took place in 1828 at the Blue Anchor, and there was no suspicion of foul play.

The Sapient Hog is a recurring character in the history of the eighteenth and nineteenth centuries, and I am not the first novelist to find him irresistible. The Sapient Hog of this period was coming to the end of his long career under the tutelage of Mr Nicholson, while the first such pig to be named Toby really performed in the 1810s and wrote an autobiography, *The Life and Adventures of Toby, the Sapient Pig*. Thereafter, all subsequent Sapient Pigs traditionally took that name.

Piggy's medical textbooks include *The Dispensatory of the Royal College of Physicians*, 1748; *The Compleat Family Physician* by Hugh Smythson, 1781 and *A Treatise of the Materia Medica* published in two volumes by William

Cullen in 1789. Nutmeg is indeed a narcotic if taken in sufficient quantity, and the description of its effects is taken verbatim from Cullen. Nutmeg gained notoriety in the late nineteenth and early twentieth centuries when it was erroneously rumoured to procure abortion, and a number of unfortunate women fell very ill.

Piggy is inspired by Dr Stephen Luke of Penzance, who took up a position in Helston in July 1790, under Dr Johns. Luke would later marry Harriet Vyvyan of the landed gentry at Trelowarren near Helston, and then remove for a number of years to Exeter where he had a successful practice. The 1861 *Roll of the Royal College of Physicians* describes his remarkable advancement, and he ended his career – as Laurence fancies Piggy might do – as physician extraordinary to George IV.

The story of the rival Helston factions is told by Spencer Toy in *The History of Helston*, 1936. John Dirring's account of Cornish banking on the website *Cornish Story* was particularly helpful to illuminate that forgotten corner of Helston history, while as before, I have relied heavily on *The Ancient Language and the Dialect of Cornwall* by Fred W. P. Jago, published in 1882. I could not have rebuilt a picture of Helston without the free online database of parish records provided by *opc-cornwall.org* and the *Cornwall Online Census Project*. The term *red herring*, in its present-day meaning, is popularly supposed to have been coined in 1807 by William Cobbett, the real-life journalist on whom the character of William

Philpott is based. Finally, I have tweaked the lyrics of the 'Tol de Rol', which was written in 1784 about the Duchess of Devonshire, who canvassed energetically for Charles James Fox and was rumoured to give kisses for votes. The original is collected in the admirably titled *The Wit of the Day or The Humours of Westminster, being a complete collection of the Advertisements, Handbills, Puffs, Paragraphs, Squibs, Songs, Ballads &c. Which have been Written and Circulated during the late Remarkable Contest for that City*, 1784.

ACKNOWLEDGEMENTS

Having lived very close to Helston for twenty years, *Scarlet Town* was great fun to write, and I only hope the inhabitants will forgive any mistakes, or any tweaking of the facts I have included for the exigencies of the story.

The Museum of Cornish Life in Helston is a really wonderful place, jammed full of the stuff of everyday life in past times, and I have spent many a happy hour looking at its collections of veterinary equipment and farm implements among so much else. Mark Dungey kindly searched through their records for old pictures, and Isobel Bloomfield was very helpful on the old Market Hall and Guildhall which is now long gone, replaced by a very handsome Victorian building.

Emily Rainsford drew the delightful map of the town, only very slightly tweaked from reality to fit neatly on one page; while Eloise Logan read multiple drafts and made her usual invaluable comments.

Huge thanks to my brilliant editor Miranda Jewess,

copy-editor Alison Tulett, and proof-reader Fiona Brown. I have been blessed with the most stunning book covers designed by Steve Panton and supported by all the fantastic team at Viper, especially Emily Frisella, Drew Jerrison and Rosie Parnham. Huge thanks, too, to my agent Nicola Barr for all her support and wisdom in general, and for helping to bring *Scarlet Town* into the world in particular.

Finally, thanks to Mark for drinking with me in the various establishments named in the town, just to check the architecture and layout naturally; to Will for joining me on the Town Trail a number of years ago which sparked so much of my interest in Helston's history; and to Geoff and Bramble for their very articulate commentary on everything.

ABOUT THE AUTHOR

Leonora Nattrass studied eighteenth-century literature and politics, and spent ten years lecturing in English and publishing works on William Cobbett. She lives in Cornwall, in a seventeenth-century house with seventeenth-century draughts, and spins the fleeces of her Ryeland sheep into yarn. Her first novel, *Black Drop*, was published in 2021 and was a *Times* Book of the Year. Her second, *Blue Water*, was published in 2022 and was a Waterstones Thriller of the Month and shortlisted for the CWA Historical Dagger Award. Her fourth novel, standalone historical mystery *The Bells of Westminster*, will be published by Viper in 2024. Find her on X @LeonoraNattrass.

COMING SOON

From the bestselling author of
Black Drop, *Blue Water* and *Scarlet Town*

London, 1774.
The opening of a royal tomb will end in murder…

AVAILABLE NOW

Jane Eyre meets Amy Dunne in this
Sunday Times Historical Fiction Book of the Year

'A dark, inventive story'
The Times

'A gloriously foreboding gothic tale'
Heat